THE CARDINAL IN EXILE

To
Anthea

CONTENTS

History has taught me that rulers are much the same in all ages and under all forms of government; they are as bad as they dare to be.

—*Samuel Taylor Coleridge*

I

The Great Debate

The summer heat was not yet sufficiently advanced to make Rome unendurable, yet the three who sat in the shaded garden of the Convent of San Silvestro welcomed the occasional breeze. Michelangelo appeared the most uncomfortable, but that was because he was still partially lame from a fall from the scaffolding in the Sistine Chapel where he was painting an immense fresco of *The Last Judgement*. His two friends were so used, in the course of their meetings, to his thin, wiry form pacing restlessly about during the conversation that his present immobility was almost disturbing. Once or twice he instinctively tried to hobble about, but the pain soon drove him back to his seat.

Vittoria Colonna made in her dress no concession to the season. At a distance she might have been taken for one of the nuns; but her heavy garments were more discommoding than their coarse serge. On her part this was intentional. It was the last vestige of her *penchant* for self-mortification. It was also, though it is probable that she did not consciously realise it, a kind of silent protest against the Pope's refusal to allow her to wear a nun's habit.

Vittoria Colonna was now forty-nine and had been a widow for sixteen years. She was justly considered Italy's most famous woman. That she was a Colonna, a member of the leading family of Rome whose story was the history of Rome itself, counted for much; that her husband, the Marchese di Pescara had been in command of the Papal-Imperial troops at the victory of Pavia, which had changed the balance of power in Europe, counted for more; yet it was her own personality, rather than her lineage and her great possessions, which set her at the centre of the artistic and religious ferment of sixteenth-century Italy.

After her husband's death from the delayed effects of Pavia where he had fought hand-to-hand to the end, though bleeding from three wounds, she had obtained Papal permission to be received in the convent of St. Catherine in Viterbo (though not to be clothed as a nun), and there she made her home, in the sense of the base to which she always returned from her constant visits —to her castle at Ischia, to Naples, to Ferrara, to Orvieto and above all to Rome. In the capital she always stayed in San Silvestro in Capite which, two and a half centuries earlier, had been given by the Pope of the day to the Poor Clares, particularly those of the house of Colonna.[1]

Despite many suitors, Vittoria had refused to marry again but had devoted herself to celebrating in sonnet after sonnet the excellencies of her dead husband (who had never loved her and had only seen her once during the last three years of his life). The eventual publication of these tributes and some religious poems, which went quickly through three editions, gave her poetic fame and a recognised place in the literary firmament.

Yet it was inevitable, for one of her temperament, that her ultimate interest would be religion. Having gained the world and found it dust and ashes, she made haste to renounce it. 'I seem unbound and unencumbered,' she wrote in one of her sonnets, 'yet my heart is buried in narrow soil.' She started to mortify her body to such an extent that she reduced herself to skin and bone, a living corpse, with only her great, liquid eyes, accentuated beyond measure in her emaciated face, vivid with life.

[1] They remained until 1840 when they were driven out by Garibaldi. The monastic buildings are now the main post and telegraphic office of the city.

Thus she had first met Reginald Pole, the third of the group now in the garden of San Silvestro, when, reluctantly, he had come to Rome at the age of thirty-six, to be made a Cardinal. The understanding between them was immediate. Though he was not a priest, she asked him to become her spiritual director, with the result, as she put on record, that 'to him I owe the health of my soul and the health of my body, for the one through superstition and the other through ill-government stood in peril'.

Pole gradually brought her to understand that Christianity is not ascetic and that she was mistaken in supposing that physical mortification was a part of piety. She 'rather offended God than otherwise by treating her body with such rigour'. In the religion of the Incarnation, the human body was a precious thing, to be treated with care until it pleased God to release the spirit from it for a while, to be reunited with it at its resurrection.

'So that lady,' wrote one of her circle, 'began to mitigate the great austerity of her life and brought it, little by little, to a reasonable and honest moderation.'

Something of the spiritual comfort which Pole had given to Vittoria, she had given to Michelangelo, when that tormented genius disillusioned by his past, harassed by the present, had finally abandoned his native Florence and taken up residence in Rome to be with his last and enduring lover, Tommaso de' Cavalieri. In this young nobleman, Michelangelo, confessing 'a thousand times love has forced me under its yoke and exhausted me' had found at last one who could hold him, not only by beauty of body but by nobility of soul. 'I believe,' he confessed to a friend, 'I should instantly fall dead were he ever absent from my thoughts.' He who had in the past prostrated himself to so many worthless youths whose bodies he had immortalised in marble had at length found peace in subjection to a single master. And this calm certainty of a human love had brought a new awareness of divine love. In one of his sonnets, he wrote:

Painting and sculpture cannot any more

Quicken the soul that turns to God again:
To God who, on the Cross, for us was set.

And this conversion from Apollo to Christ was in great part due
to Vittoria Collonna.

She had sent him a copy of her poems with an accompanying
letter which said: 'So great is the fame which your ability confers
that you probably never have believed that Time or anything else
could bring it to an end. But when the Divine Light enters your
heart, you know that earthly fame, however long-lived, suffers a
second death. If, therefore, in your works you behold the goodness
of Him who has made you a unique master, you may realise
that in my almost lifeless verses I merely thank God that while
writing them I offended Him less than I do in my leisure and
beg you to accept this as a pledge for future works.'

This marked the beginning of a friendship which, in its passionate passionlessness, recalled the devotion of a mediaeval
troubadour to his lady. In an answering sonnet to her, he likened
himself to the rough model which a sculptor makes in cheap
material before beginning his final work in valuable marble.

First I was born a model of myself
That later as a perfect work of art
You, gracious lady, might create me new.

Michelangelo, Vittoria and Pole had thus become bound to one
another by inseparable links in their common quest for God and
the meaning of life and art and the conduct by which they might
attain supernatural salvation. It was this they were discussing.

'There is nothing more dangerous,' the Cardinal said, 'than to
delude oneself that one is saved. And few things, unfortunately,
easier.'

'On the contrary,' retorted Michelangelo, 'there is so much
ugliness in mankind that sometimes I find it difficult to believe
that anyone will be saved.'

14

Vittoria, pursuing her own thoughts, said: 'It is the manner of salvation that still eludes my understanding. How hold the balance between faith and works?'

'It is quite simple,' Pole answered. 'Believe as if everything hangs on faith; behave as if everything depends on works. Then Heaven will not elude you.'

'You know how honestly I strive to do so,' she said, 'yet I know that my faith is not yet firm enough or my works good enough.'

'As for me,' said Michelangelo, 'my works no longer seem at all good. Once I might have thrown a good statue or picture in the scales against damnation. But not now.'

'But how,' asked Pole, 'would you construe "good" in that respect?'

'The best copy of God's perfection; the nearest imitation of His painting.'

'And the subject? Has that nothing to do with it?'

'Nothing in the world. It is the labour for perfection that sanctifies art.'

'Yet is it not possible that when you are at work on holy things you may be aided by supernatural grace?'

Michelangelo was disinclined to reply. The artist's vision of God is not easily translated into the terms of the theologian. All that he knew certainly was that his creation at its best fell so immeasureably short of the Creator's that he was in despair. An argument on these lines with the Cardinal would not be fruitful, but Vittoria, by virtue of her poetic gift, might understand. He turned to her and said abruptly: 'Your sacred poems, dear lady, edifying as they are, are not your finest work, even though you may credit them to inspiration.'

'You must know,' she replied, 'that I should never think of my poor poems as "works" which might aid the saving of my soul.'

'As I account my works now.'

'It seems to me,' said Pole gently, 'that both of you lack humility.'

'You are pleased to be paradoxical,' said Vittoria.

'No,' said Pole. 'Humility is to accept what you are. No one can deny that Michelangelo is the greatest artist in Italy, probably in Christendom. And your poems, Vittoria, are rightly praised. For either of you to pretend otherwise is a falsity that springs from a hidden pride.'

'But in the eyes of God,' said Michelangelo, 'our gifts, such as they are, are nothing.'

'How can you say that,' Pole answered, 'when they are His gifts?'

'Then let me put it,' said Vittoria, after a moment's thought, 'that we are unworthy stewards of His bounty.'

'If you mean,' the Cardinal replied, 'that you have sometimes fallen short of what you might have done, yes. We are all guilty of that. That is the doom of our humanity. But you are not like the unworthy steward who did not use his talent and was sent to Hell for it. You have used your talents and it will stand you in stead for Heaven.'

'I will dare to pray so,' said Michelangelo.

The subject which the three were discussing, 'How can a man be saved?', though of deep personal importance to them, was also the fashionable topic of the day. For the first and last time in the history of Europe, theology, at every level, was the only wear. Great personages and the most humble, princes and poets and politicians, men of the world usually unaccustomed to think of such things, joined in the discussions. 'There does not appear to be any gallant gentleman or any good courtier,' wrote an impatient ecclesiastic, 'who has not some little erroneous opinion of his own.' A young duchess, hitherto occupied with nothing more weighty than dancing and other amusements now spent her time in discussing the Bible and questions of Grace with theologians. She confided to her cousin that 'were it not for those who discourse with me about the Scriptures and Free Will until I hardly know whether I am a Christian or a Jew, I should fall into melancholy.' And a riotous undergraduate informed his guardian: 'I am now reading the Scriptures wherein I find the way to true happiness. Your Excellency cannot imagine the number of persons here who, leaving other studies, are giving themselves to Sacred Letters.'

The great debate affected more than the piety of the simple and the intellectual attitudes of the fashionable. It invaded high politics. The Emperor Charles V, to strengthen himself in his ceaseless military and diplomatic struggle with Francis I, King of France, needed the support of the Lutheran princes of Germany. For this severely practical reason he insisted on arranging a theological conference at Ratisbon to attempt to reconcile the Lutheran view that 'salvation is by faith alone' with the traditional Catholic view that 'faith without works is dead'. Though ultimately the belief that one can gain Heaven merely by believing one was 'saved' was incompatible with the belief that Heaven is to be won by evincing one's faith in God by doing works of piety, charity and mercy, a compromise formula was devised and—though Luther himself considered it 'a roundabout and patched affair'—it might have been adopted had not the French party, scenting the danger which would arise from the achievement of unity, injected fresh bitterness into the controversy.

'The enemies of the Emperor,' it was reported, 'dreading the power he would obtain by the union of all Germany, have begun to sow tares of discord among the theologians. Carnal envy has interrupted the Conference.'

The tool of the French party was a thirty-two-year old French lawyer, John Calvin, already consumed with fanaticism and, even as a student, so stern and unbending that he was known at his university as 'the accusative case'. He was the inventor of the most extreme interpretation of 'salvation by faith alone' as meaning that a good action was impossible and, unless one were predestined to salvation before one's birth, a life of exemplary holiness would still lead to everlasting torture in Hell. Calvin, realising that an effective way of wrecking the Ratisbon Conference would be to arouse national passions, circulated a document urging the Germans to resist 'the bloodthirsty Roman tyranny and its bepurpled, godless company'.

The collapse of the Conference became now only a matter of time. The compromise formula was uncompromisingly rejected by all parties. The theologians in Ratisbon, the Pope in Rome, Luther at Wittenberg, the Catholic and the Protestant Estates of Germany were unanimous in one thing—their refusal to be reconciled.

The failure of the Conference, though he did not attend it, had been of some personal consequence to Cardinal Pole. The Papal Legate at Ratisbon had been Cardinal Contarini whom he loved and revered as a second father.[2] Contarini, who was the leader of the party of reform within the Church, had been chosen as legate as much for his character and outlook as for his learning. If anyone could reconcile conflicting claims, it was he. 'If we wish to put an end to the Lutheran troubles and errors,' he had proclaimed, 'we need not muster against them heaps of books, Ciceronian orations or subtle arguments. Let us rely rather on the probity of our lives and a humble spirit, desiring nothing but the good of Christ and our neighbours.'

And his first charge to the Catholic theologians at Ratisbon had been: 'It is our duty to continue steadfast in prayer to the God of peace and unity that He may send His Holy Spirit into our hearts and restore the unity of the Church. Our part is to strive, by goodwill and well-doing, to bring our opponents to think shame of themselves for separating from brethren who are filled with love.'

In his formulation of the compromise between 'faith alone' and 'faith and works', Contarini had naturally gone to the limit of orthodox concession. He had, in fact, gone so far that he was

[2] Pole's own father had died when he was five. For Contarini's earlier career see 'A Matter of Martyrdom', Chapter XII.

uneasy without the approval of Pole, whom he recognised as the profounder theologian and he had sent a copy of his statement to the younger Cardinal, asking his opinion on it.

Pole had been enthusiastic. 'You always show yourself logical and clear in the development of the subject,' he wrote, 'and the conclusions you draw are such that everyone must understand you. The examples from Holy Writ and the Fathers are excellently worked out. All objections are refuted. In short, your statement of the doctrine is like a partly-concealed pearl, always possessed by the Church but now accessible to everyone.'

Thus the rejection of the formula, which was not only stigmatised on all sides as untenable, time-serving and ambiguous but which even led Catholic rigorists to doubt Contarini's orthodoxy, had been a bitter blow to Pole and the sting was the more hurtful because the decision came on the heels of the news of his mother's death.

On May 27 in that year 1541 the Cardinal's mother, the Countess of Salisbury in her seventieth year, had been summarily executed in the Tower of London, by order of her cousin, King Henry VIII, for her fidelity to the Catholic faith.

The shock of her killing was the greater because it was impossible for her son not to blame himself in part for her death. King Henry had sent to Pole, living in Rome, a request for a treatise on the religious situation in England and the theological aspect of his divorce of his queen, Catherine of Aragon. 'Disregard all affection and leave all dangerous results to my wisdom and policy,' Henry had ordered him, 'and declare your opinion truly and plainly, without dissimulation.'

With a culpable simplicity, Pole had obeyed, supposing that the King would accept unpalatable truth when he desired accomodating falsehood and violent denunciation where he expected conventional flattery.[3] The immediate result was that the incensed King made several attempts to have the Cardinal assassinated

[3] For Pole's treatise see 'A Matter of Martyrdom' Chapter XIV.

19

and, when these failed, took his revenge by killing Pole's mother and elder brother who were in his power in England.

Now, though Pole might say, as he did: 'To be the son of a martyr is a greater honour than royal birth,' he was haunted by the question of his own responsibility; nor was it any solace to realise that his tragic misjudgement of Henry sprang from his incapability of imagining him so evil. Such simplicity was surely itself a great sin?

Yet, despite these doubts and an ever-increasing sorrow for his mother's death, the Cardinal had so mastered himself that, when in company of others, he appeared quite calm. His tears he kept for his oratory.

So now, in the garden of San Silvestro, hardly six weeks after he had received the bitter news, Pole might have appeared to a stranger as one serenely remote from the cares of the world. Though the youngest of the group—he was now forty-one—he seemed effortlessly to dominate it. But both his friends knew the immensity of the strain which lay behind the calm appearance.

What they did not allow for was his vulnerability over the lesser matter of the Ratisbon Conference. This, which seemed to them—and, indeed, to him—so infinitely small a thing in comparison with the cause and manner of his mother's death, had assumed an altogether disproportionate importance. In his mind, the repudiation of the formula destroyed him as a theologian and, so, increased his self-distrust. All refuges seemed assailed. Consequently, when Vittoria mentioned Ratisbon, he dismissed the subject sharply with: 'It is better not to speak of this till Contarini himself comes to tell us of it.'

Vittoria, intending sympathy, asked: 'There will be another conference to put it to right?'

'His Holiness has promised to call an Ecumenical Council. Then Peter will speak and we can cease debate.'

Michelangelo said: 'I have already ceased. I rest on what you have already taught us. I read the second book.'

The old artist had, at this moment, a greater sensitivity than

20

Vittoria to Pole's mood and was intent to comfort him. Michelangelo was referring to the Cardinal's teaching that at first God had revealed His mysteries in a book given to all, the Book of Creation. But men, in their foolish pride, did not understand and obey the natural law and would have been lost had not God given them a second book—'the Book of the Cross of Jesus Christ, whose contents are more absurd, more remote from human wisdom than anything that can be imagined'.

'I too,' said Pole, 'find that my only solace.'

When Michelangelo returned home, because he was unable to work on his fresco and unwilling to remain idle, he took up some red chalk and started a drawing of Christ on the Cross. As a rule, he gave all his drawings to Tommaso, but this he intended as a gift to Pole. The moment he chose to portray was Christ's cry of dereliction.

2

The Governor of Patrimony

The Patrimony of Peter was the most important of the Papal States. Bounded by the Tiber on the east and the Mediterranean on the west, it ran from Rome to the border of Tuscany just north of Lake Bolsena. Its greatest extent from east to west was about forty-five miles: from north to south nearly sixty. It was part of ancient Etruria, famous for its fertility and its great harvests of corn, wine and oil which, even in the pre-Christian centuries had saved Rome from famine and now caused the Pope to give thanks that Rome had not only abundance for herself but could come to the aid of other states, like Naples and Genoa, and even of foreigners. The Patrimony had been church land for four hundred years, since the great Matilda, Countess of Tuscany—an ancestress, as he was never tired of insisting, of Michelangelo—had, at the beginning of the twelfth century, bequeathed it to the Holy See.

Its centre and capital was Viterbo, on the site of the ancient Etruscan Temple of Volturnus, the god of wine and gardens, the 'changeable god', at whose shrine the twelve Princes of Etruria were accustomed to repair to deliberate any necessary changes in their policies. The church of Our Lady-in-Volturna was still a reminder of the older pantheon. The alteration of the name was said to have been due to Desiderius, the last King of the Lombards, the father-in-law of Charlemagne, who, in the eighth century, decreed that Volturna should henceforth be known as Viterbum.[1]

Just south of the walled city, Monte Cimino rose 3,000 feet, clad in the forest of oaks and chestnuts which had been a place of nameless terror to the Romans, and from its summit the traveller could on a clear day see Rome itself.

The nearness to Rome was one of the reasons which Pope Paul III gave to Cardinal Pole for appointing him, in the August of 1541, Papal Legate for the Patrimony and Governor of Viterbo. 'I do not wish you to be too far away,' said the septuagenarian Pope. 'As Viterbo is an easy day's journey, you can come to advise me in any sudden need. Nor shall I fail to visit you.' Viterbo was Paul III's birthplace and he was accustomed to stay in his family mansion there, the Farnese Palace, on his way to the summer residence of the Popes at Orvieto.

Pole was profuse in this thanks for the honour but the Pope cut him short. 'It will benefit us both,' the old man said. 'I shall have the best Governor for the Patrimony and you will be able to lead the life of quietness and study which is agreeable to you.'

He naturally made no mention of his true reason for the appointment which was that, in his affection for Pole, he realised that his paramount need at the moment was new work and responsibilities.

As another mark of his consideration, the Pope ordered Perino del Vaga, to whom he allowed a monthly pension provided he served only the Farnese, to paint a portrait of him giving the Cardinal the authorisation of his new Governorship.[2]

[1] The authenticity of the decree has been disputed, though not disproved. It was, however, certainly not questioned in 1541 when the work of Annio di Viterbo, a Dominican friar of the fifteenth century, was accepted as genuine history. Only in later centuries was Annio discovered to be 'a wholesale and crafty forger'. Nevertheless the marble tablet with the decree of Desiderius is still shown in the Museum at Viterbo.

[2] This double portrait is now in the sacristy (not, as guide books say, the church) of Santa Francesca Romana in Rome.

Five days after Pole's appointment to Viterbo, Europe was shaken by the news that Hungary had fallen to the Turks. Suleiman the Magnificent had captured Buda, turned its cathedral into a mosque and proclaimed the country a Turkish province. In Rome the news caused such consternation that it seemed to many that the infidel was actually at the gates of the Eternal City. All eyes turned to the Emperor Charles V to show himself in deed the champion of Christendom.

But the failure of the Ratisbon conference had lessened the Emperor's effective power. He could not, as he had hoped the conference would have enabled him to, rely on a united Germany, where Luther summed up the dichotomy in the first lines of a new hymn he wrote for the occasion:

> Lord, shield us with Thy word, our hope,
> And smite the Moslem and the Pope.

Francis I, the 'Most Christian King', made matters worse by actually supporting the Turk. Any enemy of the Emperor was, by definition, a friend of his. He offered Suleiman Toulon as a harbour for his fleet, ordered a mosque to be built in Marseilles, issued coins stamped with the fleur-de-lys on one side and the Crescent on the other, with the disarming inscription *Non contra fidem sed contra Carolum*—'Not against the Faith but against Charles'—and, announcing himself the 'Protector of German Liberties' against 'the ignominious Roman yoke', epitomised his attitude in the slogan 'Better a Turkish Germany than a Papal one!' When two of his secret envoys to the Sultan were murdered by Imperialists near Pavia, Francis determined to declare war on Charles—his fourth—as soon as it was convenient.

The Emperor, remarking that 'all my life has been spent in trying to mend the discord in the Church and in saving Christendom from the infidels; all his life has been spent in supporting the infidels and perpetuating the troubles of the Church', hoped, not unreasonably, for the support of the Pope. Charles had determined to make a diversionary attack on Algiers and, on the way to embark at Genoa, met Paul at Lucca. He found the Pope unhelpful. Paul refused to excommunicate Francis or even to deprive him of his title of 'Most Christian King' on the grounds that, should he do so, 'there would be a danger that the King of France, who does such appalling things, might himself turn Turk like the King of England.'

Paul also advised Charles to postpone the attack on Algiers until the time—and the probable weather—should be more propitious. Charles, however, refused, relying on the advice of Hernando Cortés, who was with him, and who considered any possible obstacle minimal compared with those he had overcome in conquering Mexico. Altogether the meeting at Lucca was unsatisfactory, except that the attendance of the Pope's illegitimate son and his wife, the Emperor's illegitimate daughter, indicated a certain family solidarity.

The Emperor's only diplomatic success was to detach the most vigorous of the German Protestant princes, Philip, Landgrave of Hesse, from his allegiance to the Schmalkaldic League, the confederation of Lutheran rulers united against the Emperor. This minor triumph, however, could hardly be attributed to Charles's own initiative.

The Landgrave, a handsome debauchee now in his mid-thirties, was avid to rid himself of the unamiable and ailing woman he had married when he was nineteen. As divorce was forbidden, it seemed an impossible aspiration. Philip was, however, an industrious reader of the Bible, as became one who announced his intention to compel his subjects 'either to confess Christ or to emigrate', and in the course of his Biblical studies, he discovered that the Old Testament patriarchs were allowed more than one wife and that the New Testament contained no explicit prohibition of polygamy. He put this point to Luther who was forced to admit 'what was allowed in respect of marriage by the law of Moses was not actually forbidden in the Gospel' and, with some reluctance, gave the Landgrave permission to have two wives, provided that the arrangement remained a closely-kept secret.

When, inevitably, the truth, with its consequent odium, leaked out, to the consternation of the Protestants everywhere, Luther saw no alternative to lying. 'The secret "yea",' he observed, 'must for the sake of Christ's Church be a public "nay"' and justified his dictum by explaining that Christ, on occasion, told politic lies, as when He said that He was ignorant of the date of His Second Coming.

Unfortunately, the public 'nay' was disbelieved and the Protestant princes, in measureless anger and indignation, refused to guarantee Philip of Hesse's immunity from the legal penalty for bigamy which, in that godly land, was death. Now, therefore, for the pressing motive of personal safety, the Landgrave hastened to make his peace with the Emperor, abandoned the Schmalkaldic League and even promised as a last resort to return to Catholicism provided the Pope would grant him a dispensation.

The detaching of Hesse from the ranks of his enemies was a minor matter which could hardly compensate the Emperor for the general failure of his policies. Yet, as Charles regarded it as his paramount duty, as the temporal head of Christendom, to attack the infidel and to lead the attack in person, nothing could alter his determination to proceed against Algiers. At the beginning of September he embarked at Genoa with a number of galleys manned by German, Spanish and Italian troops and sailed slowly through the Mediterranean, pausing at Sardinia and Corsica, to Majorca, the nearest base to Algiers, where he had ordered his main force to await him. But already the storms had begun and his more experienced seamen echoed the Pope's advice to postpone the expedition to a more propitious time of year. When Algiers was at last sighted, on October 20, it was in a sea so wild that any attempt at a landing would have been mass-suicide.

In Viterbo, that October, Cardinal Pole had at last settled with his entourage and 'familia' in his official residence, the Governor's

26

Palace, at the northern edge of the city by St. Lucy's Gate. The palace was, in fact, a fortress which had been built in the turbulent times at the end of the fourteenth century for the safety of the Governor, and had subsequently been made magnificent by painters and sculptors appointed by Julius II and Leo X and, more particularly, the present Pope, Paul III.

Viterbo was, *par excellence*, a Papal city. Popes and Antipopes had, in the strife-torn twelfth and thirteen centuries, taken up their residence there in the Palace of the Popes which, with its fountain and its staircase and its exquisite traceried arches adjoined the Cathedral. Here Adrian IV, the only English Pope, had met the formidable Frederick Barbarossa and made him ceremonially hold his stirrup as a practical demonstration of the relative status of spiritual and temporal power. Here the Papal court had remained continuously for twenty years. Here the conclaves were held which chose six successive popes, including Gregory X whose election took place only after more than two-and-a-half years of wrangling, brought to an end by the angry Viterbese confining the Cardinals to the Papal Palace and keeping them short of food until they arrived at a decision.

In more recent times and within living memory, two popes, Nicholas II and Paul II, had come in search of health in the waters of Viterbo's little sulphur lake, Il Bullicame. And now that a Viterbo-born Pope occupied the Chair of St. Peter, there was a continuous stream of workmen and engineers and artists and officials from the Vatican at work on Paul's own Farnese Palace, near the Papal Palace; on the Governor's Palace; on the Palace of the Priors, in the centre of the city, which was the administrative headquarters of the Patrimony; and on the little church of St. Mary of the Oak, an object of Paul III's especial devotion, which was a short distance outside the city and to which he had ordered the construction of a new road.

The Cardinal had left the overseeing of the practical preparations of his installation at Viterbo to Alvise Priuli, the young Venetian nobleman who was to him, emotionally if not physically, all that Tommaso Cavalieri was to Michelangelo. On Priuli, during the ten years they had known one another, Pole had come to rely completely both at the centre and at the circumference of his life. At the centre, Alvise's understanding love was, in all chances and changes, his abiding solace—and never more than now in the desolation of his grief for his mother. At the circumference, Priuli relieved him of the nagging irritations of practicality. In the early days the young Venetian had provided for him a perfect retreat from the world, when he needed it, in his villa at Treviso. Now that he lived with him always, he saw to it that the Cardinal, wherever he might be, had round him the circumstances and simplicities he needed. Priuli had that rarest of gifts of so anticipating wishes that requests were unnecessary, and his combination of charm and efficiency was such that even Sandro, Pole's house-steward, who had at first bitterly resented him, gave him an admiring obedience.

While preparations were in train, the Cardinal decided to visit some of the towns in the Patrimony over which he was to rule. He went first to Civita Vecchia, where the Papal galleys, in no wise aiding the Emperor, lay peacefully at anchor. In this dreary and dirty town he had, though he was careful not to allow it to be seen, little genuine interest. He was glad to leave it and proceed north to Bolsena, in which his interest was intense.

Bolsena, the ancient Volsini, still deserving Juvenal's description 'set among wooded hills', with their lower slopes rich with olives and grapes and chestnuts and figs round the shores of its great lake whose waters were darkened by myriads of waterfowl, had once been the scene of a miracle.

In its church of St. Christina (herself miraculously preserved from drowning in the lake), a Bohemian priest, who had secret doubts about the Real Presence of Christ in the Blessed Sacrament, had been saying Mass one day in the year 1263. His secret questionings were answered by drops of blood suddenly issuing from the Host and falling on the corporal.[3] The immediate result of the 'Miracle of Bolsena' was the institution, the following year of the Feast of Corpus Christi, for which Thomas Aquinas was appointed to write the Office.

Now, with the controversy about Transubstantiation raging even more fiercely than it had three hundred years earlier—Luther had just described the Mass as 'the greatest and most horrible abomination of the Papacy'—and with theologians so divided on the correct interpretation of Christ's words at the Last Supper: 'This is my Body' that even had the formula for Justification been accepted at Ratisbon, reconciliation would still have been impossible on the doctrine of the Eucharist, Pole particularly wanted to visit again the scene of the miracle which had such far-reaching fame. For the 'Mass of Bolsena' had become, in popular belief, increasingly prominent in accepted history and recently Raphael had made a great fresco of it in the room in the Vatican which he had devoted to examples of the direct intervention of God in affairs of the Church, beginning with the release of St. Peter from prison by an angel.

The corporal itself, still stained with reddish spots in the shape of a profile of the type of face traditionally attributed to Christ, was now in the cathedral of Orvieto, whose building had been begun almost immediately after the miracle for the sole purpose of enshrining the relic and which was now—a reliquary in stone—one of the most beautiful churches in Italy. On visits to Orvieto with the Pope in past summers Pole had more than once examined the corporal. Though he did not openly question the miraculous occurrence, he was not privately inclined to believe it and was grateful for the Church's ruling that no miracle after the death of the last apostle demanded the assent of faith. Reputed miracles after the end of the first century were to be accepted or rejected on the same grounds of historical evidence as would apply to any secular event. Yet because the Bolsena Host had become, in popular understanding, so much part of the true

[3] The piece of linen on which are put the Host and Chalice at Mass.

29

doctrine of the Blessed Sacrament which was under such fierce attack from the Lutherans, Pole hardly dared voice his disbelief even to himself.

As far as he was concerned, he gave the full assent of his will and understanding to the doctrine of transubstantiation because his reading of Scripture and his training in theology made no other credible to him. A bleeding Host, by confusing accidents with essence, attacked rather than strengthened his faith. But with his habitual humility he accepted that to many of the simple, unversed in theological formulations, it might be a saving sign and that he had no right to assume that his own temperament and perceptions formed a criterion of universal truth.

So now he went to Bolsena to pray before the altar where the supposed miracle had happened beseeching certainty and enlightenment. But, though he spent a very great time there on his knees, he was vouchsafed neither.

He decided not to go on to Orvieto, as he had at first intended, but returned to Viterbo by way of Bagnarea, where, finding the inhabitants disinclined for anything but lying in the sun and singing to a guitar, he lent them a considerable sum from his own purse to set up woollen manufacture; and through Montefiascone, whose potent wine, *Est-est-est*, was famous far beyond Italy and whose natives, consequently, were prosperous and hard-working even if they too tended to lie happily about the streets.

In Viterbo, on his return, one of his first visits was to another church for a different reason. Just opposite the Governor's Palace was the Franciscan Church and friary where Dante had stayed, where St. Bernadino had preached and where lay buried 'the Pope of a day', an elderly invalid cardinal[4] who had died of a stroke in

[4] Cardinal Vicedomino Vicedomini took the name of Gregory XI, but as this title was also taken a century later by the last French pope, Roger de Beaufort, the use of it tends to confusion.

30

the Papal Palace the day after his election to the Papacy. But it was none of these things which aroused Pole's special interest. He went to look at a picture which was the latest acquisition of the Church and was still arousing some controversy. It was a *Pietà*—Our Lady with the dead body of her Son—but painted in a controversial style. Instead of the conventional pattern, with Christ in His mother's arms and the Cross in the background, the dead body is stretched out at the feet of the Virgin, who looks up to the Cross (which is out of the picture and presumed to be where the spectator is standing), and in the background, under a wild, dark sky, lies Jerusalem—'a much-admired shaded landscape' by a master of *chiarascuro*.

The artist, Sebastian Luciano, was an old friend of Pole's—he had painted the first portrait of him when he became a Cardinal—and of Michelangelo's, who let it be known that he regarded Sebastian as the finest colourist and, indeed, the best painter of the day (though the cynical regarded this as merely a way of additionally denigrating Raphael). It was said that the idea of the *Pietà* as well as the original sketch for it were in fact Michelangelo's, though Pole had been unable to get conformation of this from either artist, who agreed to say that painting had its mysteries no less than theology, and refused further to enlighten him.

As he left Rome for the Patrimony, Pole had called on Sebastian, who lived in luxury by the gate from which the Via Cassia ran to Viterbo. The visit was actuated by several motives. One was to try to heal the breach which had recently opened between Sebastian and Michelangelo; another was to urge the painter to work; a third was mere friendship.

Sebastian had been granted the office of the Piombo[5] and as it was a Franciscan perquisite had had to become a Friar. The appointment had had one most unfortunate result. As he now

---

[5] The holder of the office affixed the leaden seals to Papal documents (*piomba* from the Latin *plumbum*, lead) and Sebastian is known to history as Sebastiano del Piombo.

had more than enough to satisfy his desires, the artist who, when he was poor and in competition with Raphael, never ceased working, would now not trouble to lift a brush and even the youths who came to him to study art found they learned little from his example but good living.

The coolness with Michelangelo had arisen from a misunderstanding (although, once Raphael was dead, the sculptor had in any case found less occasion to praise the painter). Sebastian had discovered a process of preparing stone so that it would take colouring with oils and had prepared the wall of the Sistine Chapel on which Michelangelo was to paint his *Last Judgement* with the necessary incrustation. Unfortunately, though he had the Pope's permission he had omitted to consult Michelangelo, with the result that the artist told him sharply that he would only do it in fresco, that oil-painting was a woman's art fit only for lazy people like Fra Sebastiano and that he had wasted considerable time first by putting the incrustation on and then by the labour of taking it off.

Now, as Pole took his leave of Sebastian, he expressed a hope that the two artists had resolved their differences.

'You should know, my Lord Reynold,' said Sebastian, 'that every artist must of necessity differ with every other artist, however we publicly pretend to admire each other. But I am sure that, when we are all allowed to see *The Last Judgement*, my real admiration will drive me to renew my affection.'

'And will not you yourself give us some new painting to admire?'

'Like all the rest, you reproach me with indolence without understanding the cause of it.'

'Then enlighten me, Sebastian.'

'There are men now living,' the artist replied, 'who can do in two months what used to take me two years. And these do so much that it is just as well that there should be some, like me, who do nothing, so that they may have employment.'

He smiled and blinked contentedly, while Pole searched the

happy, rubicund face and tried to estimate how far he was serious.

'Besides,' said Sebastian, 'I have done my best work and have no mind for men to rejoice at my decline. You must promise me that as soon as you arrive in Viterbo you will visit my *Pietà* to see how splendid I was. Though I hear that the friars have not hung it in the best light.'

After the Cardinal left the Church of St. Francis he continued his walk across Viterbo to the convent of St. Catherine, by the Gate of Truth, where Vittoria Colonna was awaiting him.

They had not seen each other since Pole's appointment to the Patrimony.

'My son and my Lord,' she said, 'I congratulate you on your honour less than myself on my good fortune that you will now always be so near me.'

'A quarter-of-an-hour's walk,' he answered.

'Yet you grieve me by walking in so dangerous a fashion. You gave me your promise to take no risks.'

'I am not likely to be murdered in the streets of my own city,' he replied smilingly. 'I have not had time to give the Viterbese reason to hate me.'

'There are English here,' said Vittoria, 'and I hold you to your promise. You must never move without your guard.'

Pole nodded assent. 'You echo Alvise,' he said. 'But now we have a longer journey than across the way.'

'Where?'

'To Rome.'

He told her that Michelangelo had at last finished his great work, that the scaffolding was down and that *The Last Judgement* was to be seen, appropriately, on All Saints' Eve. 'His message is,' said the Cardinal, 'that he knows our friendship will not fail him and that the Pope is coming back from Bologna so that he himself may say the Mass.'

33

'Then when His Holiness reaches Viterbo,' said Vittoria, 'we will ask that we may join his company. There will be safety there.'

Just before they reached Rome, news was brought to the Pope that disaster had befallen the Emperor. After Charles had sighted Algiers, the sea remained so rough that it was three days before a landing could be attempted. Eventually, during a lull in the storm, 22,000 men were put ashore on a half-submerged spit of land to the east of the city. But at night the storm broke again and lasted till morning. Torrents of rain submerged the camp so that the troops were wading knee-deep in slush and water. In the dawn, the storm rose to hurricane force and in a very short time annihilated before the eyes of the army ten great galleys and more than a hundred transport vessels.

The troops had brought ashore provisions for only two days and they were reduced to gathering what fruit they could from palm trees, eating toads and at last slaughtering their horses for meat. Yet, even so, they all but captured the town. But the storm did not abate and at last Charles bowed to the inevitable.

With tears in his eyes he mourned the loss of 'a great number of noble men who came from all nations to fight the Infidels with me' and he was heard to murmur, again and again, 'Thy will be done'. Indomitably he led his men, weak from lack of food, harassed by the continuous skirmishing of the Moors, until they managed to re-establish communication with what was left of the scattered fleet at Cape Matifou. There they re-embarked, with the Emperor, lest the troops should lose their trust in him, the last on board.

As the Papal party entered Rome, they found a city in panic at the news, dreading some greater catastrophe to come, a foretaste of the end of the world.

34

3
A Vision of Judgement

When, on the Vigil of All Saints, the Pope entered the Sistine Chapel and for the first time saw above the altar Michelangelo's immense fresco of *The Last Judgement*, he prostrated himself in prayer and lay there on the marble floor, beseeching forgiveness for his sins, while the choir of the Vatican sang the introit: 'It is for God's faithful servants to sit in judgement on the nations while He, the Lord their God, reigns for eternity.'

Such was the immediate impact on Paul III of the *terribilità*, the awe-inspiring intensity, of the masterpiece. But mingled with his homage was a sense of gratitude. He, who had waited thirty years for the Triple Crown, had throughout all that time yearned, as he admitted, for that day as the one when, as Pope, he could command Michelangelo's service; and almost his first act on attaining the Papacy had been to appoint him supreme architect, sculptor and painter of the apostolic palace and to commission him to paint *The Last Judgement* on the east wall of the papal chapel. And now his choice had been splendidly justified.

Within a very short time, a chronicler was to write: 'This great painting is sent by God to men to show what can be done when supreme intellects descend upon the earth. Happy indeed is he who has seen this stupendous marvel of our century! Happy

35

and most fortunate is Paul III in that God has consented to confer this triumph under his rule. How much more are his merits enhanced by the artist's skill!' The verdict was to be confirmed throughout the centuries, but Paul realised immediately at first glance that Michelangelo had bestowed on him a kind of immortality and the old Farnese sang the Mass with an overflowing heart.

There had been many renderings, by many artists, of the predicted day when 'the powers of Heaven will be shaken and the Son of Man will come upon the clouds of heaven with great power and glory; and he will send out his angels with a loud blast of the trumpet to gather his elect from the four winds from one end of heaven to the other. They shall separate all things that offend and them which do iniquity and shall cast them in the furnace of fire; but the righteous shall shine forth as the sun in the Kingdom of their Father.'

Michelangelo, however broke with tradition in several ways and in particular by representing all the men and most of the women in complete nakedness. He who had always considered the nude male body as the perfection of created beauty, and thus the only object worthy of great art, had taken this opportunity of demonstrating his mastery and understanding of it.[1]

[1] *The Last Judgement* the visitor now sees in the Sistine is not the fresco as Paul III saw it. A month before Michelangelo's death in 1564 the Council of Trent decreed that certain 'objectionable nudities' should be painted over. The work was entrusted to Daniele da Volterra, who was thereupon named 'Il brachettone' —'the breeches maker'. In 1572 further emendations were made; and later the painting was in danger of being completely destroyed when El Greco offered to replace it by one of his own which would be 'decent and pious and no less well painted'. In 1586, Cesare Nebbia was paid for providing more clothes for the risen, and further overpainting was done in 1626, 1712 and 1762.

Changes other than those in the interests of supposed 'decency' were made. The two lunettes of the Instruments of the Passion were altered and 'by the alteration of the background this portion seems now entirely separated from the

Bodies were shown in every imaginable attitude—lying, sitting, kneeling, standing, walking, climbing; twisting and leaping, soaring and plunging; at full stretch, resting, inert, awakening; flying upward, propelled downward; grappling and striking out, contorted with fear and pain, ecstatic in bliss, straining for beatitude and cringing in torment. Every age was there: boyish beauty, assured maturity, and the achieved nobility of old age. And every angle of vision was included, from the boldest foreshortening to the simplest stance.

Dominating the entire composition, was Christ the Judge, on a cloud ablaze with glory, his right hand upraised in a gesture of omnipotence at that moment of divine decision when the blessed inherit Heaven and the unrepentant are banished to irrevocable Hell.

The nail-prints in his hands and his feet and the wound in his side, to which his left hand points, signal his identity, though his appearance—again defying all tradition—is rather that of an Apollo, beardless, his hair in loose fair curls and his naked, muscular body that of a man in his thirties at his physical best. At his side, beneath the shelter of his upraised arm, sits his mother looking downwards to a slender pink-beaded rosary which is the rope by which an angel is hauling two of the risen to Heaven. Opposite her and nearest to Christ among the surrounding saints is John the Beloved, depicted, not as the aged man of Patmos, but golden-haired, in all the beauty of his youth, gazing raptly at

central group, with which it was in close combination. Still worse is the disappearance of the bank of cloud which separated the upper from the lower section of the picture, whereby the figures of the saints have lost their foothold. In consequence of all these disfigurements and alterations a judgement on the pictorial qualities of the fresco is no longer possible. The distribution of light and shade, calculated by the antemeridian light, which brought all the masses of figures into a clearly organised membership, can now only be guessed at.' (Pastor) As Thode put it: 'The state in which the gigantic work has come down to us is one of such mutilation that it is impossible to form an opinion of its artistic qualities.' Or, as Michelangelo himself said: 'What a crop of fools this work of mine will produce!'

Jesus, whose eyes meet his. Standing behind John is the white-bearded Peter, handing back the Keys of the Kingdom, that of gold and that of iron, whose use, now that the gates of Heaven and Hell are no more, is at an end.

Immediately surrounding Christ, a group of martyrs display the instruments of their deaths as if they were their passports to Heaven—Andrew his cross, Paul the sword which beheaded him, Simon Zelotes the saw with which he was sawn asunder, Bartholomew the knife that flayed him, Lawrence the grid-iron on which he was roasted, Sebastian the arrows that made him their target, Catherine the spiked wheel on which she was broken, Erasmus the windlass which wound his entrails and Blaise the steel comb which tore his flesh. These were they who, in the words of the Apocalypse, 'were slain for the word of God and testimony which they held and who cried : "How long, O Lord, holy and true, dost thou not judge and avenge our blood on them that dwell on earth?" ' And now their justification was accomplished as, below them, the complacent citizens of the world that had persecuted them tumbled to damnation.

For his portrayal of Hell Michelangelo had followed his fellow-Florentine Dante's description of the entrance to the *Inferno*. It was the supreme painter's tribute to the supreme poet but, insofar as it introduced classical legend into Christian prophecy, it formed another break with tradition. There, with the red glow in the background, was Charon the ferryman, having crossed Acheron, the 'joyless river', first of the rivers of Hades, emptying his boat and driving its cargo to the feet of Minos, the cruel judge of Hell with his huge serpent-tail. The painting was an exact illustration of the poetry.

'Then all of them together, sorely weeping, drew to the accursed shore which awaits every man who fears not God. Charon, the demon, with eyes of glowing coal, beckoning collects them all and smites with his oar whoever lingers. As the leaves of autumn fall off one after another, till the branch sees all its spoils upon the ground, so one by one the evil seed of Adam cast themselves on that shore.[2] Minos sits horrific and grins, examines the crimes upon entrance; judges and sends according as he girds himself. I say that, when the ill-born spirit comes before him, it confesses all and that sin-discerner sees what place in Hell is for it, and with his tail makes as many circles round himself as the degrees he will have to descend.'[3]

On Charon's right hand was a cavernous glimpse into Hell's mouth where one man was seen plunging into the fire while a devil, claw-footed and horned, whispered gleefully to another that his time had come to follow him.

Michelangelo had followed Dante also in the main group of the saved who were born before the advent of Christ to earth and whom, by his descent into Hell, he had made free of Heaven. In this vision Dante had questioned Virgil in Limbo: 'Tell me, Master; tell me, Sir', I began, desiring to be assured of that Faith which conquers every error, 'did ever any, by his own merit or others,' go out from hence that afterwards was blessed?' And he,

[2] Poi si ritrasser tutte quante insieme,
  forte piangendo, alla riva malvagia,
  che attende ciascun uom, che Dio non teme.
Caron dimonio, con occhi di bragia
  loro accennanda, tutte le raccoglie;
  batte col remo qualunque s'adagia.
Come d'autunno si levan le foglie
  l'una appresso dell' altra, infin che il ramo
  vede alla terra tutte le sue spoglie:
Similemente il mal seme d'Adamo
  gittansi di quel lito ad una ad una,
  per cenni, come augel per suo richiamo.
                              (Inferno III. 106-117)
[3] Stavvi Minos orribilómente, e ringhia;
  esamina le colpe nell' entrata,
  giudica e manda, secondo che avvinghia.
Dico, che quando l'anima mal nata
  li vien dinanzi, tutta si confessa;
  e quel conoscitor delle peccata
Vede qual loco d'inferno è da essa:
  cignesi colla coda tante volte,
  quantunque gradi vuol che giù sia messa.
                              (Inferno V. 4-12)

understanding my convert speech, replied: 'I was new in this condition when I saw a Mighty One come to us, crowned with the sign of victory. He took away from us the shade of our First Parent, of Abel his son, and that of Noah; of Moses the Legislator and obedient; Abraham the Patriarch: David the King; Israel with his father and his children and with Rachel, for whom he did so much; and many others and made them blessed. . . .'[4]

This group, led by Adam, balancing Peter on the opposite side, showed David, not as the king but as the young shepherd, pointing to a throng of the pre-Christian blessed hastening to the realisation of beatitude.

Islanded on a cloud between Heaven and Hell, the seven angels of the Apocalypse sound their summoning trumpets. With them are the Recording Angels, holding the books containing the names of the saved and damned. The Book of Life is very small; the Book of Death so large and heavy that it needs two to hold it.

Below the angels, on their right, the dead rise from their graves at the blast of the trumpets. Here flesh is seen clothing skeletal bones; here gravestones are lifted as corpses crawl out; here a grinning skull, still in cerements, gazes at one whose flesh has returned to it. At the edge of the fresco presiding over the event,

---

[4] 'Dimmi, maestro mio, dimmi, signore',
   cominciai io, per voler esser certo
   di quella fede che vinci ogni errore;
'Uscicci mai alcuno; o per suo merto,
   o per altrui, che poi fosse beato?'
   E quei, che intese il mio parlar coverto.
Pispose: 'Io era nuovo in questo stato,
   quando ci vidi venire un possente
   con segno di vittoria coronato.
Trasseci l'ombra del primo parente,
   d'Abel suo figlio, e quella di Noè,
   di Moisè Legista, e ubbidiente;
Abraam patriarca, e David re,
   Israel con lo padre, e co'suoi nati,
   e con Rachele, per cui tanto fe',
Ed altri molti; e fecegli beati:
                (Inferno IV 46-61)

is Ezekiel, the prophet who was commanded to say in the Valley of Dry Bones: 'Thus saith the Lord God, Behold, I will cause breath to enter into you and ye shall live; and I will lay sinews upon you and will bring up flesh upon you and cover you with skin and ye shall live and know that I am the Lord. O my people, I will open your graves and cause you to come up out of your graves.'

High above the scene, in the two terminal half-circles of the wall, where Michelangelo when he had painted the ceiling twenty-nine years before[5] had put the Ancestors of Christ, were now the Instruments of the Passion. Bands of naked youths, borne along as if by a tempest of wind, carry, on the one hand, the cross and the crown of thorns, on the other, the pillar at which Christ was scourged, with the hammer for the nails. The remainder of the instruments are distributed, though not prominently, between them.

The depicting of the Instruments of the Passion in a Doom was in accordance with convention. Michelangelo, from his youth in Florence had been familiar with it in a *Last Judgement* painted two centuries earlier by Andrea Orcagna (himself a Florentine sculptor, painter and poet and a devotee of Dante) where winged angels carried them in procession above the throne of God. Their presence was theologically required because, according to the Scriptures, the *Last Judgement* was heralded by the appearance of the Cross—the 'sign of the Son of Man'—in the Heavens.

Yet even here Michelangelo had departed from tradition. The column was, whether by accident or design, more prominent than the cross. This was generally interpreted by the *cognoscenti* as a tribute to Vittoria Colonna, to whom he owed his conversion.

Vittoria herself, overwhelmed as she was by the first sight of

---

[5] The first Mass said in the Chapel after the completion of the ceiling was on All Saints Eve 1512. All Saints Eve, 1541, was obviously chosen, apart from its appropriateness to the theme of the Last Judgement, as an anniversary.

the fresco, soon began to see it in a personal light. Her recognition of herself as Our Lady and Tommaso as Christ made this inevitable. St. Peter was a portrait of the Pope, Paul III, as Adam was of the Emperor, Charles V. On the flayed skin which St. Bartholomew was holding was a rough self-portrait of Michelangelo himself.[6] And Ezekiel was very recognisably Reginald Pole.

She laughed, with the rest of Rome, at the careful portraiture as Minos (who, most unclassically, had been given long ass's ears) of the Papal Master of Ceremonies Biagio da Cesena. He, in the course of his duties, had seen the upper part of the fresco earlier in the year and had described it as 'a stew of nudes' more fitting for a brothel than a chapel. Now when he saw himself exhibited, twitchy-nosed and asinine for posterity, he hastened to the Pope and indignantly demanded that His Holiness should order Michelangelo to alter it. Paul replied that, had it been a mere matter of purgatory, he might have been able to do something but over Hell not even the Papal writ had any authority. And Rome quoted the quip with delight.

But Vittoria was more interested in another aspect of Minos. He had wound his tail round his body twice to indicate that one of his victims was consigned to the second circle of Inferno. Who? The second circle was that of carnal lovers, where Paolo and Francesca were and Tristan and Iseult and Antony and Cleopatra and Paris and Helen and 'great Achilles', the lover of Patroclus, and many other slaves of desire. And Michelangelo? Surely this was his confession of the sin that made him captive, as plain to those who understood his condition as his terrible statue 'Victory' in which he had represented himself as an aged bowed prisoner with his lover of the moment, naked, beautiful and ruthless, straddling his neck?

---

[6] The oft-repeated suggestion that Bartholomew is a portrait of Aretino rests on no firmer basis that his head has a slight resemblance to Titian's portrait of that scurrilous writer—the only one in existence. This seems improbable on several grounds; for one thing because Michelangelo was unlikely to put him among the saints, for another because Aretino's attack on the fresco (which might be called a 'flaying') did not come till some years after the painting was completed.

Sebastian del Piombo, examining *The Last Judgement* as an artist, surrendered less to the greatness of the theme than to the greatness of the painter.

He had, of course, unvoiced reservations. He would have been less than human had he not looked for and found places where the fresco appeared patchy,[7] an effect which would not have occurred had the painting been in oils as he had wished.

And because fresco limited the number of colours that could be used, Michelangelo's intentionally sombre blues and greys and browns lacked, in Sebastian's opinion, something of the brilliance of contrast that oils might have given it.

He noticed, too, that the sculptor, who had proclaimed that painting was related to sculpture as the moon to the sun, had used many of his foreshortenings to gain the effect of relief; and that he had, moreover, dispensed with the painter's conventional aids of geometrical construction and perspective, but had used the walls of the chapel themselves as the completion of the total effect in leading the eye immediately to the focal point of Christ in glory.

But the more Sebastian studied it the more subdued he became. If it was a reproach to his own lassitude to realise that this gigantic picture—over 2000 square feet—was the work of one man in his sixties who had refused to allow any pupil to give him the least help on it, it was also a kind of justification of his idleness in that *The Last Judgement*, for the moment, obliterated all other art. Painting itself had been judged and had been given a new destiny.

To Reginald Pole the fresco was, behind and beyond everything else, an assertion of belief. Here, at Christendom's centre, was now set, tremendous and inescapable, a defence of controverted doctrine. Pole recognised immediately that the core of Michel-

[7] In fresco painting—painting on damp lime wash—the artist applied as much plaster as was needed for one day's work. If the plaster was allowed to stand for longer than a day, a film of lime would form which gave a patchy appearance to the painting.

angelo's interpretation was that salvation was not by faith alone but that works were of paramount importance. The saints, exhibiting the means of their martyrdoms, proclaimed this almost defiantly. It was as if they were asking their Master whether their steadfastness and their agony had been in vain and he was replying by pointing to the wound in his side made by the spear which, after his long torture, had killed him. Because of their actions, issuing from their faith, they were sharers of Christ's passion and, so, inheritors of Heaven.

And everything in the picture, seen by this light, confirmed the doctrine. For saved and damned alike there was individual responsibility leading to reward or punishment, not a capricious predestination where character and action were unrelated to the final reckoning.

The Cardinal paid tribute also to the artist's charity and understanding. In his youth in Florence, Michelangelo had fallen under the spell of Savonarola. Now, in age, though the Friar had long ago been burnt for heresy, the painter could not bring himself to deny that early loyalty and put Savonarola among the damned. Yet neither, in obedience to the Church, could he include him among the saved. So he had painted him, prominent and recognisable, among those just coming out of their graves.

And, in his own portrayal as Ezekiel, Pole, recognised a tribute to his position in the Church at the moment. For the Hebrew prophet in the Valley of Dry Bones was commanded to say, in God's name: 'O my people I have brought you up out of your graves and I shall put my spirit in you and ye shall live and I shall place you in your own land of Israel and ye shall know that I am the Lord who hath spoken.' Now in the Church, the 'Israel of God', the Cardinal, as leader of the movement for reform, was engaged on just such a mission to revivify it.

He prayed that, when he came to render his account at the Judgement, he would not have failed.

4
The Viterbo Society

At Viterbo, it could be observed that Cardinal Pole ruled and Vittoria Colonna reigned. From the Governor's Palace where he lived with his *familia* of about thirty persons, for the most part friends and servants who had been with him for many years, he administered the Patrimony. From the Convent of St. Catherine, where she performed her religious duties, she honoured the *familia* with regular visits and transformed it into a literary circle which, as the 'Viterbo Society', became famous throughout Italy.[1] And because the literature with which it was preoccupied was mainly mystical theology, its members were also dubbed the *Spirituali* and, as such, became an object of suspicion in rigidly orthodox circles.

In a letter to Contarini, Pole wrote: 'The contentment I find in my present station is above anything I could have hoped, yet, if I might judge the future by God's dealings with me in the past, this happy time will not last long, for I have always found that some bitterness or other soon comes to sour the cup of felicity . . .' For the moment, however, things could not be more satisfactory. 'Although a certain amount of business presents itself, it does not

---

[1] This Society an historian has described as 'one of the rarest literary gatherings that ever flourished in Italy, or elsewhere, as befitted a circle of which Vittoria Colonna was queen.'

interfere with my plan of life, but rather improves it. I need not say anything of the administration of justice where I hope I benefit those who stand in need of it. I can keep my morning hours for private study and I try to use them to the best advantage. All government business is deferred till after dinner, except cases which are urgent, but there are not many of these and, when they occur, they do not take up more than an hour or two.

'The rest of the day I spend in good and useful company, especially that of our Messer Marco Antonio Flaminio. I call it useful because, in the evening, Marco Antonio gives me and the greater part of the *familia* a portion of that food that does not perish and in such a manner that I do not remember ever having received greater consolation and edification.'

Marco Antonio Flaminio had been Master of Eloquence and Philosophy at the University of Padua when Pole was studying there. He was also a poet with a passion for classical Rome, (as his adoption of 'Mark Antony') betokened, and like Pole and their mutual friend, Christophe de Longueil, was a member of the brilliant set which gathered round Cardinal Bembo[2] in his villa at Padua. Gradually the poet turned from classics to religion and 'having had a great share in Reginald Pole's friendship, he was the first of the Italians who, at his instance, attempted in Latin metre the divine strength and harmony of the Psalms.'

Religion effected in Flaminio hardly less of a transformation than it had in Vittoria Colonna, whom he knew both as friend and fellow-poet. And, like her, he went to extremes. Leaving Pole's household, where he had lived after his retirement from teaching at the University, he went to Naples, the centre of a revivalist movement which, in many of its aspects, was heretical and, in all, dangerously emotional.

The equivocal mysticism of the Neapolitan school had been epitomised in the little treatise entitled *The Benefits of Christ Crucfiied*. This book Flaminio edited, chiefly improving the

[2] See 'The Marriage made in Blood' pp. 211, 212; 'A Matter of Martyrdom' pp. 52, 53.

46

style but occasionally emending the doctrine. It sold over 40,000 copies and became one of the most discussed books in Italy. Having supervised its publication in Venice, Flaminio returned to Pole's household and became, as far as Vittoria allowed, the lion of the Viterbo Society.

It was, inevitably, *The Benefits* which he made the basis of his homilies in which the Cardinal found so much edification. But it had to be admitted that Pole also found occasion for a considerable amount of argument and gentle correction, since it was his function within the group to insist on a measure of theological precision. This, after all, was the main matter of the European debate and, at any further conference that might be held in succession to Ratisbon, it was on the hard plane of the intellect, not of mystical apprehension or emotional need, that agreement would have to be reached.

No Christians, of any variety, would disagree that their first duty was to love God Who had redeemed them 'by sending His only-begotten Son to suffer death upon the Cross'. Divisions only began with the questions: What is 'God'? How does one 'love' Him? What exactly is meant by 'redemption' and in what way does 'the Cross' redeem? Without the accumulated wisdom of theology in the background (and St. Thomas Aquinas had, after all, written twenty-two difficult volumes to answer the question 'What is God?'), the simple statement had the wrong kind of simplicity. It could mean anything or nothing.

So although, because of their understanding of each other at the deepest level, the members of the Viterbo Society could discuss matters of belief with a freedom which the uninitiated might well have mistaken for the wilder flights of heresy, Pole was scrupulous to ensure, as far as he could, that their own conclusions were never heretical and that they understood which cloudy passages in Flaminio's book could not be safely endorsed.

If the technicalities of theology were thus essential in the study, they were, in the Cardinal's opinion, completely out of place in the pulpit. There the emotion aroused by the Cross should be given the fullest expression. There St. Paul's injunction to preach 'nothing but Christ crucified' should be passionately followed. Unfortunately it was not. One of the main weaknesses of the Church was the aridity of the tedious discourses by which preachers, academically trained but lacking urgency or fervour or even, apparently, any sense of the love of God, were alienating their congregations.

Michelangelo, when the matter was under discussion, was never slow to quote Savonarola's dictum: 'They make such mournful music that not only do they fail to bring dead souls to life, but they go near to killing living ones,' and the layman, Cardinal Bembo, was moved to complain to the Pope: 'What can I hear in a sermon? Nothing but Doctor Subtilis striving with Doctor Angelicus and at last Aristotle coming in as a third to decide the quarrel!'

Pope Paul had taken the matter seriously enough to ask Cardinal Contarini, immediately after his return from Ratisbon, to prepare some *Instructions for Preachers* and Pole, in answer to Contarini's request—for in everything the elder Cardinal preferred to have his English friend's opinion—was trying to formulate his own thoughts on the subject.

The revival of preaching was also a particular care of a new religious order which the Pope had authorised the previous year—the Society of Jesus. The founder was a Spanish nobleman, Inigo Lopéz de Loyola, who was to be known in history as St. Ignatius Loyola. His small stature—he was only just over five feet—predisposed him to self-assertion. 'Up to his twenty-sixth year,' he admitted, 'he was entirely given up to the vanities of the world and especially delighted in martial exercises, being led thereto by an ardent desire of military glory'.[3] But these dreams were

[3] Ignatius always wrote of himself in the third person.

brought to an end by wounds received in a siege and during his long convalescence his thoughts turned to religion. Because his mind had a soldierly disposition, he saw in his imagination two camps, one at Jerusalem, the other at Babylon; the one Christ's, the other Satan's; in the one all that was good, in the other, all that was vicious. Man had a choice of which standard he would serve under; but whoever chose Christ's must be fed with the same food and wear the same garments, must endure the same hardships as 'Christ in His poverty and ignominy'; and according to the measure of his deeds would he be admitted to share in the rewards of His victory.

Gradually Ignatius, in the world again but never again of the world, attracted to himself a few like-minded young men and they all became priests. The military metaphor remained. They called themselves a Company and, as a company was always known by the name of its commander, they took the name of the Company of Jesus. They looked for recruits from 'whoever will serve as a soldier in our society, characterised by the name of Jesus, under God's standard of the Cross, and devote himself to our Lord alone and to His Vicar upon earth.'

Their unquestioning obedience to the Pope personally, as soldiers to a Commander-in-Chief, was emphasised in their vow 'to perform whatever the reigning Pontiff should command them, to go forth into all lands, among Turks, heathens or heretics, wherever he might be pleased to send them, without hesitation or delay, without question, condition or reward'. To make immediacy of action easier, they dispensed with certain customs common to Religious, such as wearing a particular habit or singing the Office together in choir.

Pope Paul, though 'Company' was changed to 'Society', respected their forms of thought and entitled his Bull confirming them *Regimini Militantis Ecclesiae*, 'For the Government of the Fighting Church'. And their head was to be known as 'The General'.

In the beginning the Jesuits were merely mission-priests, preaching and teaching throughout the countryside, with the sermon, inevitably, as their principal weapon. It was, Ignatius ordered, to be short, it was to be centred on Christ crucified, it was to be simple and directed at the ordinary hearer and it was to be judged not by its eloquence but by its effectiveness in obtaining conversions.

When Pole arrived in Viterbo he found one of the Jesuits giving a mission there and greatly regretted his recall to Rome to receive instructions before proceeding to Germany. The Cardinal wrote to Ignatius that his preaching 'had borne much good fruit by the grace of God and his laudable life. My regret at losing him would be the greater did I not know that he has been called to labour elsewhere by the Pope's wish and for the good of the Church. I offer my services to you and to all your company and pray you to remember me in your prayers'.

In the spring, another member of the Society appeared in Viterbo but only on his way to complete his education at the University of Paris. Pedro Ribadaneira was seventeen and had been a page in the household of the Pope's grandson, Cardinal Farnese. The young Jesuit, exploring the city, went up into the pulpit of one of the churches in which there was no one, at the moment, but the sacristan. The sacristan, for a joke, rang the bell. The congregation thus summoned insisted on a sermon and the youth repeated one which he had preached for practice during his novitiate in Rome. So great was its effect that one old man, who had long been contemplating an act of revenge, immediately sought the confessional.

The most famous preacher in Italy, the fifty-four-year-old Bernadino Ochino, was Vicar-General of another new Order, the Capuchins, who had now been in existence for fifteen years. They were Franciscans who had reformed themselves by returning to the primitive rule of the Little Poor Man of Assisi and, as an outward and visible sign of it, wore the original head-dress of the order, a long pointed hood sewn on to the habit.

Ochino, according to the Emperor Charles V who had heard

50

him one Lent in Venice, could preach so as to make the very stones weep. When he appeared in Rome, his sermons were invariably attended by many Cardinals and Pope Paul himself had, on one occasion, planned his itinerary through cities in which he was preaching. Vittoria Colonna was one of Fra Bernadino's most fervent admirers and had induced him to preach in Ferrara while she was visiting it. At Viterbo she remained in constant correspondence with him and, though he was actually in Naples, adulated by the excitable children of Vesuvius, he was regarded as an honoured and influential member of the Viterbo Society.

So also was his intimate friend, Peter Martyr Vermigli, an Augustinian Prior in Naples, who, the same age as Pole, had been with the Cardinal at the University of Padua. As a preacher, Vermigli ranked second only to Ochino, though as a thinker—an Augustinian like Luther—he tended towards heresy.

Surrounded by so many friends, her intellect involved on so many planes, Vittoria Colonna had seldom been so happy. She also acquired a new status. She officially adopted Pole as her son and as his 'second mother' she did her utmost to make up a little for the death of the Countess.

5

Cardinal Caraffa objects

There was one man in particular who was profoundly suspicious of the Viterbo Society—Cardinal Caraffa.[1] This Neapolitan nobleman, who had been Bishop of Chieti since he was eighteen, was now sixty-six. Immensely tall and thin, with the burning eyes of a fanatic, tirelessly energetic and torrentially eloquent, he spoke five languages fluently and was reputed to know the whole of the Bible, Homer and Virgil by heart. This alone would have accounted for his dislike of those he considered *dilettanti*; but his deeper concern was spiritual. As a priest, he had a passionate concern for souls—and the souls not only of *spirituali* and poets and artists but of the great mass of poor, silly sinners. These were 'the little ones' of the Church and the religious imperative that thundered in Caraffa's consciousness was Christ's warning that 'whosoever causeth one of these little ones to stumble, it were better for him that a mill-stone were hanged about his neck and he were drowned in the depths of the sea'.

His was not a temperament which found satisfaction in discussing theological niceties, especially those on the fringe of heresy; and as he watched the exponents of the new doctrines lead the simple stumbling to destruction by believing that they were saved if they thought they were or, worse, that it was im-

[1] For his earlier career see 'A Matter of Martyrdom' pp. 155-57.

material how they behaved since their salvation or damnation was predestined, he became impatient of learned debate. Where Pole's instinct was to try to understand divergencies, to define them in argument and then, by his charity, to bring back to safety the soul in danger of heresy—as he had in the case of Flaminio—Caraffa's was to seek out heretics and punish them. He would not have discussed Flaminio's *The Benefits of Christ Crucified*. He would have burnt it.

In this he revealed himself hardly abreast of the times, but, as the printing-press was no older than himself[2] he might be pardoned for not grasping the full implications of that revolutionary invention. He understood well enough that the dissemination of propaganda by printing accounted for the pace at which heresy was spreading, but he did not immediately see that the centuries-old remedy of burning manuscript works hardly applied to books which could be quickly reprinted.

Consequently when, shortly after the failure of the conference at Ratisbon, the Pope asked Caraffa what remedy he would suggest to counter the spread of heresy, the Cardinal replied unhesitatingly that the only efficient course would be the establishment of a searching inquisition with powers of punishment. Where the Faith was in question, there must be no delay in resorting to vigorous measures; no special consideration must be shown to any prince or prelate; severity should be exercised against any who tried to shelter under the protection of a potentate, but those who admitted they had, for whatever reason, fallen into error must be treated with gentleness and fatherly compassion; yet there must be no toleration of heretics, particularly those who taught predestination. The centre of a tribunal of inquisition, Caraffa continued, must be in Rome. 'As St. Peter,' he said, 'subdued the first heresiarchs in no other place than Rome, so must the successor of Peter destroy all the heresies of the whole world in Rome.'

[2] Roughly speaking. Caxton set up his printing-press in London in 1476, the year of Caraffa's birth.

The Pope was impressed and officially appointed six Cardinals, with Caraffa at their head, as 'Inquisitors general and universal in matters of faith on both sides of the Alps' with powers of delegation. Caraffa, circumventing the delays of official action, immediately hired a house which he made the headquarters of the Inquisition in Rome and appointed his own chaplain, on whom he could rely, as Commissioner-General.

One of the first targets was, inevitably, the Viterbo Society—or, at least, the 'corresponding members,' Vermigli and Ochino who, Caraffa was certain, were secret heretics. He had become suspicious even of Pole and Contarini because they had recently visited Vermigli in his monastry and, after a long discussion, decided to vouch for his orthodoxy to the Pope and, by so doing, had obtained the removal of the interdict prohibiting him from preaching in Naples which had been issued on the denunciation of the Order of Theatines, which Caraffa had founded.

As for Ochino, he, having realised that it was now improbable that he would be raised to the purple to which he considered his fame and talents entitled him, was throwing discretion to the winds and publicly asserting that good works were not necessary to salvation. 'God who made you without your help,' he told sympathetic audiences in Venice, 'will also save you without your help.' After a temporary suspension of his licence to preach by the Papal Nuncio in Venice, he received a courteous letter from the Pope asking him to come to Rome to explain himself more fully . . .

Ochino excused himself on the grounds of the heat and went instead to Verona, the model diocese of the reforming movement ruled by the great bishop Gian Giberti.[3] Here another missive from the Pope arrived, this time a peremptory summons. Giberti urged him to obey it and Ochino set out intending to do so. But

[3] For his career, see 'A Matter of Martyrdom' pp. 151-153.

he changed his mind and instead went to consult Vermigli, who had also been summoned to Rome.

From Montaghi, near Florence, Ochino wrote to Vittoria Colonna: 'I find myself here in no small trouble of mind, having come here with the intention of going to Rome. But, understanding better every day the way things are going, I am most particularly persuaded by Peter Martyr Vermigli not to go because I should have either to deny Christ or to be crucified myself. The first I will not do; the second, yes, but with His grace and when it shall be His will. I have not now the spirit to go voluntarily to death. When God requires me, He will be able to find me anywhere. Christ teaches me to flee by his flight into Egypt and into Samaria; so also does Paul tell me when I am not received in one city to flee into another.

'After this, what more could I do in Italy? On the other hand it is hard for me. I know you will think so. The flesh recoils from leaving everything behind and thinking what will be said. It would have been more than welcome to me to speak with you and to have had your opinion and that of the reverend Monsignor Pole. Pray to Our Lord for me: I desire more than ever to serve Him with His grace. Salute everybody.'

On the next day he fled to Calvin in Geneva. Vermigli followed him two days later.

The sensation in Rome was immense. The 'great light', as Vittoria had once dubbed Ochino, had been put out. More practically, Caraffa had been spectacularly proved right. And in Viterbo there was at first incredulity, followed by dismay and a grief almost beyond bearing at some other news. On the same day that the unmasked heretics had fled, Contarini had died.

His sudden death was due to a fever, though none could be sure how far his will to live had been weakened by the reverses and disappointments of the last two years.

The unexpectedness of the double blow almost prostrated

55

Pole. Vittoria, in her letter of condolence to Contarini's sister wrote, 'The Cardinal of England, your brother's most intimate and truest friend, feels this loss so much that his strong, pious mind, unvanquished by so many troubles, seems to have given itself over to grief more than ever before. It is almost as if the spirit of consolation, which habitually dwells in him, were allowing him thus to suffer as a testimony to the afflictions of the just.'

Pole needed no such lesson. Life had already reiterated it and from the beginning he had never expected any happiness to last. Yet now the one man on whose judgement he was accustomed to rely had been taken from him at the moment when his already formidable self-distrust reached a new peak. Years ago, his elder brother, Montagu, with his courtier's outlook, had told him that his main weaknesses were, in the first place, to assume that all men were as honest as himself and, in the second, to suppose that any man really wanted to be told the truth.

Reginald was being forced to consider whether Montagu had not after all been right. He had perhaps—he still clung desperately to the 'perhaps'—brought Montagu as well as their mother to death by telling Henry VIII the truth when he had asked for it. And now, by his blindness in trusting the honesty of Vermigli and Ochino, he had dangerously compromised the cause of Catholic Reform for which he and Contarini had so long and so devotedly laboured and which now seemed to depend on him alone.

Yet, when his grief for his friend had spent itself a little, he found the courage to act uncompromisingly as Contarini, so he considered, would have had him act. When Caraffa, whom he still considered personally his friend, wrote suggesting that under his Governorship of the Patrimony there had been so far no executions and that it was now Pole's duty to leave argument for action and hunt down heresy with all the rigours of the law, he replied: 'The arguments I choose to make use of to convince the minds of those in error, though they may appear to you to be less vigorous than the case requires, are in reality far more effective.

It is not the countenance armed with terror, but the exposition of truth and, above everything, the compassion of the Christian spirit which draws from misguided men the confession of error in which the heart has a greater share than the tongue.'

Caraffa remained unconvinced. In his secret notes for the Inquisition, he wrote 'Heretics' against the names of Reginald Cardinal Pole and Vittoria Colonna, Marchesa di Pescara, and in the Index of Forbidden Books which he had started to compile he gave first place to Marco Antonio Flaminio's edition of *The Benefits of Christ's Death*.[4]

[4] His eventual suppression of this was successful enough. As Ranke writes: 'Though many thousands of the work were disseminated, not one was suffered to escape; the book entirely disappeared and is no longer to be found. Whole piles of confiscated copies were burnt in Rome'. It could still be found, of course, in other countries and an English translation of it was made six years later by Pole's cousin, Edward Courtenay.

6

Henry at fifty

On the first anniversary of Margaret Pole's execution, 27 May 1542, King Henry VIII had a month left of his fiftieth year. On June 28, the Eve of the Feast of St. Peter and St. Paul, this self-styled 'King, Emperor and Pope in his dominions' would pass into what he considered his old age.

Youth was, indeed, far behind. The nonsuch paragon of thirty years ago in whom, according to the Venetian Ambassador of the day, 'God had combined such corporal and mental beauty as not merely to impress but to astonish all men' was hardly recognisable in the twenty-stone syphilitic[1] hulk which had to be carried from room to room in a sedan chair and hoisted upstairs or on horse-back by machinery.

The flat, fat, florid face accentuated the smallness of the malicious eyes and the cruel lines about the mouth. The nose was coarsened by a swelling the size of an almond. A mass of jewelled rings drew attention to the thickening fingers. The ulcerated legs, despite frequent treatment with an ointment containing ground pearls, were worse than ever and prevented exercise. The erstwhile mighty hunter now sat at a butt to shoot the game the

[1] The question of Henry's syphilis continues to be argued, though it seems to me to have been finally dealt with by Dr. Ove Brinch in his paper *The Medical Problems of Henry VIII*, read to the Danish Medico-Historical Society and published in *Centaurus*, 1958 (Ejner Muskgaard, Copenhagen.)

beaters drove past, accounting on one recent occasion for two hundred deer 'as near as if they had been domestic cattle' and enough young swans to fill two river boats. For edible purposes this was satisfactory enough. The King's gluttony had, if anything, increased and a visitor noticed, exaggeratedly, the inevitable result: 'The King is so fat that such a man has never been seen; three of the biggest men that could be found could get inside his doublet.'

Periodically the pain from the legs was violent enough to endanger the King's sanity, if not his life. When one of the fistulas closed, 'the humours which had no outlet were like to have stiffled him, so that he was some time without speaking, black in the face and in great danger.' He was just recovering from one such attack which had come on in March and he was still in the throes of the depression which was its aftermath. Accentuating it was the gloom which had left him only fitfully since St. Valentine's Day on which festival he had chosen to have executed his fifth wife, the eighteen-year-old Catherine Howard. The reason was that, as her uncle, the Duke of Norfolk, had put it to the French Ambassador, 'she had prostituted herself to seven or eight persons.' That wound to Henry's pride, if not to his affection, showed no signs of healing.

The whole episode had bristled with hurt. The King had proclaimed publicly: 'After so many strange accidents that have befallen my marriages, God has given me a jewel of womanhood and perfect love.' Less than twenty-four hours after this announcement, Thomas Cranmer, the Archbishop of Canterbury, had felt it his duty to point out to his sovereign the kind of girl (she had had her first lover at fourteen) he had in fact married. The King, after stigmatising her as 'abominable, base, carnal, voluptuous and vicious', called for a sword so that he might kill her immediately and then burst into tears. As the chronicle of her lovers was unrolled, he threatened: 'That wicked woman! She never had such delight in her lovers as she shall have torture in her death!'

Yet, in the end, it was she who was merciless. At the block on Tower Green—placed where it had been placed for her cousin, Anne Boleyn, six years earlier—she announced to the crowd assembled to watch her die: 'Long before the King took me, I loved Culpepper. I would rather have had him for a husband than be mistress of the world, but sin blinded me and greed of grandeur.' And her last words were: 'I die a Queen, but I would rather die the wife of Culpepper. God have mercy on my soul!'

Henry had, for the moment, no intention of seeking a sixth wife. For one thing, his new enactment, which made it high treason for such a one to conceal any irregularity in her past, had severely limited the supply of potential candidates at home. And abroad he was not really wanted. The week after Catherine's execution he had, indeed, entertained in one of his palaces the ladies of the court, personally overseeing the arrangement of their rooms, providing them in the evening with 'great and hearty cheer' at a banquet and ordering them all to stay the night. But this was no more than a required bravado.

The King's greatest anxiety was the health of his four-year-old son and heir, Prince Edward. The boy had had a bad attack of malaria and though the doctors cheered Henry by telling him that the Prince's natural strength would probably pull him through, they confided to the French Ambassador that 'the Prince is so fat, unhealthy and overfed that he cannot live long.' Nevertheless Edward rallied and was able to admonish one of the physicians, fussing with over-anxiety: 'Go away, fool'. He was now convalescing in the country at Ashridge in the care of his elder step-sister, the Princess Mary.

Mary was glad to be away from Court. Her father had long ago killed her love for him. She was twenty-six now and, except for the brief spell when Edward's mother, Jane Seymour, was Queen, she had from the age of fifteen lived in misery and despair. Henry had used all that spite and callousness could devise to break her. She had been separated from her mother, dying of cancer, in spite of Catherine of Aragon's heart-broken pleas to be allowed to see her only child before she died. She had been relentlessly ill-treated and threatened, living in daily fear of poisoning, until, in a moment of nervous prostration, she had consented to acknowledge her mother's twenty-seven-year-long marriage to Henry invalid and herself, in consequence, a bastard. This she had been proclaimed, her title of Princess taken from her and herself made a servant of Anne Boleyn's child, Elizabeth.

Yet Mary was not, except in her affection, broken. Not for nothing was she the grand-daughter of Isabella the Catholic. The rigid Spanish honour which she had inherited from her mother held her to her royal duty. She moved about the court, a small, bustling figure with her father's red hair and a mannish voice almost as deep as his, the once-more-acknowledged First Lady. Even her latest step-mother—eight years her junior—could not displace her. Catherine Howard had complained bitterly to Henry that the courtiers paid greater homage to the Princess than to her and, in pique, had tried to deprive her of two of her Maids-of-Honour.

The King, fearing his son's death, was diplomatically bound to treat his daughter royally. She was his one counter in the international marriage-game and he busied himself in trying to arrange a match for her. The Duke of Orléans, Don Luiz of Portugal, Philip 'the Fighter', Palatine of Bavaria, who had defended Vienna against the Turks, the Duke of Milan, who had lost the use of both arms and feet—these, and several more, were canvassed. More importantly, the Emperor himself was seriously considered. Years ago, he had broken his engagement to her to marry Isabella of Portugal and now that Isabella had died of her seventh child there seemed no reason why the original plan should not be carried out.

Mary would have greatly welcomed it, for she had never been able to forget Charles and, in secret touch with him through his ambassador in England, Eustache Chapuys, she had regarded him as her and her mother's champion during the days of her father's most bitter persecution. Yet she had no illusions. Although in Paris that year, 1542, with negotiations for her marriage with the Duke of Orléans at their height, heavy wagers were being offered daily that she would be given to the Emperor, all that Mary said was: 'There is nothing to be got but fine words and while my father lives I shall only be the Lady Mary, the most unhappy lady in Christendom.'

In the background, tacitly ignored but forgotten by no one, was the plan that she should marry her other cousin, Reginald Pole.

It was ten years since Mary had seen him. He had come to Richmond on her sixteenth birthday to take farewell of his mother who was her Governess and also—so she had liked to think—of her. He was then nearly thirty-two (his birthday was a fortnight after hers) and she saw him always in her mind as he had been then, with a new hardness in his eyes and the mouth, not hidden by his short beard, grimly set. Tall, elegant, graceful as a leopard, looking every inch the Plantagenet prince he was, he seemed the embodiment of impersonal courtesy, remote even in crisis. He had refused the Archbishopric of York, her father's offered bribe for complaisance in the putting away of her mother, and, by threatening to denounce the King's policy in Convocation, he had obtained Henry's hurried permission to return to his studies in Italy. As he went, thankfully, into his self-imposed exile, Mary had realised that another chapter of her youth had ended. He would not come back. She would not be his wife, after all.

If her disappointment had not had the edge of Charles's rejection of her in favour of Isabella of Portugal, it was more pervasive, for the figure of Reynold had filled the interim of those seven years of girlhood after the Emperor's defection. The fact that he was a man, a week younger than Charles, was to her no draw-back, for that was the age she had come to imagine her husband. And if she had seen Pole seldom, because of his earlier studies in Italy, it was, even so, oftener than she had seen Charles . . . Moreover, the marriage to Pole had been planned even before her father's diplomatic needs had dictated the choice of the Emperor. When she was in her cradle her mother and Pole's had planned it.

Yet she was not insensible that Reynold's attitude to her was remote. His one unspoken concession to the arrangement was that, though in deacon's orders and a prebendary of Salisbury Cathedral—and, now, a Cardinal—he had no intention of becoming a priest. He was charming to her but, even in her early teens, she had been quite aware that he behaved as an elder brother rather than as a prospective bridegroom. And so, indeed, she had responded. It was only later, in conversations with his mother, her Governess, that she seriously began to think in other terms.

The year after Reginald had left England, the match had suddenly become a matter of international politics and Eustache Chapuys had written to enlist the support of the Emperor: 'Your Majesty should use all means possible to draw to you the son of the Princess's Governess, who is now studying at Padua. The great and singular virtue of Pole is that he is of the King's kindred on both his father's and his mother's side,[2] and to him, according to the opinion of many, the kingdom should belong. The Queen would like to bestow the Princess on him in marriage; and the Princess would not refuse.'

Though Charles, who had at that moment other matters to attend to, made no definite move, the possibility remained until, four years later, the north of England rose in revolt against

[2] His father, Sir Richard Pole, was Henry VII's first cousin; his mother, Margaret Plantagenet, Countess of Salisbury, was first cousin to Henry VII's wife, Elizabeth of York. Henry VIII and Reginald Pole were thus second cousins on both sides.

Henry's ecclesiastical policy and, in the Pilgrimage of Grace, shook the throne. Then, had Henry fallen, Mary married to Pole, thus uniting Plantagenet and Tudor, would have taken the Crown. But it happened far otherwise. The King, by the simple expedient of breaking his pledged word, had triumphed and had celebrated his victory by the destruction of the Plantagenets. The aged Countess of Salisbury was summarily executed after nearly two years' imprisonment in the Tower of a rigour intended to kill her and Henry had cynically used as evidence of her high treason a piece of needlework she had done many years before, anticipating Mary's marriage to Reginald, showing the marigolds of Mary intertwined with the pansies of Pole.

This judicial murder of her beloved Governess, who had been to her not only a second mother but the most potent and enduring influence of her life, had finally turned Mary implacably against her father. As the Princess examined her conscience of this first anniversary of that May morning when Margaret Pole had been hacked to death by a blundering youth of an executioner, Mary knew that she hated Henry. His cruelty to her mother, though she could not forgive it, she could at least understand, because he had been caught in the toils of his overmastering lust for Anne Boleyn, whom Mary—and not Mary alone—considered a witch. His cruelty to herself she forgave freely, because to do so was an imperative of her religion. But the insensate killing of an old woman—a woman whom, in the days of his sanity, Henry himself had described as 'the saintliest woman in England'—was something of another order. That she did not forgive, nor would.

Henry himself had neither scruples nor regrets. His megalomania was absolute. As Martin Luther had put it: 'Squire Harry will be God and does whatever he lusts.'[3] The King's accredited

---

[3] Das Juncker Heintz wil Gott sein und thun was in gelüstet.

omniscience was such that Catherine Howard, when she became Queen, had warned Culpepper not to seek absolution for their adultery. Even the confessional was not safe. He 'should never shrive him of any such things as should pass betwixt him and her, for if he did, surely the King, being supreme head of the church, should hear of it.'

As Henry's acts had the *imprimatur* of divinity, how should he repent of his judgements? Yet, though he could have no contrition for what Christendom called a crime, he was troubled by a certain mundane restriction of his justice. He was unable to reach Reginald Pole. And to have Pole killed had become his obsession of obsessions. He no longer troubled to conceal it. That spring, Eustache Chapuys, writing to the Emperor of the sudden arrival at court of two Italians who were trying to ingratiate themselves with the King by saying that they were on bad terms with the Pope, remarked pertinently: 'They will not get much reward for this if they do not offer to murder Cardinal Pole.'

For six years Henry had been employing assassins of every variety, from his own intimate friends like Sir Francis Bryan, his 'Vicar of Hell', and Sir Thomas Wyatt, his ambassador to France, to hired ruffians in the Low Countries and in Italy and English criminals who had fled overseas to escape the penalty for manslaughter. And still Reginald lived. And not only lived but acted in a way which increased Henry's hatred.

Only six months earlier, when two would-be murderers had been detected by the vigilance of Priuli and, on arrest, had made a full confession, Pole refused to allow them to be put to death, saying that as the injury was only personal to himself, he had the right to spare their lives. In consequence they were merely sent to the galleys—and that 'for no long time'. On another occasion, just after his mother's death, the Cardinal—so it was reported to Henry—had described two other emissaries from England 'as if coming to help a man ardently desirous of rest to divest himself of his raiment'. It was impossible to intimidate a man so spiritually disciplined that he could put into action the precept: 'A Christian must learn to contemplate life with patience and death with desire.'

On that particular morning, the King was celebrating the anniversary of Margaret Pole's death by inaugurating a new effort to remove her son. Henry's old and tried friend, Sir Gregory Casale, a member of a great Bologna family but himself long resident in London, had recommended to the King a certain Alessandro who, he said, was engaging young Englishmen for service in the household of his brother, Francesco, in Italy. Sir Gregory wondered whether the King would care to nominate two candidates. Once in Rome, with unimpeachable *bona fides*, they might be able to render His Majesty the service he so urgently required. Tentatively, he was sending two youths whom he thought might be suitable, though, of course, neither he nor Alessandro had broached the secret matter to them. That was for the King to decide.

Henry, looking at them kneeling before him, found them personable enough. Both were the youngest sons of good families, who were anxious to visit Italy, partly for adventure, partly to acquire those niceties of civilisation which should facilitate advancement when they returned.

'So you wish to leave my dominions?' Henry barked at them.

'Only, sire,' replied the elder who was the more ready of thought and tongue, 'that we may return to them the better able to serve Your Majesty.'

'In what way?'

'In whatever way Your Majesty might wish.'

'You would swear that?'

'By the strongest oath we can,' said the younger. 'By the—'

The elder quickly interrupted him, fearing lest, in his simplicity, his companion might propose a religious oath of a nature which might be unacceptable to Henry's beliefs of the moment.

66

'We should swear "by the King's life",' he said.[4]

Henry smiled approvingly

'In that case,' he said, 'you would not spare those who tried to take the King's life?'

They agreed vehemently but doubted if such traitors really existed.

'There is one in Rome, a cankered serpent of a Cardinal, who for many years has tried to compass my death. Should you meet him, remember your oath.'

'Your Majesty will be pleased to give us fuller instructions?' asked the younger, who had never heard of Pole.

'Sir Gregory will tell you more of the matter,' said the King, 'and I shall not be forgetful of your service when you return.'

Two months later Pole, from Viterbo, wrote to the Cardinal-Archbishop of Bologna: 'A certain Alessandro of Bologna arrived here this morning with two young Englishmen who call themselves Flemish, and as Alessandro's answers varied and he was recognised by some of my people as a messenger of the King of England, I am having him detained while I send word to Your Eminence that enquiry may be made if Messer Francesco Casale has really, as this man says, ordered him to bring these young men for his service. I do not suspect them, as they seem simple youths, but I do suspect that man.'

When Francesco Casale denied all knowledge of Alessandro, except that he had been in his brother's service in England, and said that he had certainly given no commission to recruit men for his household, Pole sent the three under escort to Rome, but took no further proceedings against them.

The news of the failure threw Henry into such a frenzy

[4] Nicander Nucius in his *Second Book of Travels* noted that 'the most binding oath taken by the English is that by which "the King's life" is pledged.'

that for a fortnight Sir Gregory Casale dared not appear at court. When at last he ventured to return, it was to offer a new plan. As individual attempts to destroy Pole seemed so prone to miscarry, why not arrange for a stronger means of attack? Three noted Italian *condottieri*, Ludovico de l'Armi of Bologna, Count Bernard di Bonifacio of Verona and Filippo Pini of Lucca would, Casale was certain, be willing to organise the matter as they would one of their predatory campaigns, provided the King would pay for the soldiers they hired.

Henry assured Sir Gregory that, in a matter of such importance, he was willing to pay to the limit and then and there gave Casale £1,000 from the Privy Purse as a first instalment.

7

The Calling of the Council

When Pope Paul III had made Pole, Contarini and Caraffa Cardinals, he had asked from them and other reforming colleagues an analysis of the prevalent weaknesses of the Church. Pole had actually drawn up and written the Plan for Reforming the Church—*Consilium de Emendanda Ecclesia*—and the others had signed it. It had been presented to the Pope in the spring 1537—five years ago.

The *Consilium* was uncompromising. It laid squarely on the Papacy the blame for the present plight of the Church—on those Popes who, by their laxity or their greed, had encouraged nepotism and simony, who had shown so little care for the welfare of their flock that they had appointed flagrantly unsuitable pastors, and who, apparently regarding the property of the Church as their personal possession, 'imagined that their will was law and that they were the owners instead of the custodians of all benefices.

A drastic reorganisation was needed. Bishoprics must be awarded on the grounds of merit and suitability, not to provide an income for some friend or relative. Benefices must not be given to those who either would not or could not reside in them, and priests who had obviously no vocation or who were inadequately educated and trained should be refused ordination.

"Numberless evils flow from the great carelessness with which the sacred offices are bestowed—contempt for the spiritual state, the neglect of the worship of God."

The scathing attack on abuses—an exhaustive list, including even the dirty and unkempt appearance of some of the clergy in St. Peter's—was a reminder, if anyone needed it, that it was from the same pen as that which had recently castigated Henry VIII. Indeed, in retrospect, Caraffa was inclined to wonder whether, unwittingly, Pole had not done more damage to the Papacy by the *Consilium* than he had to his own family by the *De Unitate*, for a sybaritic Cardinal fearing reform above all things, had surreptitiously sent a copy of the *Consilium* to Luther, who had immediately published a German translation of it, embellished with scurrilous and sarcastic comments, which had rapidly run into thirteen editions.

The document had concluded with the hope that, under Paul III the Church would be cleansed. 'You have taken the name of Paul: you will, we trust, follow the example of St. Paul. He was chosen to carry the name of Christ to the heathen: you, we hope, are chosen to make that almost-forgotten Name live again in the hearts, not only of the heathen, but of some Christians, to heal our disorders, to bring back straying sheep to the fold, and to turn away the anger of God, which we have so deserved.'

Paul—'our good old man', as Contarini was accustomed to call him—was, though genuinely determined on reform, the victim of one besetting sin, nepotism. Almost in spite of himself, the Farnese tended to act as a 'Rennaissance Pope' (which, indeed, he was) and use his office for the aggrandisement of his family. Yet this weakness—which he recognised—in no way lessened his intention to cleanse the Church. He was prepared immediately to initiate the necessary reforms by promulgating them in a Papal Bull, but a majority of the College of Cardinals pointed out that this might fail in its intention because should it be widely disobeyed, as was probable, the Church would be brought into even more disrepute. The only safe and effective way was to summon an Ecumenical Council.

The practical difficulties in the way of such a Council were immense. The first necessity for its meeting was peace in Europe in order that the representatives from all countries could safely attend it. The second was the support of the secular rulers, without whose permission none of the bishops who owed them allegiance would dare to attend it. The third was agreement on where it should be held. With the Emperor and the King of France perpetually at war or, if technically at peace, engaged in a diplomatic struggle in which the one would automatically oppose whatever the other proposed and with the Lutheran states of Germany refusing in any circumstances to acknowledge the Pope's writ, all the conditions were likely to remain indefinitely unfulfilled.

Nevertheless, the Pope, undaunted, had called for a Council to assemble in Mantua in the June of 1537, three months after he had received the *Consilium*. The French and the Germans, as the most economical way of wrecking it, immediately brought pressure to bear on the Duke of Mantua, who complained that his capital had been selected without any prior consultation with him and demanded 1500 foot and 100 horse, to be provided and paid for by the Pope, as a guard for the town.

Pole, on hearing this, had protested: 'This will bring calumny on us and make people say we do not want a free Council.' The Pope agreed and prorogued the meeting till November at some place to be announced later.

Vicenza, in Venetian territory, had been eventually chosen and the date put forward to May 1, 1538. On May 1, only one prelate appeared, the Archbishop of Uppsala who had been driven out of his see by the Lutherans and was now living in Italy. The Council was postponed for the third time and no date was set for its meeting. The project was abandoned for four years, though the Pope's efforts never ceased.

The failure of the conference at Ratisbon, however, revived

the matter as one of great urgency, for now to the reform of ecclesiastical abuses was added the necessity for an authoritative definition of the doctrine of Justification. On July 22, 1542— the day after he had established the Inquisition—Pope Paul reconvened the Council despite the fact that Charles V and Francis I had just started their fourth war. The date of meeting was to be All Saints' Day, November 1; the place, Trent, a town about seventy-five miles north-west of Venice.

The selection of Trent had been made with the greatest care. It was a free city, ruled by its local Prince-Bishop, Cardinal Christoph von Madrutz, and subject to no European sovereign. It was just within the boundaries of the Empire, yet predominantly Italian in population and tradition. Standing, as it were, at the centre of Germany, France and Italy, no place could have been more convenient for an Ecumenical Council. The town itself, surrounded by high mountains known as the Alps of Trent, was large and well-built and, being at the frontier, a trading centre with an ample sufficiency of goods and merchandise. The splendid Romanesque cathedral, whose building had been begun in the twelfth century by one of Trent's crusader-bishops, was easily able to accommodate in session all the delegates, who could find comfortable lodgings in the town. The Papal Legates and their suites, as well as the more important bishops, were offered the personal hospitality of the Prince-Bishop in his great castle which was known, it might be hoped as a good omen, Castello del Buon Consilio.

The choice of the principal Legate, who would preside over the Council, was, in the circumstances, inevitable; and Pole, with Alvise Priuli, his chaplain, Thomas Goldwell and two or three others of the *familia*, in October left Viterbo for his new responsibilities at Trent.

Hardly had they departed than Vittoria Colonna received a long, self-justificatory letter from Ochino with a copy of some of his sermons which had been printed in Geneva. In that city, John Calvin was in the process of making himself a virtual dictator and was enforcing a rule as arbitrary and merciless as his doctrine of predestination. A house-to-house visitation had been established to enquire into the private lives and beliefs of the Genevans, who were also exhorted to spy and report upon each other. Any criticism of the Protestant Reformers was regarded—and punished—as blasphemy. Plays and games were forbidden and even secular reading was discouraged and psalm-singing substituted as an alternative pastime. (One exasperated citizen who, hearing an ass bray, remarked: 'What a fine psalm!' was instantly committed to prison.)

Calvin, after an exhaustive catechising, approved of Ochino to the extent of allowing him a licence to preach to the Italian colony in Geneva; and the ex-Capuchin completed his enfranchisement from his monastic vows by following his conscience and marrying his housekeeper. He settled down to write a Latin play showing the Pope under the direct control of the Devil and followed his theological speculations to their logical conclusions by denying the divinity of Christ.

Pole, before he left Viterbo, had anticipated that Ochino would try to get in touch with Vittoria and, knowing how completely, at an earlier period of her life, she had been under his influence, he was a little apprehensive as to what might happen in his absence. He advised her, should she hear from Ochino, to send the correspondence to Cardinal Cervini in Rome. Marcello Cervini, a year younger than himself, was, now that Contarini was dead, the Cardinal whom Pole trusted most. He managed to combine the inflexibility of Caraffa with the charity of Contarini and his diplomatic skill was such that the Pope had entrusted him with missions to both Charles V and Francis I to try to gain their co-operation in the opening of the Council.

When the packet arrived from Ochino, Vittoria, who considered that he had put himself deliberately 'outside the ark of salvation', sent it immediately to Cervini with a note dated

73

4 December 1542: 'The more I see of the actions of the Cardinal of England, the more I realise how true and sincere a servant of God he is and that I cannot err in following his advice. And because he told me that should letters come to me from Fra Bernadino not to answer them but to let Your Lordship have them, I send you the enclosed letters and little book which have arrived today.'

At Trent that December Pole was suffering from the coldness of its climate. The snow and the wind sweeping from the surrounding mountains made life for him, who always craved the sun, nearly intolerable. His spirits became as depressed as his body when none but a mere handful of lesser prelates arrived in Trent and it became clear that, once more, the Council would have to be postponed. Time was extended because the Emperor had promised to attend in person; but his new war gave him an excuse and the opposition to the Council of the German Lutherans from whom he hoped to get money gave him a reason for absenting himself.

At last, in the spring, the Pope, who was at Bologna, asked Pole to visit him 'in order that he might be better informed of the state of things in Trent.' The Cardinal set out immdiately and advised Paul that, 'if the idea of summoning an Ecumenical Council was persisted in much longer, the only result would be to make the disobedience of Catholics appear the more culpable and increasingly diminish respect for Papal authority. The lesser evil would be to dissolve the assembly immediately, promising a resumption at some later date when Christians might feel more disposed to attend.'

Reluctantly the Pope agreed. The Council, it seemed, was fated not to be.

8

A Visitor from England

Before returning to Viterbo, Pole accompanied the Pope back to Rome and for a few days remained in the apartments which he was accustomed to occupy in the Vatican. Here he was able once more to enjoy the company of Michelangelo. Pope Paul, as a practical answer to the mounting criticisms of *The Last Judgement* in the Sistine Chapel, had ordered the artist to paint two new frescoes on the walls of the new Pauline Chapel which he had just had built for his private use on the south-east side of the Sistine, separated from it by the Sala Regia. The subjects chosen were the Crucifixion of St. Peter and the Conversion of St. Paul.

Michelangelo, who had now been at work for over a year, had already completed the upper part of the Paul fresco, a concourse of naked angels attending a descending Christ, saying 'Saul, Saul, why persecutest thou me?'

The artist was about to begin the figure of the saint himself lying blinded on the ground, his hand to his brow, stunned and dazed by his vision. He showed Pole his drawing of it.

'You are making him an old man?' the Cardinal asked in surprise.

'Yes. Why should I not? Is there anything in Holy Writ against it?'

'Certainly the Bible does not mention his age,' Pole conceded, 'but he is generally thought of as young at Damascus.'

'For me,' said the artist, 'he must be old. The young understand nothing.'

'Yet you were only twenty-four when you sculpted your great *Pietà*.'

'I did most of it when I was twenty-three,' said Michelangelo. 'And that is why I speak as I do. I was paid 450 golden ducats for it. They asked me for the finest work I could do in marble. I fulfilled the bargain. It is a good statue. But it is not a *Pietà*. It is a young woman with a young man lying dead across her knees. Not Our Lady and Our Lord. Only now at seventy do I begin to understand what that means and if God is good to me and gives me a few more years I may yet be able to do a less unworthy *Pietà*.'

The conversation was interrupted by the entrance of Priuli with the news that a visitor from England was asking to see the Cardinal.

'Who is he?'

'How can I tell?' Priuli retorted. 'They give what names they please. All I know is who he says he is. He calls himself Master Geoffrey and says he was a yeoman on one of your father's estates in Buckinghamshire. When you see him—so he says—you will know him.'

'By your tone, Alvise, I can hear you think he's another of the King's murderers.'

'No, Reynold, I make no judgment on that; but at least he is not armed.'

'If he has travelled so, he will be a man of peace.'

'He did not travel so. We took his sword from him. I take responsibility for that. He was loth to give it up, but I told him that as the King sent so many wasps to buzz about you, it was my duty to see they came without their stings.'

When Pole met his visitor, unkempt, travel-stained, with staring eyes and obviously under great mental strain, he did not for a second or two recognise his brother. When he realised it he went towards him with outstretched arms: 'Geoffrey! After so many years. My dear brother!'

But Sir Geoffrey Pole refused the embrace and, instead, fell at Reginald's feet with: 'One brother shouldn't embrace the murderer of another.'

'Boy,' said the Cardinal, reverting to his childhood name for him, 'get up. You didn't kill Harry.'

'With my tongue and this weak body, yes, I did. I must tell you. Before we can talk, I must tell you. Let me, Reynold.'

Priuli said: 'Now there is no danger, Reynold, I will leave you alone.'

Geoffrey, however, attempted to stop him. 'No, not for me. Stay, whoever you are, stay and listen. All England knows. Every Embassy. Why not you?'

'This is my friend, Alvise Priuli,' said the Cardinal. 'He is not ignorant of what has happened.'

'We had the news here at the time,' said Priuli, 'how Lord Montagu was done to death and you, Sir Geoffrey, were tortured to give evidence against him.'

'They put me in the Tower,' Geoffrey broke out, his words tumbling over each other, 'because they said I'd not shown my brother Reynold's letters to the King. Why should I? You know, Reynold, they were simply family things, asking how we were and saying how you fared here.'

The Cardinal nodded assent, as his brother continued: 'But they said it was treason to hold communication with the arch-traitor who'd flaunted a Red Hat against his liege lord—that's you, Reynold—and a double treason not to reveal it. So they arrested me and kept me alone in a dungeon for eight weeks—'

'Eight weeks—'

'To the day. Fifty-six days. That's over a thousand hours, all in suspense. . . . It will be now and now and now; but yet it never comes; and you're almost brave and think they've forgotten. And then they strike. . . . They starved me too.

77

Cromwell was clever—clever as the devil.'

'I know,' said the Cardinal. 'If ever man deserved Hell it was Thomas Cromwell.'

'Then,' continued Geoffrey, 'after too much quiet, no quiet. In one short week, twice tortured, seven inquisitions and sixty different questionings. No rest. No sleep. Only the everlasting "Answer! Answer!" to questions that are traps however answered. And promises of pardon, if I'd give evidence of treason. . . . Twice I tried to kill myself so that I couldn't answer if I would. But they foiled that.'

'But, Geoffrey,' said the Cardinal, 'you told them nothing.'

'But I did, I did. Harry died because of me. It was the pain. And my brains had been broken too, I think. I didn't see all the traps. . . . You believe that, don't you? You'll forgive—'

'Of course, boy. Now, listen to me,' said Reginald, speaking slowly and emphatically. 'Nothing you said brought about our brother's death—or our mother's.'

'Of that, thank God, I am not guilty. But Harry—'

'Nothing you said brought about our brother's death. They'd planned that before you were arrested. Montagu was too near the throne—as I am, now he's dead; as you will be when they kill me.'

'You told them nothing, Sir Geoffrey,' said Priuli, seeing him so near to hysteria and thinking that his intervention might add to the Cardinal's firmness. 'All you said was that you'd heard from your brother; that you'd sent Hugh Holland to warn him of King Henry's assassins; that Lord Montagu had in his library all the works of Sir Thomas More; that—'

'You know I said all this?' said Geoffrey, surprised into practicality.

'You said yourself it's through the Embassies,' said the Cardinal. 'We had news of it here and Alvise is in my confidence. So you see there's nothing for us to learn, nothing to blame you for, nothing to forgive. Only joy that you are here—and safe.'

Sir Geoffrey, however, refused the easy comfort. 'But there

78

is, I tell you. There is, there is, there is. If I'd not spoken Harry'd be alive. They told me that, you see; they told me. They said I'd served them by ridding the state of a traitor and they would pay my price—my freedom. So I'm Judas and Cain . . . and there's no forgiveness.'

'In half-an-hour,' said the Cardinal, 'I have an audience with the Pope. I shall take you with me and ask that you may confess to His Holiness himself. And I have no doubt that he will give you absolution.'

'And before you go, Sir Geoffrey,' said Priuli, 'I crave the honour humbly to give you back your sword.'

In the days that followed, the two brothers had much to say to one another. It was Geoffrey's wish to become a member of the household at Viterbo, but Reginald insisted that, with his wife and children still in England, he was imperilling their safety, if not their lives.

'The King of England's spies are everywhere; though it doesn't need them to give him the news that you're with me. He'll get that through the embassies. And when he does, he'll take revenge by killing the rest of the family. You must leave me. It may be you have already been here too long.'

'Where can I go, Reynold? Not back to England. That's cut off for ever. Am I to wander over the face of the earth . . . like Cain.'

'Get such thoughts out of your head for ever. They should have no place after your absolution. You will go to Liége, where the Bishop will protect you, as he protected me once, against the King of England's murderers. He will see you are housed properly and I will allow you as much as I can spare for your support. You will be safe and will find, please God, some happiness.'

'An exile.'

'As I am.'

'But you have always loved Italy. I was only a boy when you first came here and when you came back to visit us, you were always longing for Venice. It's Italy that's your home.'

'No,' said the Cardinal quickly, as if rebutting an accusation which was true and needed prompt and emphatic denial, 'only my second home.'

'What do you miss most?'

'You'll laugh at me if I tell you.'

'No.'

'The English trees.'

'*Trees?*'

Reginald nodded. He saw in his mind the beech and hazel in the woods of his father's Buckinghamshire estates; the great oaks and elms near Canterbury; he smelt the scent of the limes in Oxford and the apple-trees in the orchards of Stourton Castle, where he was born and, at all corners of his memory, what he considered the queen of trees, the English ash. They overwhelmed the sharp cypresses and the harsh ilex of Rome. But he doubted whether Geoffrey would understand even if he tried to explain and merely said in a clipped voice: 'Yes; in the matter of trees I am not yet free of worldly affections.'

'Sometimes,' said his brother, 'I do not understand you at all, Reynold.'

'I will instruct you, boy, when we get back to England.'

'You're certain we shall go home.'

'Yes.'

'When?'

'In God's time.'

In diplomatic circles, there were rumours that Pole's return to England would not be long delayed. King Henry had decided to participate in the war. The Emperor, considering that the French king was allied with the Turk, saw no reason why he should not seek the help of the heretic and had consequently invited Henry to join with him in the conquest of France. The plan, according so well with traditional English policy, appealed to Henry, though one of his courtiers commented that this would be the fourth 'voyage' of the King into France 'and yet he has not a foot more ground in that kingdom than he had forty years before.'

The strategy envisaged was simple. Charles would advance through Champagne, Henry through Picardy and they would meet under the walls of Paris to deliver the *coup-de-grâce*. What was not so simple—and what in fact took six months to accomplish—was a formula for the treaty. Charles, regarding himself as the unbending champion of the Catholic Church, could not allow Henry to describe himself either as 'Supreme Head of the Church' or as 'Defender of the Faith'. Both titles the King stubbornly refused to have excluded from the document until practical matters became so urgent that compromise was essential and it was agreed to style him 'King of England etc.'

Once England had entered the war, the name of Reginald Pole was inevitably raised. Chapuys, Charles's ambassador in London, wrote to his master that the French were unlikely to invade the south-west of England as he feared 'unless they should have Cardinal Pole with them, by whose means affairs in this realm might be altered,' while the English agent in Venice reported that not only was Pole going into France but that 'the Pope was sending with him one of his chief captains at the head of 6000 men to be employed in an invasion.'

The rumour was quite unfounded, though the new situation had to be discussed at the Vatican and Pole was kept in Rome for consultation for some weeks after he had planned to return to Viterbo. Even his monumental patience started to wear thin and when, in the middle of July, he received a letter from Vittoria Colonna, he asked the Pope for permission to return to his duties in the Patrimony.

Vittoria had been very ill. 'Our Lord knows that I desire extremely to speak to you,' she wrote to her 'son', 'for no

81

stronger reason than that I see in you an order of mind, which the mind alone can appreciate, which always leads me on to such a plenitude of light that I no longer feel my own misery. If, by His grace, I am hastening towards Him, all the more do I need to speak to you, not out of anxiety of the Divine love, it is as if I spoke with an intimate friend of the Bridegroom sent to prepare and call me to Him, to fortify and console me. So may you quickly and in good health be here, though your travelling in these times gives me anxiety. May God guard you, as I pray, and our coming be joyful and secure.

'I say little of myself, for I cannot say I am quite well, in order not to contradict the doctors; nor can I say that I am not well; so I will say only that I am very much better, most of all in the consolation of your coming, which would be supreme, did I not fear the journey. The goodness of God protect you.'

Priuli, fearing that the recent visit of Geoffrey would precipitate more intensive attempts at assassination even on the comparatively short road from Rome to Viterbo, arranged for a special guard; but there was no attempt made to disturb the peace of an uneventful journey. In Viterbo, Pole went immediately to St. Catherine's Convent and, to his relief, found Vittoria out of danger.

In England, that week, in the chapel at Hampton Court, Henry VIII privately married his sixth wife, an already twice-married gentlewoman of 31, Katherine Parr, tiny, red-headed, with evasive eyes and a prim yet sensual mouth. She had been married at the age of 13 to an elderly nobleman who, within two years, left her a wealthy widow. She then married—as his third wife—another elderly peer who, at the beginning of 1543, left her even wealthier one. She had fallen in love with the lecherous, exuberant, ambitious Thomas Seymour, the King's brother-in-law, Prince Edward's younger uncle and when the King informed her that her destiny was royal as he wanted her for himself, she gave an involuntary gasp of horror and said: 'It would be better to be your mistress than your wife.'

Nevertheless Henry persisted and she, assuming that he had not long to live and that Seymour would still be available after his death, capitulated. She was encouraged in her decision by the Archbishop of Canterbury, who, knowing her Lutheran leanings, considered that she might, as Queen, be able to influence Henry in that direction. Remarking that 'God is a marvellous man' she sacrificed her own inclinations to Him—and Cranmer—and allowed herself to be married to Henry in the presence of the Princesses Mary and Elizabeth.

She had once as a child remarked to her mother, when told to do some sewing: 'My hands are ordained to touch crowns and sceptres, not needles and spindles.' She was now, in spite of obvious drawbacks, on the whole delighted that she had been right.

9

The Road to Trent

The short unnecessary war was not a success, except for Henry VIII. As those who knew him expected, he broke his word for his own advantage and while the Emperor was, according to their compact, advancing towards Paris, Henry refused to go further than Boulogne, which he besieged. On September 14, 1544, it surrendered to him, the French marching out with all the honours of war. Four days later, Charles V and Francis I made peace, without troubling to inform Henry.

Neither the Emperor nor the French King had much heart for a fight. Charles, ill and racked with gout, had found himself, after his dash through Champagne, isolated with a mercenary army and, because of his ally's defection, without money and provisions. Francis lay sick near Paris, remonstrating with God: 'Thou hast made me pay dearly for this crown which I supposed I had received as a gift at Thy hands' and saying that he would place no obstacle in the Emperor's way. His one desire was to die in St. Denis by the tombs of his ancestors. In this mood of depression, he remembered that he was the 'Most Christian King' and not only renounced the Turk, but returned to the active service of the Church. By the secret clauses of the Treaty of Crépy, he agreed to help the Emperor in making possible the meeting of the Council of Trent and in endeavouring, by peaceful persuasion, to bring the Lutherans back into the Church so that they could attend it. If such persuasion was unavailing, he would aid Charles in war against them. He would also do his best to restore the Faith in Geneva by returning what had become 'Calvin's city' to its proper overlord, the Duke of Savoy.

In fulfilling these new obligations and officially requesting the Pope to re-open the Council, the French King made it possible for Paul to reconvene Trent with, at last, some hope of success. To allow ample time for preparation, the date chosen was March 15, 1545—the fourth Sunday in Lent, known as *Laetare*, from the first word of the introit: 'Rejoice, Jerusalem: gather together all you who love her; rejoice and be glad, you that were in sadness; that you may exult and be suckled plentifully with the consolations she offers you.' It was hoped that it would be appropriate.

Unfortunately at the moment when the reunion of Christendom seemed once more within grasp, the Lutherans made it unequivocally clear that nothing would induce them to attend an Ecumenical Council. Lest any doubts should remain in any quarter, Luther issued a pamphlet entitled *Against the Popedom of Rome, instituted by the Devil,* addressing Pope Paul as 'Most Hellish Father' and calling on all good Christians 'with all available weapons to attack the Pope, Cardinals and the whole ulcer of the Roman Sodom and to wash their hands in their blood. This devilish Popery is the supreme evil on earth, the one is which all the devils combine together.'

In place of a Council summoned by the Pope in a place of his choosing there should be 'a free Christian Council in some German Protestant city like Worms or Spires whose object was 'to overthrow the Man of Sin, the Antichrist, the Pope, who has set himself in the temple of God' and to expound the doctrine of Justification by Faith Alone.[1]

---

[1] It was the more important to Luther that there should be no external criticism, since he had inserted the word 'alone' in his vernacular translation of the New Testament. It has no place in the original Biblical text of the *Epistle to the*

The Emperor was caught in a continuing dilemma. Had Charles been a private citizen, he might well have been the model Catholic layman of his times. His cast of thought, his personal piety, his good works, his informed conscience were typical of the devout life of the day. But he was also the supreme ruler of most of Europe, including among his subjects the fanatical Catholics of Spain, the equally fanatical Protestants of Germany and the great mass of indifferents who could be stirred up on either side by persuasive propaganda. And his duty, for which he considered himself answerable to God, was to govern them for their good.

So now, though he allowed himself to stigmatize Luther's latest outburst as 'a raging piece of defamation' (which was his personal *cri de cœur*), he also came to Worms (which was his political necessity) to make a last endeavour to obtain Protestant assent for the conclusions to be reached at Trent. He was still far from well, with his gouty arm in a sling, and his failure was almost a foregone conclusion; yet he was not altogether prepared for seeing himself lampooned as the puppet of the Devil, especially as the Pope was also reproaching him for having, by his temporising action, once more delayed the meeting of the Council.

Meanwhile, though it now seemed certain that *Laetare* Sunday would be too early a date for the reassembly at Trent, the Papal Legates continued their preparations. Of the original three, only Pole was retained. Paul considered his presence essential for several reasons. Primarily, he represented, uniquely, the party of the Reform; but he was also unchallenged as a theologian. His defence of the unity of the Church, in the famous and ill-fated letter to Henry VIII; his understanding of the subtleties

Romans. This, like the deliberate mistranslations of Tyndale (see *A Matter of Martyrdom* pp. 128-130), explains the enthusiasm of the anti-Catholic forces, then and later, for the vernacular.

86

of the key-doctrine of Justification, as shown in his co-operation with Contarini in the arguments at Ratisbon; his historical knowledge of the ways of previous Councils—Trent would be the nineteenth Ecumenical Council of the Church—which he was now epitomising, at the Pope's request, in a lengthy essay in the form of eighty-six questions and answers—all were contributory reasons for the choice of him. And, finally, there was both his previous experience of Trent and the fund of goodwill which the charm of his personality had drawn from the inhabitants, from the Prince-Bishop himself to the lowliest of the ecclesiastical officials.

The two Cardinals chosen to accompany him this time were Cervini and del Monte,[2] who were appointed for quite different reasons. Cervini, the saint-like friend to whom Reginald had entrusted Vittoria during his previous absence at Trent, was indeed a reformer no less ardent than Pole himself; but the Pope's motive in sending him to Trent was a more personal one. Cervini had been trained as the mentor and adviser of the Pope's grandson and namesake, the twenty-five-year-old Allessandro Farnese who at the age of fourteen had been made a Cardinal, Vice-Chancellor of the Holy Roman Church, Governor of Tivoli, Archpriest of Santa Maria Maggiore, Archpriest of St. Peter's, Administrator of Jaen in Spain, of Vizieu in Portugal, of Wurzburg in Germany and of Avignon in France. At sixteen, he was additionally made Bishop of Monreale in Sicily.

If Paul was at times uneasily aware that the boy was a living advertisement of his besetting sin of nepotism, he determined at least to make him eventually worthy of his high offices and for this purpose had appointed Cervini to be perpetually at his side. The result had been satisfactory and young Farnese was already noted for his zeal in the service of the poor, for his natural administrative ability—at 21 he undertook the entire organisation of Avignon during an appalling plague—and for

[2] Both eventually became popes, del Monte as Julius III and Cervini as Marcelius II. On the latter's death in 1555, Caraffa succeeded as Paul IV.

his own learning and his patronage of art and literature. 'There is nothing more despicable,' he used to say, 'than a cowardly soldier or an ignorant priest.' The influence of Cervini on him had made him wholeheartedly behind the reforms; but the old Pope was shrewd enough to guess that, as influence is apt to be reciprocal, Cervini might equally be trusted to safeguard the interests of the Farnese.

The third legate was a man of a very different stamp from either Pole or Cervini. He was nearing sixty—their senior by thirteen years—and the greatest canonist in Rome. Ciocchi del Monte was the son of a famous Roman jurist and had studied jurisprudence at Perugia and Siena. Brought up by his uncle, a Cardinal, he had at an early age been made Chamberlain to Pope Julius II and had continued in favour with Pope Clement VII. But here the closeness had had unexpected and unfortunate results.

At the sack of Rome, del Monte (who was forty at the time) had been one of the hostages for payment of the Pope's ransom. As, in spite of his efforts, Clement had been unable to raise the full sum by the time appointed, del Monte and the other hostages had been seized by the barbarous mercenaries and led out in chains to the gallows erected in the Campo de' Fiori and prepared for death. At the last moment, they had been reprieved and taken back to prison. The grim farce appealed to the mercenaries, who repeated it two days later; but this time the reprieve was accompanied by the warning that a third performance would proceed to its mortal end. The hostages avoided this at the last moment by making their keepers drunk and so escaping: but del Monte never forgot the agony and suspense of those terrible days and always celebrated St. Andrew's Day, the anniversary of the escape, with more devotion than he accorded to any other feast of the Church.

Not that del Monte, who was a lawyer first and last, had any particular interest in religion; and of theology he knew practically nothing. But as a canonist he was invaluable. His tempera-

88

ment, erratic, excitable, subject to bursts of great anger and periods of immovable depression, bore the scars of his dominating experience. His appearance was such that artists found difficulty in painting his portrait, for his face, framed in a long, grey beard, gave the impression of a coarse peasant—a comparison enforced by his perpetual indulgence in his favourite dish of onions in any form, which he had supplied to him in enormous quantities from Gaeta. His manners also were reminiscent of the peasantry.

Yet he was by no means untouched by the Renaissance. He was fond of music, delighted in staging plays and, as far as his circumstances allowed him, was a patron of architecture. His most alarming idiosyncrasy was a passion for practical jokes which annoyed even his closest friends. And, not alone among the Cardinals, he preferred boys to women.

On Ash Wednesday, a week before the date set for the departure of the Legates, Cardinal Ardinghelli, head of the Papal secret service, laid before the Pope details of the plot to murder Pole. The three *condottieri*, Ludovico de l'Armi, Count Bernard di Bonifacio and Filippo Pini, had received urgent instructions from Henry VIII, by one of his Privy Chamber sent from England specially for that purpose, that the assassination was to take place somewhere on the road to Trent or, failing that, in Trent itself.

By this timing, the English King would be able to turn an act of personal hatred into a spectacular blow for Protestantism. Though still assiduously burning heretics at home, Henry found his sympathies gradually inclining, under the influence of his sixth wife, to the Lutherans and he had approved the recent Protestant assertion at the Diet of Worms that 'they had England, Denmark, Sweden, Norway and most of Germany with them'. If the murder of Pole, which would inevitably postpone the opening session of Trent, could alter the course of theological diplomacy, Henry would be delighted to have achieved so inexpensive a triumph.

The Pope, on being made aware of the situation, ordered immediate counter-measures. In the first place, Pole must not travel with Cervini and del Monte, though he must appear to and a substitute must go, wearing his clothes. Secondly, Pole must be given a guard of at least twenty-five picked soldiers, who were to be responsible for his safety even in Rome, to which Bonifacio was reported to be travelling with some of his captains. Thirdly, every effort must be made to arrest de l'Armi, who was the principal—and by far the most dangerous—of the murderers. He was at the moment domiciled in Venice, ostensibly recruiting soldiers for the English army, but, as a native of Bologna, he was legally the Pope's subject, and, so, under his jurisdiction.

Ludovico de l'Armi, (whose mother was a sister of that Cardinal Campeggio who, with Wolsey, had presided over the 'trial' of Catherine of Aragon) had spent much of his early life in France, where he had sold his sword indifferently to Francis I or Charles V. Having obtained a taste less for fighting than for plundering, he came back to Italy to organise one of those 'bands' which plagued the countryside.[3] To cite him to appear now before a Papal Court was, as everyone realised, a farcical waste of time; and, though it was done in order that the ordinary processes of law should not be neglected, a more effective measure was taken. His father, a law-abiding citizen of Bologna, was summoned to Rome as a surety, in the sum of 50,000 crowns, for Ludovico's good behaviour. At the same time the Signory of Venice was, through ordinary diplomatic channels, informed of de l'Armi's real purpose and was requested to expel him from their boundaries.

Neither move met with any success. Ludovico's filial instincts were not prominent and the Venetians were so proud of their

[3] He was eventually captured and executed two years later for a variety of proved crimes.

liberal way of life which, if possible, interfered with nobody, not even murderers, that they refused to disturb him and explained that they wished to maintain good relations with the King of England. The English Agent in Venice, writing to Henry, predicted rightly that any attempts to impede de l'Armi would fail; but when he added that 'Pole must go in perpetual fear' he was very wide of the mark.

Pole was so little afraid that it needed the Pope's absolute command for him to agree to the travelling precautions. He was particularly disturbed that one of his servants should have to run the risk of impersonating him.

'Set your mind at ease,' said del Monte. 'We will see that he's protected as if he were you yourself.'

'I thank you for that,' Pole answered, 'but if such is the case why should it not be me myself?'

Cervini said impatiently: 'It seems that whatever we may do there is some risk. Your life is too precious to be exposed to it.'

'My life is of no more account than that of any of my servants,' Pole answered quietly.

No one doubted that he meant it, but Cervini continued: 'My lord, you must forgive me if I speak my mind on this. You know it is spoken in all charity.'

Pole nodded assent.

'God, so I see it, has given you a double burden. You are the Cardinal of England. The faith of your country's in your care when the time comes. That is responsibility enough. More, you may be king of it.'

Pole shrugged.

'I know,' said Cervini. 'I set no store by that, though others do and it's to be reckoned with. Your cousin Henry reckons with it bloodily enough. And you're the Pope's Legate with more knowledge and experience than del Monte or I have.'

'Even if I granted that,' said Pole, 'it does not seem to me of importance. I could easily be replaced at Trent. What is your drift in this?'

'The drift, my lord,' replied Cervini, 'is this. Because you are what you are, you cannot say "I am as other men" and ape the largesse of their obscurity.'

'I thank God,' Pole answered, 'that I have overcome any ambition to be other than the lowliest; though I have still far to go on the road to humility.'

This was, he knew, no answer and Cervini continued relentlessly: 'This—forgive me, my lord, if I should hurt you, but I speak as a priest—is nearer pride than humility.'

The shaft went home. This was Pole's own constant teaching, —'Humility is to accept what you are' he had reiterated, especially to Vittoria and Michelangelo—turned against himself. But in applying it to the inner things of the soul or the creative gifts of the intellect, he had omitted to give due weight to the accidents of position and power. And they, too, must be accepted, though there was, indeed, a case for considering the categories totally different. . . . That might make an interesting discussion at the Viterbo Society. . . . But, at the moment, he was not inclined to argue.

'I am indebted to Your Lordship,' he said to Cervini, 'and will be instructed by you.'

Cervini and del Monte left Rome for Trent on February 24 and arrived at Bologna on March 5. 'Not to delay our journey,' they wrote to Pole, 'we did not go by Siena or Florence, though we sent a man to learn from friends there if anything further is known about your affairs. Ludovico is said to be still in Venice and Bonifacio is still somewhere in the neighbourhood of Rome. We hope you will soon be able to be with us to share our burden: indeed, the nearer we approach Trent the more we desire your presence.'

They arrived there on Friday, March 13, two days before *Laetare* Sunday (though it was clear that the date of the Council would have to be put back again), and immediately wrote to their absent colleague: 'We have both been diligent on the way to learn the movements of Ludovico and Bonifacio, but have got no further light on them except here from the Cardinal of Trent who tells us that Ludovico was in this city for two days shortly before our arrival.'

But, because they were concerned with a matter of life and death, they naturally did not trouble to report a trivial and irrelevant incident on the way.

As they were passing through Verona, they found the crowds which were in the streets to see them being entertained by a variety of street-performers and side-shows. Among them was a performing ape. The animal, by some carelessness on the part of its keeper whose attention was for the moment riveted by the display of ecclesiastical magnificence, broke loose. Most of those near it scattered, screaming; but a ten-year-old boy stood his ground, apparently quite unconcerned, and, when the ape ambled up to him, pawing him in curiosity, talked to it as if it were human and gave the keeper the opportunity of an easy re-capture.

Amid the plaudits of the crowd, del Monte dismounted and called the boy to him.

'You are a brave lad,' said the Cardinal. 'What is your name?'

'Innocent, Your Highness.'

He managed to invest the name with overtones which made del Monte look more carefully at him. The street-arab stared back at the Cardinal with a depth of meaning in his sultry blue eyes. In such matters there is neither age nor status.

'Is your father here?' asked del Monte.

'I don't know who my father is, Eminence. Even my mother doesn't know.'

That, reflected del Monte, was fortunate. He could get his brother Baldovino, who was amenable in such matters, to adopt the boy.

'You are a brave boy,' said del Monte again, this time more loudly so that everyone might hear; 'you showed no fear.'

'I like apes,' said Innocent.

'What would you say if I bought the ape and made you keeper of it?'

'I should do my best to give Your Highness every satisfaction. May I kiss Your Highness's hand?'

The Cardinal held his hand out. The crowd saw nothing but the edifying spectacle of a Prince of the Church charitably condescending to a child. Only del Monte, as the boy's loose, thick lips slobbered on his hand, was aware of the tongue-tip and even he did not realise that, at that moment, he had sold himself into slavery.

At last, at the beginning of Passion Week, Pole obtained the Pope's reluctant permission to set out for Trent sometime after Easter—reluctant because Paul, although realising the necessity of it, was still hoping that safety would be further ensured by the arrest of de l'Armi by the Venetian authorities.

Paul had never ceased to hold himself responsible, at least in part, for Pole's danger. His insistence, eight years ago, in creating him Cardinal despite the Englishman's vehement pleas that such a step would finally alienate King Henry VIII had marked the beginning of the assassination attempts. After the arrest of Pole's family, the Pope had delayed an audience with him because, as he admitted, he could not bear to look him in the face; and when, shortly afterwards, he had sent him on a mission to Charles V, he had insisted that the Cardinal make the journey dressed as a layman, with very few attendants, to mislead those lying in wait for him. Of all things, Paul did not want Pole's blood on his hands. So now, in allowing him to leave Rome and the safety of his guard, the Pope insisted that the Cardinal should take similar precautions. He was to wear lay dress; he was to travel not by the direct route through Tuscany which Cervini and del Monte had taken but circuitously, remaining as long as possible in papal territory and avoiding Venice. He might, if he wished, spend Easter in Viterbo, but he must be accompanied thither by his guard.

Once the Easter ceremonies were over, Pole, in Viterbo, prepared for the journey to the north. Many of the *familia* clamoured to be allowed to share the danger but in the end the choice was narrowed—apart from four personal servants—to the three who refused in any circumstances to leave him, Priuli, Flaminio and Thomas Goldwell. At their request he cut almost to nothing that luxuriant beard which distinguished him in any company and which Sebastian del Piombo, when painting his portrait, had mockingly described as 'almost a landscape'. They decided that he should travel as a silk-merchant. Priuli took charge of a sumpter-mule, laden with bales; and the rarest of stuffs was used to make a doublet for Pole himself that he might the more convincingly assume the appearance of one exhibiting the best of his wares on his own person.

A fortnight after Easter they set out after a sad farewell to Vittoria Colonna whose anxiety, though she tried to master it so that it should not disquiet her 'son', was piteous. Hardly had they gone than she wrote to Cardinal Morone, who was still in Bologna and would see Pole on his arrival there, urging him to exhort Pole to take the utmost care and to impress on Priuli and Flaminio to keep the most severe guard over him, remembering that God had chosen them, out of all his other friends, to look after him.

Three days later she wrote again, considering Pole's legation to the Council as that of one sent by God, like Christ Himself, to unite Jews and Gentiles in the bond of unity and peace. All Pole's difficulties and tribulations, she said, were witnesses to his inflexible faith. 'Every opposition the world can make to his work only serves in the end to kindle the flame of his divine charity. I am only anxious that he may keep well and safe and that God will leave him with us for a long time.' She added a warning postscript: 'I must tell you that I have never feared Ludovico as much as that Bonifacio.'

Michelangelo, realising how desolate she would feel in Pole's absence, wrote, apologising that he himself was unable to leave Rome, but suggesting that frequent letters might be welcome. But Vittoria, suspecting that her illness, though temporarily stayed, was mortal, desired only the presence of the man who had saved her not of the man she had saved. 'Noble Messer Michelangelo,' she wrote in reply, 'if we keep on writing to each other, I should have to neglect the chapel of St. Catherine here and forego meeting with the company of sisters at the appointed time; while you would have to interrupt your work in the Pauline Chapel and could not before daybreak discourse with your pictures which speak to you no less naturally than the living creatures that surround me. Thus we should both offend, I against the Sisters, you against Christ's Vicar.

'Since I know your steadfast friendship for me and your devotion rooted in the bonds of Christianity, I think we need bear no witness by letter. I shall pray God to let me meet you again, his image in your soul, as you have represented him in the drawing you have given me of *The Woman of Samaria at the Well*.'

In fearing Bonifacio rather than Ludovico, Vittoria's instinct was correct. Essentially de l'Armi preferred the wide sweep of a military campaign, with its limitless opportunities for plunder, to so limited an objective as he was now being paid to undertake— one, moreover, which was attended by legal danger to his family. Count Bernard di Bonifacio on the other hand, saw in the murder of Pole an opportunity for fame. He was a petty nobleman who, perpetually discontented with what he considered the lowliness of his lot, was obsessed with aggrandising himself. As it seemed impossible, among his powerful neighbours, to do so by fair means, he had resorted to foul. With his associates—

his young cousin, Count Orlando di San Bonifacio, and three captains from Reggio; Zanelletto, Bottoni and Bellona—he had organised sufficient armed robberies to make him rich enough to excite envy. de l'Armi, as a soldier, would kill without a second thought, but Bonifacio considered it impolitic. Except in this case, where, should he succeed, he would win an imperishable name.

The Cardinal and his friends came face to face with Bonifacio and his captains shortly after they had left Viterbo and were travelling across the great Etruscan plain to Orvieto. At one of the bridges over the river Paglia, the bandits, having sighted them earlier, rode up to obstruct their crossing.

With excessive and ironical courtesy, the two Counts demanded a toll.

'I was not aware,' said Pole, 'that the Governor of the Patrimony so taxed his subjects.'

Priuli, regretting that he had not spoken first and fearing what Reginald might be tempted to say next, interposed quickly, indicating the captains: 'I see, Excellency, that you have brought with you good and full authority to collect the toll.'

Bonifacio beckoned to the captains to come nearer. 'They are indeed,' he said, 'skilled in such service.'

Flaminio, whose one desire was to get away as quickly as possible, asked: 'And how much is the toll?'

'For merchants such as you,' said Bonifacio, 'the impost is accommodated to their means. For some it is much; for others little.'

'And how is it determined?' asked Pole.

'Each man is his own assessor.'

'That is a strange rule.'

'They choose how much merchandise they carry, much or little. We take it all.' He examined the stuffs on the mule. 'You have made a satisfactory payment. Zanelletto,' he called, 'I put the mule in your charge.'

Priuli, who thought it would appear suspicious if they made

97

no protest at all, said: 'When we next see the Governor, we shall report our payment to him.'

'You know the Cardinal?'

Flaminio said: 'We have in the past provided him with silks.'

'Is he in Viterbo now?'

'He was,' said Pole, 'just before we left.'

'You are certain of this? My information was that he is on the way to Bologna.'

'I spoke to him yesterday in Viterbo,' said Priuli. 'That is all I can say. Have you some business with him?'

'It may be,' said Bonifacio. 'And you say he is a customer for silks?'

Flaminio nodded.

'Then you have paid the right toll,' said Bonifacio as he ordered his men to turn back to Viterbo.

When they were out of earshot, Goldwell, who had been praying silently throughout the encounter, said, 'May St. George of England continue to guard us!'

'Why St. George?' asked Flaminio.

'It is his feast day today. And he is a soldier.'

On May 16, the English Agent in Venice, writing to Henry VIII had to admit: 'Cardinal Pole is arrived in Trent. In Ferrara the Duke gave him an escort by water as far as Ostiglia. The Bishop of Rome has published a new Bull to summon all prelates to the Council, but the movements in Germany and the refusal of the Protestants to come to Trent will frustrate it.'

So Pole also feared; and in writing to the Pope to report his own safe arrival, he implored His Holiness for a special blessing, 'for unless the Lord build the house, their labour is in vain that build it.'

10

The Ecumenical Council

The seven months between Pole's arrival in Trent and the actual opening of the nineteenth Ecumenical Council of the Church on December 13, 1545 (the Pope had chosen *Gaudete* Sunday as being reminiscent of *Laetare*) were filled with frustrations and the pettinesses of protocol.

The Emperor's Ambassador had instructions to delay proceedings as long as possible until Charles had settled his German policy. The envoy managed to waste considerable time on a question of status, insisting that, as the Emperor's representative he should take precedence of von Madrutz, the Prince-Bishop, Cardinal of Trent, giving place only to the Legates, as representing the Pope.

When that point was eventually settled, his colleague, the Spanish Ambassador, insisted on sitting next to him. This exacerbated the French. Francis I had written to assure the Council of his veneration and of his concurrence with whatever decrees the Council should enact; but privately he had instructed his ambassador to treat political matters with the highest seriousness and to yield as little as possible to the Emperor. Consequently when the Spanish representative tried to sit next to the Imperial, the French accused him of usurping their proper place, which was immediately below the Imperial. The Spaniard, egged on by the Imperial envoy, stood firm, whereat the French announced that they were withdrawing from the Council and would call a National Synod in Paris, to settle religious affairs on a national basis as the Germans were doing in Worms. As this could in no circumstances be allowed, it was eventually agreed that the French and the Spanish would appear alternately on public occasions, so that the question of precedence would not arise.

More important was the question of voting. Should this be by heads or by nations? The Emperor, lord of so many nations, naturally desired the latter as likely to give him a majority in any disputed matter. The Pope, seeing in such a departure from custom the seeds of a national churchmanship which would finally wreck the universality of the Holy Catholic Church, insisted on the former.

The thorniest question, however, was the meaning of 'reform'. The word had become ambiguous. It now signified not only an improvement in ecclesiastical morals—on which everyone outside the Curia was agreed—but also an alteration in Christian doctrine, which only the Protestants and their sympathisers wanted. The Emperor, who was not yet ready to do without the secular support of the Lutheran princes, wished to begin with the moral issue. The Pope insisted that the primary duty of an Ecumenical Council—indeed the only reason for its calling—was to define dogma, wherever dogma was in dispute. The reform of abuses was secondary only. The enunciation of a principle must obviously precede the application of it. Eventually a compromise was proposed by Thomas Campeggio (de l'Armi's aged uncle) that the matters should be treated simultaneously, one committee dealing with faith and another with morals and then submitting their findings jointly to a plenary session.

The perpetual interference of the secular powers at every level was a source of profound irritation to Pole and Cervini, though del Monte (who as the eldest of the three acted as President) was indifferent to the order in which things were discussed, provided that the discussion was sufficiently prolonged to postpone *sine die* any effective change of morals.

Pole had already in his essay on Councils attacked secular interference in scathing terms. Were rulers, he asked, the right persons to influence religious affairs? Rich men, it was known on the authority of Christ, would find it difficult enough to enter the Kingdom of Heaven; it would be far more difficult for secular rulers who were usually puffed up with riches, honours and worldly pleasures of all kinds. What mattered now was not pomp and political interests, but humble and repentant hearts determined to confess the common guilt of Christendom and to make amends.

Now, writing in the name of all the legates, he addressed the Pope: 'Everything will be upside down if the Pope obeys and the heretics command. It would be better for Your Holiness to abandon your See and return the keys to St. Peter than to suffer secular authority to determine questions of religion.'

On the other hand, he admitted that it was impossible to open the Council against the will of the Emperor, the King of France and the other rulers for the obvious reason that none of the bishops from their countries would attend it and that, in such a case, the Council would not be truly Ecumenical. 'So, in healing one wound, we might make many.'

The Council assembled at last and, on the third Sunday in Advent, as arranged, those delegates who had troubled to come took their places in the choir of cathedral. In addition to the three Legates and the Cardinal of Trent there were four archbishops, twenty-one bishops, five heads of religious orders and the representatives of the Emperor and of his brother, Ferdinand, King of the Romans (the French had gone home) as well as forty-two theologians and nine canonists who had been summoned as consultators. del Monte sang the mass of the Holy Spirit; the Bulls establishing the Council were read and the date of the next meeting, at which business would begin, was fixed for the day after Epiphany, Wednesday, January 7, 1546. The Fathers then dispersed for the Christmas festivities.

Pole had written the text of the opening statement for the January 7 session and it was read from the pulpit by the Secretary of the Council. As the delegates settled back to receive the conventional pieties, comfortably certain that they would be expressed with all the stylistic elegance for which the author was noted, they were suddenly shocked into attention. All heads turned towards Pole as the reader started: 'Before the tribunal of God's mercy, we, the shepherds, should hold ourselves responsible for all the evils now burdening the flock of Christ. It will be found that it is our ambition, our avarice, our cupidity which have brought all these evils on the people of God and that it is because of these sins that pastors are being driven from their churches and the churches starved of the Word of God and the property of the Church, which is the property of poor, stolen, and the priesthood given to the unworthy and to men who differ from lay-folk only in dress. If God punished us as we deserve, we should long since have been as Sodom and Gomorrah.

'Any man who looks into his heart will be bound to acknowledge he has failed in his duty, which is not to seek his own glory but God in all things. Many here have seldom, if ever, visited their own churches, so that they are incapable of giving an account of them. If any good is to come from this Council it must come from God and not from men. For those who truly walk in the way of the Lord, discussions are vain and useless and it is a pity to waste time on unprofitable questions. The Catholic faith is ours already; all that is required is that we should preach and practise it better.

'Above all, do not be swayed by anger, hatred or friendship. All classes of men are prone to this and especially those who serve princes. They easily speak for love or for hate, according as they think their princes are affected, from whom they await reward. We therefore admonish the delegates that, though they must serve their princes with all required loyalty, they are to serve them as bishops, acting as the servants of God, not as the servants of men.'

In a speech at the next session, a fortnight later, Pole returned to the question of pluralities, which had become almost an obsession with him, although the subject of the debate was the relationship of faith and morals. Moral law, he said, could not be separated from dogma. As God had given Moses two tables of the law, the one dealing with faith and the other with morals, so Christ had sent His disciples to preach the Gospel and to teach right conduct.[1] Where unblemished faith was found, there was no room for bad morals. The fulfilment of public duties was far weightier than private ones. A king must not only rule his subjects, but care for them and defend them. On bishops is laid the obligation by word and deed to care for their flocks. As a first step towards discharging this duty, 'let anyone who holds two bishoprics forthwith resign one of them.'

He was listened to with great respect, but only one bishop —an Italian—resigned one of his benefices—in Spain.

Before the next session there was a slight controversy about decorum. On Shrove Tuesday, March 3, the Cardinal of Trent gave a great ball to celebrate the marriage of his niece. To this he naturally invited some of the bishops, including the nearly-octogenarian Campeggio, not as spectators but as participants and he was delighted that they joined the dance. del Monte naturally approved of the proceedings and Pole did not disapprove, but Cervini, who had been ill, protested violently. 'Some acrid remarks' wrote a correspondent, 'have passed between him and Trent. It will certainly be reported as a scandal in Rome that bishops, old Fathers of the council, have been skipping and dancing.'

But what, in that bitter March, most interested the Legates

[1] Pole here is using 'the Gospel' in its proper sense of the Good News of the Resurrection of Jesus Christ. This is quite different from the right conduct proposed in the Sermon on the Mount.

was the possibility of getting away from Trent. Not only had Cervini been incapacitated but a plague had broken out not far away; troops were continually passing through the city so that the Legates 'might find themselves locked up in Trent with soldiers billeted on them'; and Pole himself, in spite of Priuli's care of him, was fighting a return of the partial paralysis which had attacked him on his last visit. Only del Monte, for whom Innocent and the ape seemed to have provided a rejuvenating interest, was apparently indifferent to his surroundings. However, he joined with his colleagues in a plea to the Pope for release, pointing out that their legation had already lasted a year, that the Council was now established and was making good progress, that they themselves were not in very good health and that they would welcome the appointment of their successors so that they might return to their ordinary duties. The Pope took no notice of their request and at the fourth session, which opened on April 8, it fell to Pole to defend against the attacks of Lutheran-inclined bishops, the orthodox doctrine of the Church that the basis of faith was to be found not only in the Bible but in tradition.

He earned for once the enthusiastic approval of Caraffa by his comparison of the Church with an army drawn up in battle array to withstand not only the wiles of Satan striving to sift men like wheat but also the attacks of men who, in the name of 'reform', were questioning the essentials of the Faith. He urged the necessity of examining the efficacy of their weapons, quoting St. Paul's memorable passage on the whole armour of God— the breastplate of righteousness, the helmet of salvation, the sword of the Spirit which is the word of God, and 'above all, the shield of faith wherewith ye may be able to quench all the fiery darts of the wicked'.

But the 'word of God' was not the Bible alone, as the Lutherans were trying to insist. In addition to the Bible there must of necessity be certain revealed truths in which Christ had instructed the Apostles and which, under the guidance of the Holy

Spirit, were the inheritance of the teaching Church throughout the ages. Supernatural revelation, which was the ground of faith, rested on this tradition as well as on the Bible. Further, the Bible could only be interpreted by the Church. The bandying about of texts divorced from their context, which was the habit of Protestants, was not an exposition of the Scriptures.

The standard text of the Bible which was to be used for sermons and disputations was the Latin Vulgate. Pole, however, who from his undergraduate days at Oxford had been an enthusiast for Erasmus's Greek New Testament was as well aware as anyone that certain of the Vulgate renderings would no longer stand the test of scholarship and he was careful to point out that the adoption of the Vulgate as the standard did not rule out textual emendations.

Pole's speech, based on a profundity of knowledge and a clarity of judgement, won unanimous approval and the protesting bishop was left without any support. Caraffa, mollified though he was by Pole's defence of tradition, was immovably aware that this subject was only a preliminary skirmish for the main battle on the subject of Justification and here he suspected that Pole would show his true reforming colours by endeavouring to revive, though possibly in a modified form, Contarini's Ratisbon formula. Caraffa had, therefore, come to Trent with a carefully prepared treatise of his own in which, point by point, he refuted that view. Unsure how far he would be able to carry the Council with him, he had decided, despite the Spanish drawback, to avail himself of Jesuit help and, in answer to his request, Ignatius had sent two of his most trusted companions who had been with him from the beginning, both Spanish and both in their early thirties, Diego Laynez and Alfonso Salmerón. Though they were the youngest of the delegates, they came as the accredited theologians of the Holy See, with the privilege of speaking one at the opening and one at the close of the sittings.

'You must remember above all things,' Ignatius had instructed them, 'to preserve the most perfect union and entire agreement in thought and opinion. Let neither of you trust in his own prudence exclusively and, as Le Jay will join you in a few days, you will fix a time every evening to discuss what you have done during the day and what you have to do tomorrow. You will decide on the subject of your consultation by vote or in some other way. In the morning you will deliberate together on the plan of action for the day.'

The Jesuits arrived in Trent on May 18 and were received by Cervini who passed them on to the Secretary of the Council to enjoy the hospitality of his house until they could be found suitable quarters in an inn.

'He gave us all three,' Laynez wrote to Ignatius, 'for our joint apartment, a little, tiny smoky oven of a room with a bed in it and a trucklebed (which, when pulled out, did not leave space to take two steps in the room). There was no table for us to study at and, as for chairs, only one footstool, but there were lots of boots, belonging to the Secretary and his valet, and a large chest, an old harp and the valet's sword, which were kept in our oven. I said to Salmerón : "This is a little more than we bargained for; let's go and find an inn"; but Salmerón thought it was better to stay in the oven in spite of the heat in order not to show any signs of discontent. So Salmerón slept that night upon the chest and John and I upon the beds. Next day, the Secretary came and asked if we lacked anything; and I answered, with my usual foolishness, "You can see, we lack everything." And he said, "That's so, but at the present moment, what do you need?" I answered, "At least a candle to go to bed by". Then he asked "What more?" and I said, "At least a candlestick to put it in." However, the keeper of the store-closet was out, so we couldn't have a candle that night.

'After about a week, having paid visits to nearly everyone, we went to Cardinal Cervini to beg him to give us a room, for everyone was asking where we were lodging and a good many people wanted to come and see us, but we did not think we could receive visits where we were. The Cardinal said that our having no rooms was not from any lack of goodwill but because of the absence of the houseowner where he had intended to place us; and he excused the Secretary by saying that, as we were in the habit of preaching patience, we ought also to practise it. I told him truthfully that I had not mentioned it in order to escape discomfort, for last year I had spent three months in Africa under a sheet, suffering from heat by day and cold by night, whereas in the oven I could laugh and be content; but that I had spoken out because it was not fit and proper for us to have no conveniences for study, whether to prepare to preach, to read or anything else; nor fair to those who sent us, or to His Eminence, or to any members of the Council who might wish to come and see us. We have now been four days at an inn, after having spent eleven or twelve in the oven.

'I am writing this to Your Reverence, not to complain about anyone, but so that, in case complaints have been made about us, you may know the facts and be able to use them.'

While the Jesuits were still in their 'oven', a personage of far greater consequence arrived in Trent and was received with the utmost courtesy and consideration. Indeed, the Secretary's preparations for his comfort might legitimately have accounted for his delay in finding an inn for the Pope's theologians. The personage was Don Diego Hurtado Mendoza, the Emperor's personal representative.

Mendoza had been Charles's ambassador in Venice and while there he had acquired a magnificent library, spending all his money on books instead of jewellery or clothes, for which he cared little. He himself was an author. His book *Lazarillo de Tormes*, one of the first Spanish Picaresque novels, was written in the form of an autobiography of a simpleton and to those who could read behind the lines it revealed a mind which had observed the world with pitiless accuracy. A Castilian nobleman, a soldier and a scholar, Mendoza was a most formidable character and he had come to Trent now to demand of the Legates in the name of the Emperor, who was still unwilling to antagonise the Lutherans, the postponement of the debate on Justification. Dogma must be left alone.

del Monte, answering for them all, said they would convey the Emperor's wishes to the Pope, whereat Mendoza made it clear that, unless the Pope were accommodating, the Emperor 'would wash his hands of the whole business' of the Council. Pope Paul, however, had reached the limit of compliance and informed the Legates that they were to proceed with the dogmatic debate as arranged. They were overjoyed and wrote immediately to tell him how much his greatness and prudence of soul had consoled them, while warning him that 'the general meetings, to judge by the last ten days, will be tumultuous and difficult to manage, since the will of the princes is not to be acceded to'. Mendoza made an effort to gain time by requesting that the Legates should at least wait for the Emperor's reply. They refused on the grounds that, whatever the reply was, it would make no difference.

The tumults of the last ten days had been caused by a debate on the question of the residence of bishops in their sees. The Spanish Bishop of Jaen, Pedro Pachecho, had asked whether the requirement was of Divine ordinance or was merely an ecclesiastical law, humanly promulgated. It was natural that the Spaniards, who always tended to consider themselves more truly Catholic than any other nation—particularly than the Italians— should opt for severity. It was also, in the circumstances, inevitable that the Italians, reasonably contending that episcopal residence was obviously only a matter of discipline, would outvote them.

When, however, the result was announced, Pachecho accused

del Monte of falsifying the votes; del Monte thereupon refused to have him sitting near him and tempers soared among both the Spanish and the Italians; the Archbishop of Palermo, with tears in his eyes, knelt before the Legates, imploring them for the love of Christ to remember charity; Pachecho was induced to apologise to del Monte who acknowledged the *amende* only with a curt nod; the Cardinal of Trent took Pachecho's side and was greeted with a torrent of abuse by del Monte, who accused him of putting Imperial interests before those of the Church and threatened to ask the Pope to transfer the Council to Italy.

The great debate on Justification (from which Mendoza was pointedly absent), introduced by Cervini on June 21, opened in an atmosphere of even greater excitement. A Neapolitan bishop who advocated salvation by faith alone, took hold of the beard of an orthodox Greek bishop and, by way of enforcing his argument, started to pull it out. Amid the ensuing uproar, Pole rose to make his last plea for moderation. He was very obviously ill and his voice was so weak that the hubbub had to still to silence for him to be heard. He besought the Fathers to consult the Scriptures, carefully to examine the books and teaching of their opponents and to separate the chaff from the wheat. He implored them not to reject a doctrine merely because Luther held it. As poison might be mixed with the most wholesome food, so did Luther and Calvin strive to mingle the true and the false. It was therefore needful not to judge lightly nor without careful examination of all the Protestant writings contained nor necessarily to reject them as completely heretical.

He then outlined his compromise solution which, as Caraffa had assumed, was substantially that which Contarini had outlined five years earlier at Ratisbon. The Protestants taught that a man was incapable of right action, that he was a creature of total depravity and could be justified by nothing that he was or did but only by the merits of Christ 'imputed' to him. This idea of 'imputed righteousness', as distinct from right actions performed by a creature possessing free will, had become the theological

109

catchword of the century. No discussion would have been complete without it and Pole had to use it, even though he modified its meaning.

There was, he said, a two-fold Justification (justitia duplex). There was an 'inherent righteousness' and an 'imputed righteousness', Inspired by the Holy Ghost, a man becomes aware of sin, turns to God and endeavours to act rightly. This is 'justitia inhærens'. Despite the good works this produces, however, it is not enough for salvation and requires to be supplemented by 'justitia imputata', an entirely unmerited salvation imputed to him through faith in Christ's perfect sacrifice for the sins of the whole world on the Cross.

It was easy enough for Laynez to point out in his reply that 'imputed' righteousness was necessarily involved in 'inherent'. Man must indeed rely on the merits of Christ but not simply because in themselves they complete our justification, but because they produce the good works which, as well as faith, are necessary for it.[2]

The strain of the debate exhausted Pole's strength. The paralysis had now affected his left arm and shoulder and his left eye was so bad that doctors feared a loss of sight. Priuli, who had very reluctantly deferred to his friend's insistence on staying at Trent at least until he had made his speech on Justification, lest his opponents should accuse him of avoiding the issue by a 'diplomatic illness',[3] now insisted on leaving immediately and, before the week was out, he had—travelling by litter and again not without protests that he was well enough to ride—reached Priuli's country villa at Treviso which, for the last ten years, had

[2] The debate on the subject continued throughout sixty-one full sessions of the Council and forty-four committees before a final decision was reached. At the sixth regular session of the Council, on 13 January 1547, was passed the great decree on Justification, consisting of sixteen chapters and thirty-three condemnations of opposing heresies, which is still the teaching of the Church. The Council of Trent itself lasted, intermittently, for eighteen years—from December 13, 1545, to December 4, 1563, but as Pole did not again attend it, it has no further place in this story.

[3] Which, in any case, Caraffa subsequently did.

occasionally afforded them a momentary respite from the world.

'I will see what the change of air and quiet will do for me here,' he wrote to del Monte and Cervini, 'and if that does not suffice I shall go to Venice or to the baths at Padua to use that mud that Frascatoro[4] praised so highly.'

Though Pole reiterated that all he needed was a little rest and warmth, Priuli, assuming complete charge, sent to Padua for the two best doctors there, Monte and Frizimalica. They examined the Cardinal carefully and warned him that, unless he took the utmost care, he would be permanently paralysed.

[4] A celebrated physician and poet of Verona.

II

Death comes for the King

Four days after the Paduan doctors had given their opinion on the health of the Cardinal of England, King Henry VIII in London ordered the burning at Smithfield of four heretics, including a woman, Anne Askew, because they had spoken against the Mass in Lutheran terms as 'the most abominable idol in the world'. The episode, when news of it arrived in Rome, was mistaken for an affirmation of basic orthodoxy on Henry's part and the Pope, with Pole's approval, sent, three weeks later, a special envoy to discuss the possibility of England being represented at Trent.

Surprisingly enough, the envoy was granted an audience of the King and two lengthy interviews with his Principal Secretary and was able to report that, though Henry refused to send a delegate to the Ecumenical Council, he would be prepared to allow English representatives to attend a small international council, a kind of subsidiary of Trent, provided it was held on French soil. Unfortunately, Pole's illness and the Pope's absorption in an attempt to secure Parma for his family led to the letter lying unanswered for seven weeks, at the end of which time Henry, who imagined that he had been made the victim of some kind of diplomatic hoax, angrily ordered the Papal envoy to leave the country immediately.

Though it was improbable that, even in the most favourable circumstances, anything tangible would have materialised, Henry, that summer of 1546, was in a mood to explore almost any avenue. He had in June at last concluded peace with France after a disastrous war in which England had faced the threat of invasion and the French had, in fact, landed raiding parties at Seaford and in the Isle of Wight and had kept the English fleet bottled up in Portsmouth.

In France, Henry's soldiers had mutinied, his mercenaries had deserted and he had been forced to procure native galley-slaves by an edict dressed as the enforcement of morality. It was proclaimed that, notwithstanding wholesome laws to preserve people from idleness 'the mother and root of all mischiefs', there were, particularly in London, a great number of 'ruffians and vagabonds', able but disinclined to work, who preferred to live by their wits, thieving and perpetrating confidence tricks 'whereby simple young men are polled and undone'. These perpetrators of 'detestable vices and fashions commonly practised at Bankside and such-like naughty places where they much haunt and lie nightly for the accomplishment and satisfying of their vile, wretched and filthy purposes', the King intended to use for service in the galleys and so ordered all 'ruffians, vagabonds, masterless men, common players and evil disposed persons' to be rounded up by the authorities for that purpose.

In his frantic search for money, Henry found that good things could also do him service. At the dissolution of the monasteries at least one thing had been left untouched—the chantries, where priests offered mass for the souls of the dead who, for centuries, had endowed them for that service. There was a great deal of money there. By a Disendowment Act, hurried through by his obedient Parliament, the King took it. There was also church plate. Why, Henry asked his brother-in-law, Edward Seymour, on whom he had come more and more to rely, should he not 'borrow' this? Edward Seymour saw no reason. 'God's service,' he said, 'which consists not in jewels, plate or ornaments of gold and silver, cannot thereby be diminished and those things are better employed for the weal of the realm.'

So the piety of the past generations was capitalized and the money left on trust to be dedicated to prayer and the service of God was used for the payment of old debts of the Admiralty; the provision of weapons and armour, victuals and clothing, for the fighting-men; the hire of German mercenaries and Irish captains; ambassadorial salaries, and the establishment of a post for the better conveyance of letters abroad.

And, as still more money was needed, Henry decided once more to debase the coinage. He reduced gold to twenty carats and silver to two parts alloy to one of genuine silver, which inevitably had a long-term adverse effect on foreign trade.

'We are in a world,' lamented Stephen Gardiner, Bishop of Winchester, who was continually employed in negotiations with the Emperor, 'where reason and learning prevail not and covenants are little regarded.' And Henry could not but agree with him, though he could see no way certainly to mend the alliance which his 'nephew' the Emperor had so cavalierly ended. But the burning of the heretics and the reception of the Pope's envoy were intended incidentally to impress Charles who, whatever his private disagreements with the Pope, was not disposed to approve, let alone to help, Henry as long as he remained publicly outside the comity of Christendom.

In so far as Henry was personally in control of the religious situation, the essence of it was thus simple enough. He was intent on impressing the Emperor with his orthodoxy, because he needed the Emperor's help. But the more teasing question was: How far was he in control? He was becoming increasingly ill; both legs had been cauterised; politics were pivoted on the expectation that he would shortly die. Further to confuse judgement was his increasing secretiveness—if, indeed, it was possible to increase an attitude which, long ago, he had expressed by saying that if he thought his cap knew his secrets he would throw it in the fire. Now the reputation for subtlety remained when the subtlety itself had given place to forgetfulness, indifference and the other accompaniments of age and pain. What was credited as being regal diplomacy was often no more than an invalid's whim.

The case of Sir George Blagge was a pointer. This Protestant courtier was a favourite of Henry who was accustomed to address him familiarly as 'my pig'. The Catholic party thought it just as well to include him in the executions, but omitted to inform the King who only discovered it by insisting on knowing what a group of courtiers in a corner of his room were whispering about. (He detested people whispering.) When Blagge, released immediately on Henry's angry command, reappeared at court, the King greeted him joyfully with: 'Ah, my pig!'

'Yes,' said Sir George, 'and if Your Highness had not been better to me than your bishops were, your pig would by now have been roasted.'

It was even more difficult to evaluate the arrest and burning of Anne Askew, who was a friend of the Queen, Katherine Parr, and who was tortured, after sentence, in an endeavour to obtain information which would implicate the Queen. When Katherine realised that the proceedings against the heretics were—as far as she could see—really directed against her, she had a wild fit of hysterics which continued until Henry, hearing her shrieks and 'incommoded by the noise', sent to enquire the reason for it. On being told by her doctor that his wife was dangerously ill and that 'it appeared that her sickness was caused by distress of mind', the King had himself carried in his chair to her bedside and assured her (though he had in fact signed an order for proceedings against her and the betting in Amsterdam and Paris was strongly in favour of his having a seventh wife) that she had nothing to fear.

But if Henry was not in fact tired of her, he was certainly extremely bored by her habit of giving him lectures on the principles of Protestantism. 'What a thing it is,' he remarked to Cranmer, 'to come to my old days and be taught by my wife!'

The Archbishop (whom Henry had now taken to calling—jocularly it seemed and was devoutly to be hoped—'the greatest heretic in Kent') lost no time in giving Katherine the hint. She immediately took it. 'I have always held it preposterous for a woman to instruct her lord,' she told the King, 'and if I have ever presumed to differ from Your Highness on religion, it was to obtain information for my own comfort regarding certain nice points on which I stood in doubt.'

'Is it so, sweetheart?' said Henry. 'Then we are perfect friends.'

Thereafter Katherine behaved with impeccable discretion. She settled down to write a religious treatise entitled *The Lamentations of a Sinner*, showing how 'our Moses hath delivered us out of the captivity and spiritual bondage of Pharaoh. I mean by this Moses King Henry VIII, my most sovereign favourable lord and husband, one meet to be another Moses in his conquest over Pharaoh; and I mean by Pharaoh the Bishop of Rome who hath been and is a greater persecutor of true Christians than ever was Pharaoh of the Children of Israel.'

There was no possibility of any conjugal disagreement here.

Nevertheless, 'Moses' had his own disillusionments about the practical results of his spiritual leadership. In what was to prove his last address to Parliament, he was moved to say, more in sorrow than in anger: 'Charity and concord is not among you, but discord and dissension in every place, when one calleth the other "Heretic" and "Anabaptist" and he calleth him again "Papist", "Hypocrite" and "Pharisee". Are these the signs of fraternal love between you? I see and hear daily that you of the clergy preach one against another, teach one contrary to the other, inveigh one against another without charity or discretion. Some be too stiff in their old *Mumpsimus*, other be too busy and curious in their new *Sumpsimus*.[1] Thus all men almost be in variety and discord.

'You of the temporality rail on bishops, speak slanderously of priests and rebuke and taunt preachers. And although you be permitted to have the Word of God in your mother-tongue[2] you must understand that it is licensed you so to do only to inform you and your conscience and to instruct your children and family and not to dispute and make Scripture a railing and a taunting stock against priests, as many light persons do. I am very sorry to know and hear how unreverently the Word of God is disputed, rhymed, sung and jingled in every ale-house and tavern, contrary to the true doctrine and meaning of the same.

'Of this I am sure that charity was never so faint among you and virtuous and godly living was never less used and God Himself was never less reverenced, honoured or served among Christians.'

The power-struggle at court was crystallised round the feud between Edward Seymour, Earl of Hertford and Henry Howard, Earl of Surrey. Hertford at forty was, merely because of his status as the Prince of Wales's elder uncle, the most influential man in the Council and, though Chapuys and the Imperialist interests deplored it, the only man of outstanding governmental ability. Surrey, at thirty, as son and heir of the now-septuagenarian Duke of Norfolk, could rely on the support of the 'traditionalists'. Hertford was a 'new man' and a Protestant; Surrey was a Catholic and, quartering the arms of Edward the Confessor—a privilege which King Richard II had allowed to his Mowbray ancestors—was of the oldest blood in England. Hertford was a cold, calculating man of business, carefully masking his emotions and subordinating even family affection to personal

[1] This expression originated in the story that an old priest always read in his breviary *Mumpsimus, Domine* instead of *Sumpsimus, Domine*. When a young priest pointed out his error, he merely said: 'I have used "mumpsimus" for thirty years and I shall not leave my old "mumpsimus" for your new "sumpsimus".' Henry's reference would have been as immediately recognised by the House as would a reference to Mrs. Malaprop in the nineteenth century.

[2] The vernacular Scriptures were, however, expressly forbidden by law to anyone under the rank of gentleman.

117

advancement; Surrey, 'the most foolish proud boy in England', was a poet,[3] passionate and prodigal, as extravagant in his gestures as he was with his fortune and openly regarding parvenus like the Seymours as 'foul churls'.

Temperamentally the two men loathed each other to such an extent that the accident that, in their persons, they represented the opposing religious, social and political tendencies of the day was almost irrelevant.

Both held the King by his paternal instinct, Hertford as the uncle of Henry's only lawful son and heir; Surrey by the fact that he had been brought up with and was the closest friend of Henry's first and most beloved illegitimate son, the Duke of Richmond. When Richmond died, Surrey had fallen ill with grief. He still could not bear Windsor, 'where each sweet place returns a taste full sour' and after Richmond's funeral the King had given him a portrait of Richmond as well as his favourite horse, a black jennet, which Surrey continued to regard as among his most treasured possessions.

With the King forgiving Surrey peccadillo after peccadillo—as he would have forgiven Richmond—it was lost labour for Hertford to insult Surrey so violently one day when they were in the gardens at Hampton Court that Surrey hit him and thus gave him the excuse to demand that, as the blow was struck 'within the precincts', he should suffer the legal penalty of losing his right arm. Henry immediately quashed the proceedings and substituted for the maiming a short confinement in Windsor Castle, with permission to use the walks and the terraces, and the only result of Hertford's carefully-prepared plan was Surrey's poem on Windsor in memory of Richmond, in which he lamented the loss of

[3] It is as a poet that Surrey takes his place in the English story. At eighteen he had translated two books of the *Aeneid* into blank verse—a form of which he was the inventor—and in his lyrics he had shown himself, as Sir Edmund Chambers says, 'a master of the first order.'

> The secret thoughts imparted with such trust,
> The wanton talk, the divers change of play,
> The friendship sworn, each promise kept so just,
> Wherewith we passed the winter nights away.

Hertford was subsequently more successful; but for that Surrey had only himself to blame. One evening with a few friends provided with 'stone bows'—the catapults generally used for shooting rabbits—he went for a row on the Thames and fired stones through the windows of the Bankside brothels to see the whores leap out of bed with their customers.

He was brought before the Privy Council to answer for the disturbance, and Hertford, who was presiding, asked him if he had any defence. Surrey, mimicking Hertford's prim, nasal speech, explained in terms equally reminiscent of godly moralisings, that he had done what he had done for the sake of the souls of the wicked Londoners who were behaving more abominably than Papists, sitting up late and . . . playing cards. By throwing a stone or two through their windows, he hoped to arouse them to a sense of responsibility. The stones, passing silently through the night, had fallen with such awful suddenness among the sinners that they might be reminded of the Last Judgement and recalled to a proper sense of their duty to God, their king and their country.

When some of the Council, secretly amused, suggested that a fine would be sufficient punishment, Hertford objected that to let the culprit off so lightly would be 'a secret and unobserved contempt of the law' which might lead to acts of 'no restraint, no limit, if winked at', and Surrey was sent to gaol for two months. Even here Hertford managed to indulge his spite by sending Surrey's companions to the Tower but the Earl himself to the 'noisome' common prison of the Fleet where he might well catch some disease.

The next blow came when Surrey was superseded by Hertford as Lieutenant-General in France. By insisting that Surrey should

dismiss the members of his staff who were likely to prove unacceptable to his successor, Hertford hoped to provoke Surrey to a
protest so violent that it could be construed as treason. Surrey,
however, was for once amenable. He was, in any case, more
interested in fighting than in organising; his personal courage was
legendary—he had recently risked his life by remaining under
fire on the bridge of one of the Boulogne fortresses 'for the better
viewing of the same'—and he was quite content to change the
Lieutenant-Generalship for the place of danger and honour
known as 'Captain of the Rearward'.

As soon as the war was over, Hertford made his first priority
the killing of Surrey. The King was obviously dying and, though
his bullock-body made periodic rallies, there was not, Hertford
calculated, much time. Unless the Howards were disposed of
before Henry's death, it was unlikely that the Seymours,
Edward's uncles though they were, would be able to enjoy the
full spoils of the nine-year-old boy's long minority. Henry had
made a very careful will, balancing the opposing forces in the
Council to ensure that policy should continue on the lines that
he had laid down.

Hertford's problem was to find some way of turning Henry
mortally against Surrey. Surrey himself, quite unwittingly, provided the excuse. During the last weeks of his command in
Boulogne he had discovered some French glaziers who had not
lost the craft-secret of staining glass in the mediaeval manner
and he decided to employ them for the decoration of the windows
in his East Anglian mansion. Among the designs he gave them
was his escutcheon, bearing, as was his right, the arms of Edward
the Confessor.

This action, combined with the rumour that he was about to
send a confidential servant to consult his fellow-Plantagenet,
Cardinal Pole, in Italy, was his death-warrant. It was represented
to the dying King that he was aspiring to the Crown and Henry,
who could always be relied on to kill in defence of his dynasty—

and now more than ever—agreed to the arrest of both Surrey and his father.

At his trial, when Surrey was asked: 'Why did you put the arms of St. Edward in your coat?' he answered: 'Go to the church of East Winch in Norfolk and you will see them there, for they have been ours for five hundred years.'

'You would have committed treason,' said Hertford, 'and as His Highness is old, you thought to become King.'

'You catchpole,' retorted Surrey, 'what have you to do with this? The Kingdom has never been well since the King put mean creatures like you into the Government. I never sought to usurp the King's arms, for all know that my ancestors had them.'

He continued to defend himself with reckless brilliance but his condemnation was a matter of course. When finally asked if he had anything to say, he burst out: 'Of what have you found me guilty? Certainly I have transgressed no law—but I know well enough that the King denies the noble blood around him and employs none but mean creatures.'

Surrey was executed on 10 January 1547 and most of his estates given to the Seymours. Hertford, characteristically, was a model of thoroughness. He took even Surrey's personal possessions which, in courtesy, should have been left for the dead man's widow and children. The furniture, the carpets, the plate, even the pillowcases, the salted fish and the preserved fruits were carefully inventoried and transferred from Surrey's London house to Hertford's—including, of course, the black jennet which had once been Richmond's.

The execution of the old Duke of Norfolk, who by the usual evidence had been involved in his son's 'plot', did not however, take place. On 27 January 1547, the King gave his assent to a bill of attainder against him and preparations were made for his execution the following day. But it was the King who died in the early hours of that Friday morning, January 28.

When it was clear that Henry's death was imminent Cranmer was sent for from Croydon, but by the time he arrived at Westminster, the King had lost the power of speech. The Archbishop asked the dying man to give some sign that he had faith in God, through Christ, which would ensure his salvation, whereupon—according to Cranmer—the King 'holding him with his hand did wring his hand in his as hard as he was able.'

While Henry lay dying, Hertford and Paget, the Principal Secretary, paced up and down the Long Gallery trying to determine the best course of action. Eventually they decided to keep the news of the death secret for three days to give Hertford time to gain possession of the new king (who was at Enfield) and to doctor Henry's will so that the plan for a balanced Council should be subverted and all power given to the Protestant party. The exercise was carried out with Hertford's usual efficiency and he was able to appoint himself Lord Protector of England, under his new title of Duke of Somerset.

On Wednesday, February 2, Candlemas Day, the royal corpse was removed from the chamber in which Henry had died and, covered with a pall of gold tissue, brought into the palace chapel, where it remained lying in state for twelve days, while perpetual masses were said for the repose of his soul. Meanwhile workmen were busy clearing and mending the roads between Westminster and Windsor, cutting down hedges where the ways were narrow, and the priests of the parishes through which the great funeral procession would pass warned to be ready to greet the corpse with prayers and censings. The journey was to take two days, pausing for the night at Sion House, once the home of the Brigettines. In that desecrated and desolate monastery the chapel was hastily refurbished by workmen sent specially from London.

About three o'clock in the afternoon of February 15 the procession arrived at Sion and the King's body was taken into the chapel. 'At what time,' recorded a chronicler, 'the King's dead corpse was carried from London to Windsor, there to be interred, it rested the first night at the monastery of Sion. At which time, were it for the jogging and shaking of the chariot, or for any other secret cause, the coffin of lead wherein his dead corpse was put being riven and cloven, all the pavement of the church was, with the fat and the corrupt putrified blood dropped out of the said corpse, foully imbrued. Early in the morning, those that had the charge of the dressing, coffining and embalming of the body, with the plumbers, repaired thither to reform the mistake and lo! suddenly there was found among their legs a dog lapping and licking up the King's blood. One William Consett, who was there present, with much ado drove away the said dog.'

And some remembered how, fifteen years ago when the King's divorce from Catherine of Aragon was 'the great matter', Friar Peto on Easter Day had preached before the King and the court at Greenwich on the subject of King Ahab and the prophets of Baal. Turning towards Henry and making a profound reverence, the Friar had said: 'Your Highness's preachers are too much like those of Ahab's day, in whose mouths were found a false and lying spirit. They flatter and proclaim falsehoods and are consequently unfaithful to Your Highness. They dare to speak of peace when there is no peace and are not afraid to tell of licence and liberty for monarchs which no king should even dare to contemplate. I beseech Your Grace to take good heed, lest if you will need follow Ahab in his doings you will surely incur his unhappy end also and that the dogs will lick your blood, as they licked Ahab's.'

12

The Cardinal Writes to the Protector

A week before the death of King Henry VIII, Cardinal Bembo died. 'For the sake of our ancient friendship,' Pole wrote to Cardinal Cervini, reporting it, 'and at the invitation of his family, I was with him the day before his death. It was good to see him so well prepared for that passage with a pious and Christian courage.'

Before his death, Bembo, at seventy-seven, had resumed something of the sway he had had over Reginald when, twenty-seven years before, the young student at the University of Padua had fallen under the spell of the older man's Epicureanism in his *non pareil* treasure-house, the Villa Noniana—the house that, as Pole had told his mother, was 'full of roses all day long.'

The beloved Longolius, whose death had been Pole's first great sorrow, had been there too and Flaminio, who had written a youthful Latin poem on the happy leisure of those days:

> And when the insect hum is still,
> And sunbeams rest on height and hill,
> We saunter forth, and climb the steep
> That beetles o'er the purple deep;

And thence we drop the painted float,
Or idly watch each little boat
That steals upon the tranquil bay
White snow-white sail and pennon gay,
And vainly wish our life may be
As peaceful as that blessed sea.[1]

But though Pole and Bembo never ceased to correspond, the years and their separate enthusiasms had driven them a little apart. When Bembo, who in his youth had loved Lucrezia Borgia and in his middle life had taken a faithful mistress by whom he had three children, had been at the age of 69 made a Cardinal by Paul III, there was an outcry from the reforming party—especially Caraffa—that such an indefensible absurdity cast considerable doubt on the genuineness of the Pope's care for reform. Bembo, who never visited the see entrusted to him but had it administered by proxy at a safe distance, was indeed a classic example of the absentee cleric against whom Pole inveighed so bitterly at Trent.

Yet the 'ancient friendship', combined with Pole's realisation that Bembo's Hat was, in fact, little more than a Papal gesture to reconcile to orthodoxy the literary and artistic movement which had formed round Vittoria Colonna, ensured that he indulged in no criticism of Bembo himself; and after Reginald had recovered a little from his illness, early in the October of 1546, he had gone with Priuli and Flaminio, to stay with Bembo at the Villa Noniana to complete his convalescence.

Here it seemed that time had stood still and that he, hollow-cheeked and with his face stamped with suffering, far older in spirit though four years younger by the calendar than Bembo had been when they had first met, was a *revenant* drawn to a once-loved spot. Flaminio felt it less keenly and saw it differently. In those days he had been obsessed by a classicism which, in the years between, had given way to a Christian fanaticism. From

[1] The translation from the Latin is by E. W. Barnard (1829).

the safety of his present refuge he could savour the past with a curious detachment as if it concerned someone else. As for Priuli, his relationship with Bembo was different from the others'. He knew him as a fellow-Venetian, from his childhood a friend of his family and an ornament of his city.

Bembo himself, ageing gracefully, was less changed than the others. His beard was white now and he was a little hard of hearing, but he did not need spectacles and, above all, his intellect was undimmed. He had not abandoned his Platonism and Beauty was still his way to God.

During one of their conversations, a shaft of sunlight happened to fall on one of his treasures, an exquisite vase of polished gold, set with a variety of jewels, and the old Cardinal immediately took it for a parable. 'The light of the sun', he said, 'is everywhere. Like the spirit of God, which is Beauty. But you only realise it in its perfection when it strikes something itself beautiful, like that vase. And therein lies the trap.'

'Explain,' said Pole, who knew Bembo in this mood of old and remembered that he liked to be invited to continue.

'The trap is that you fall in love with the vase instead of with the sun. The vase is like the body—a beautiful body. Thus if the mind is suddenly seized by desire for beauty, which it recognises as good, and, if it allows itself to be guided by what the senses tell it, it falls into the gravest error. It thinks that the body is the chief cause of the beauty which it enshrines and so to enjoy that beauty it must achieve with it as intimate a union as possible. But this is untrue and anyone who thinks he will enjoy the beauty by possessing the body is deceiving himself and is moved not by true knowledge, arrived at by reason, but by a false opinion derived from the desire of the senses.'

'And where,' asked Flaminio, 'would you lead us from this?'

'That the old can love more happily than the young, Marc-Antonio. And for two reasons. As the sensual lure of the body fades, true lovers will find a greater beauty residing in their

126

minds and affections towards each other and so be led to share the noblest part of love which is the intellect. Also, they will have taken the first step on the rung of the ladder which leads from the image of sensual beauty to the sublime mansions where the celestial, adorable and true beauty lies hidden in the secret places of God.'

They all understood that, within the courtesy of generalisation, Bembo was speaking of Pole and Priuli. Pole, remembering del Monte, said: 'But sensual love does not always die with youth.'

Bembo, unaware of the reason for the question and interpreting it as an equally generalised enquiry about himself, replied: 'In my opinion they should be condemned who, when they are old, still allow the fires of passion to burn in their hearts and make strong reason obey their feeble senses. They are like idiots or animals which lack reason.'

No one disagreed. Only Priuli in his mind violently dissented, because he was thinking not of del Monte and the ape-boy (as they tended to refer to him) but of Michelangelo and Tomasso and of the tangible beauty that that passion continued to inspire.

'Once, long ago,' said Flaminio, breaking the short silence, 'I remember you made a prayer to Love. It ran something like this—forgive me if my memory is a little at fault: "Pour yourself into our hearts and illumine our darkness. Correct the falsity of our senses and, after our long mistaking, give us the true substance of goodness."'

Bembo, smiling at him, continued it: ' "With the rays of your light cleanse our eyes of their misty ignorance so that they no longer prize mortal beauty but know that the things they first sought to see are not and that those they did not see truly are." I still do not disown the invocation.'

'But now, dear friend,' said Pole, 'your eyes see only the Cross?'

Priuli looked across at Pole in surprise. The suddenness of

the transition, in spite of the affection in his tone, sounded to him like one of Reynold's unnecessary tactlessnesses. Even Flaminio would not have put it so bluntly. But Bembo understood and answered him: 'Not only the Cross, but also those who for *love*—the love of Christ—have cared nothing for their own life and feared no manner of death, however cruel.' Then, for once particularising, he added quietly: 'It is one of my regrets that I did not know the Countess your mother.'

During his stay at the Villa Noniana, Pole learnt that Vittoria Colonna was now seriously ill. 'It is with much greater distress than I ever experienced for my own infirmities,' he wrote to her, 'that I hear you have been ill since August,' and hastened to Viterbo. Though the Pope had requested him, were he well enough in health, to return to Rome during October, he remained with Vittoria till the middle of November. Before he left for the Vatican, he inaugurated, in the presence of the magistrates and notabilities of Viterbo, a Philosophical Lectureship in Vittoria's honour, though she was too ill to attend the ceremony.

When, as soon as he arrived in Rome, he told Michelangelo the artist set off immediately for Viterbo. At first the nuns were unwilling to let him see her, but a momentary blaze of the angry power which had cowed Popes made them change their minds. Michelangelo's only regret, he afterwards told Tommaso, was that he did not kiss the dying woman on the forehead and face, but only her hand.

When at last he could bring himself to continue his work on the fresco of the *Crucifixion of St. Peter* in the Pauline Chapel, the first thing he did was to paint her as she had appeared when he entered her room, her mouth fallen open in surprise and her great eyes gazing at him, part wondering, part apprehensive, as if he were the messenger of Death.

The news of the death of Henry VIII, coming on the heels

of Pole's greater bereavements of Bembo and Vittoria, affected the Cardinal in an unexpected manner. In two urgent letters he implored the Pope to send an envoy to the Emperor (he suggested the Cardinal of Trent as *persona gratissima*) asking Charles to make a supreme effort to bring England back into the unity of the Church. As he read through the draft of the earlier letter, Reginald realised that, for the first time in sixteen years, he had written the words 'King Henry'. The King's death, it seemed, had released an unconscious stop in his mind. On the many occasions on which he had had to refer to his cousin since he had left England, he had always avoided his name. According to the nature and status of his correspondents, Henry had been 'the King of England' or 'Your master' or 'That tyrant' or even simply 'He who . . .' Never 'King Henry'. It was as if the Cardinal had separated the early paragon of a king, under whose understanding and bounty he had grown up and to whom he had given unquestioning loyalty, gratitude and love, from the monster with the blood of martyrs and kinsmen on his hands.

Now that the King was facing ultimate judgement, Reginald found the earlier Henry haunting his thoughts and his immediate response to the news of his death was the memory of how, years ago, while his family was still unmolested though he himself was the object of assassination attempts, he had made a pilgrimage to the rock-cave of Sainte-Beaune, where tradition had it that Mary Magdalene spent many years weeping for her sins, to pray for Henry who himself saw no need to pray. Here he had found what mystical theology calls 'the gift of tears'. . . . As if motivated by some force outside himself, he had started to cry uncontrollably and had found it impossible to restrain his tears even after he had left the shrine and resumed his journey. When Priuli had asked him the cause of such incontinent grief, he had replied: 'The tears have been lent to me by Him who, Himself sinless, prayed for His enemies and I offer them to God for Henry's salvation.'

Yet, whatever the complexity of his personal feelings, Pole

had no illusions about the effect of the King's death on the situation in England. It was necessary indeed to grasp at any diplomatic opportunity to bring about a religious reconciliation, but it was foolish to suppose that it would be any easier than it had been when the excommunicated King was alive. When the Pope asked him why he did not rejoice with the rest of the Curia at removal of the great enemy of the Church who was also the murderer of his mother, Pole replied: 'Nothing, Your Holiness, will be improved. Young King Edward has been brought up by heretics; the Council of Regency is controlled by heretics and, to crown everything, the Seymours and the Queen-Dowager, Katherine Parr, are more obstinate in heresy than all the rest.' Nevertheless, he did what he considered his duty, although he was quite aware that as practical politics it was risible. He wrote to Edward and to Somerset.

That April of 1547 was fought the battle of Mühlberg.[2] The Schmalkaldic League, now the strongest group of states and cities in Germany, was prepared to try conclusions with the Emperor, whom its leader, John Frederick, Elector of Saxony, now openly referred to as 'Charles of Ghent' or 'Charles of Spain'. Charles, at last realising that this militant Protestantism, in spite of all efforts at theological accommodation, threatened not only the unity of the Church but the survival of the Empire, accepted the challenge. When the states of the League renounced their allegiance to him and denied his Imperial title, he pronounced the 'ban of the empire' against their leaders, thus designating them outlaws, and at the end of March he set out from Nuremberg for Meissen on the Elbe, 200 miles away, where the Elector and his troops were encamped. He was exhausted

[2] To those whose main interest is modern history, Mühlberg may not even be a name, so it may be worth mentioning that the battle of Mühlberg is at least as important as, if not more important than, the battle of Waterloo in its effects on Europe.

and ill and in great pain from his gout and had to be carried in a litter.

At Eger, about half-way to Meissen, he joined forces with the Bohemians under his brother King Ferdinand, and thereafter insisted on abandoning the litter and riding with the army as was his custom.

The Elector John Frederick, hearing of the Emperor's approach, crossed the Elbe, thinking the unbridged river a sufficient barrier between him and his enemy—though he left a few boats manned with Saxon troops to guard against a possible attack—and started a leisurely march towards Wittenberg where he intended to fortify himself.

Charles determined to cross the Elbe and to attack immediately. On St. George's Day he made ready to lead the attempt in person. 'When he was being armed,' according to his Spanish biographer, 'it was observed that he trembled all over; but when he was ready he was calm and so full of mettle that it looked as though he were flaunting the fact that no Emperor had ever yet been shot down.' In the thick mist of the April dawn, Charles, riding among his men, gave the order to capture the boats and, under his eye, the Spanish troops threw themselves into the water and, their daggers between their teeth, swam to the attack. Bohemian gunners, up to their armpits in water, returned the fire of the defenders of the boats. Horsemen swam the river, three hundred paces wide, not knowing, in the mist, whether they would have to face the full strength of the Schmalkaldic army. Meanwhile a peasant had shown the Emperor where, at the little village of Schimenitz, there was a ford and Charles himself led his cavalry across, though, by this time, the boats had been captured and were being used for the transportation of the infantry and the baggage.

As the Emperor made the opposite bank, the mist suddenly cleared and each side saw its enemies. Before the main body of Imperialists could be marshalled in order, the Elector ordered an immediate retreat and the army of League, as fast as possible, endeavoured to reach the comparative shelter of the Mühlberg woods. But the Imperialists quickly overtook them and hurled themselves into a most bloody fray, the Spaniards calling on their patron saint, St. James, and the Bohemians marking the season with shouts of 'St. George for the Empire'.

The result was an overwhelming victory for the Emperor. The Elector John Frederick was taken prisoner and led to Charles by the Duke of Alva.

'Most gracious and all-merciful Emperor,' said the Elector, trying to make a deep bow (which, as the fattest man in Europe, he found difficult), 'I am your prisoner—'

Charles interrupted him with: 'Am I now indeed your Emperor and not Charles of Ghent? It would have been better had you realised it earlier.'

But the Emperor did not, as his brother Ferdinand urged him, execute the Elector for his high treason. Charles, according to one of his courtiers, 'began to incline more and more to mercy out of pity for a great prince in such misfortune' and he contented himself with depriving John Frederick of his territory and title in favour of his nephew, Maurice of Saxony.

After the battle when, pale with exhaustion and pain, Charles faced the congratulations of the elated army, he replied with a simple 'God has conquered'. Mülhberg, as he saw it, was a religious victory.[3]

The Pope, however, was less enthusiastic than the Emperor had a right to expect. Now that Charles was the undisputed master of Europe, Paul foresaw that he might try to dictate to the Council theological terms which would soothe his defeated

---

[3] Titian's famous equestrian portrait of Charles V at Mühlberg was painted at the request of the Emperor's allies after Charles had returned to Augsburg. Titian, who was then seventy, was in Venice but made the journey across the Alps at Charles's request. Many stories are told of its painting—one, how Charles himself moved a table and helped Titian to climb on it when the artist wanted to make an alteration at the top of the canvas. The great picture is now in the Prado in Madrid and the Emperor's armour and the caparison of his black charger depicted there are preserved in the Armoury.

Protestant subjects rather than sustain the Catholic Faith. The Pope therefore, using an outbreak of plague in Trent as a convenient excuse, moved the Council to Bologna where Imperial pressure could not be exerted. Charles retaliated by forbidding the Imperialist bishops to leave Trent and by summoning a Diet at Augsburg to draw up a declaration of faith which should serve for the time being (*ad interim*) until the Ecumenical Council reached its final decisions.

The Augsburg Diet was attended by all seven Electors and nearly all the ecclesiastical and secular princes of the Empire and was inaugurated with great splendour by the Emperor who, in his opening address, spoke of 'the necessity for peaceful Christian measures to get rid of the harmful and distressing division and rift of the German people.' It took five months to draw up 'the declaration of his Imperial Roman Majesty on how things are to be as regards religion in the Holy Empire until the decision of the Ecumenical Council.'

The *Interim* (as it came more succinctly to be called) contained, as Cardinal Farnese endeavoured to explain to Charles, at least six heresies, including a redefinition of the decree on Justification in the direction of 'by faith alone' and a lessening of the sacrificial aspect of the Mass, as well as the relaxation of two disciplinary rules to allow the marriage of priests and the communion of the people in both kinds.[4]

On the other hand it insisted on retaining the traditional forms of religion with its veneration of the Mother of God, its Corpus Christi procession, its feast days of the saints and its 'altars, vestments, sacred vessels, crosses, statues and paintings', though, in deference to the Protestants who wanted them all destroyed, it was emphasised that 'they are simple reminders and no honour is to be done to them.'

The *Interim* was, in fact, another equivocal compromise and

[4] As these matters are still being discussed (1969), it may be as well to point out that they concern usage not doctrine. St. Peter was married and Christ transubstantiated and distributed both the bread and the wine.

to the Emperor's surprise and irritation it was fiercely rejected by both sides just as Contarini's Ratisbon formula on Justification had been. On the Protestant side, there was a flood of derisive verses and satirical lampoons—'I, Lucifer, have had a child born to me by my Papist wife,' one popular song began —while, on the Catholic, the Pope, having told the Emperor that it was a scandal that a lay ruler should presume to meddle in matters of doctrine, appointed a Commission under the presidency of Cardinal Pole to refute the *Interim* point by point.

Meanwhile, the Emperor sent the formidable Mendoza to Rome to voice his protest against the removal of the Council to Bologna and to insist that, until it returned to Trent, he would recognise none of its decrees.

Again it was Pole who was deputed to receive and answer the envoy with whom he and his fellow-Legates had already crossed swords at Trent. But now Reginald was alone and his innate self-distrust was intensified by the realisation of how greatly he had relied on del Monte's canonical erudition and Cervini's diplomatic experience to reinforce his own theological acumen. Nevertheless, he would do what he could.

When Mendoza charged the Pope with having delayed calling the Ecumenical Council, Pole retorted that, if in fact there had been any delay, it was the fault of the Emperor, whose perpetual wars of aggrandisement made it impossible for most prelates to attend it.

Mendoza then attributed a political motive to the bishops who had now gone to Bologna. They were pro-Italian and anti-Imperialist. If, replied Pole, the ambassador intended this as a reproach to the bishops who had obeyed the Pope, it might be as well to remember that the schism which the Council had been called to heal owed its origin to a lack of deference to the Holy See.

Mendoza then suggested that the removal of the Council from Trent was unlawful.

But, countered Pole, the removal had been proposed to the

whole assembly and assented to by an overwhelming majority. If the Imperialists were outvoted had they anyone but themselves to blame? The Council had met twice at Trent. On the first occasion few, if any, Germans troubled to come, though Pole and his fellow-Legates waited seven months for them. At the second meeting, it was painfully obvious how few had come and not even one of those in Lutheran sees, for whose welfare the Council had been called.

Mendoza, without actually specifying the Augsburg Diet, threatened that, if the Pope were remiss in his duty, the Christian cause would not lack a protector.

It was unfortunate, replied Pole, with unaccustomed asperity, that Mendoza was not more cautious and respectful in his expressions. If His Holiness—though it was unthinkable—failed to fulfil the duties of his high station, it was comforting to know that the Emperor's well-known vigilance would supply any deficiency.

'You accept my master's right?' said Mendoza.

'Most certainly,' said Pole.

The Ambassador smiled expansively at having at last gained a major point; but the smile faded as the Cardinal added: 'As far, that is, as it is agreeable to equity and is allowed by the laws of the Church, the teaching of the Fathers and the universal consent of Christendom.'

It seemed impossible that the relations between Pope and Emperor could deteriorate further. Charles, however (whom, long ago Contarini had described as 'revengeful') saw to it that they did. He allowed[5] the assassination of the Pope's beloved son,

[5] I have used the word 'allowed' as the most accurate in this tangled and disputed matter. It is improbable that Charles planned it (though the Pope thought he had); it is impossible that he was ignorant of it and it is certain that he neither disavowed his viceroy nor apologized to the Pope for the crime. Thus, at 47, the Emperor 'allowed' the murder as, at 27, he had 'allowed' the sack of Rome.

Pier Luigi, the ruler of Piacenza, by the Imperial viceroy of Milan.

In Rome, at the centre of the crisis produced by these events, England seemed very far away—almost, again, *ultima Thule*— and Pole returned to Viterbo where, in semi-seclusion, he could see more clearly the needs of his own land. Yet, ultimately, the issues were everywhere the same. Before things could be put to rights, it was necessary to restore the unity of the Church, the broken Body of Christ.

This was the burden of the letter Reginald wrote to the boy-king. Edward was to emulate not his father in his later, dreadful years, but the Henry who had been truly the 'Defender of the Faith' of his ancestors. And to Somerset, Pole offered any help he could in healing the breach which 'that person to whom you and your forebears, before you lapsed from the ecclesiastical law, always assigned the chief authority for the well-being of the Church, that is to say, the High Pontiff.' But he warned the Protector that 'he who confirms and approves impious statutes is no less culpable than he who makes them.'

Somerset intercepted Edward's letter and, for the moment, ignored his own. He had more important things to attend to. In particular he was concerned with building himself a palace, Somerset House, in the Strand which should be consonant with his dignity as Lord Protector of England. To facilitate the work by the provision of already-hewn stone and to clear the site on which he had decided to build, he had confiscated and destroyed the London residence of four bishops, had pulled own St. Mary's Church and the cloisters and two chapels of St. Paul's Cathedral and blown up the walls of the Church of the Knights of St. John. Having thus laid the foundations of his budding greatness, he was now engaged in making himself the beginnings of a library by seizing all the books belonging to the City of London.

The activities of his younger brother, Thomas, were also

causing him some anxiety. Sir Thomas Seymour, who had married the doting Katherine Parr as soon as Henry VIII was dead, would, in his own opinion, make a better Protector than his elder brother. Endowed with a personal charm which Somerset conspicuously lacked, Sir Thomas was engaged in gaining a dangerous hold over the boy-king. Fortunately for the Protector, he over-reached himself and Somerset managed to persuade the Council of Regency to have him executed—an act of fratricide which surprised no one who knew him but which was not well looked on abroad.

A month or two after the judicial murder, the Protector at last found time to write to Pole saying that he would be pleased to welcome him to England so that the Cardinal could see for himself how 'the purity of the word of God and the doctrine of Christ is, by our means, set forth and taught more purely than it ever was formerly.'

Pole replied that, if that were true, it would indeed be an inducement to come to England but that Somerset's actions had failed to convince him of it. 'You have neither the Faith,' he wrote, 'nor any true religious feeling and are therefore unfit to be in charge of the King, though it seems that no one has dared to tell you so.'

Alvise Priuli, when Reginald showed him the letter, thought that it might be more courteously expressed, but Thomas Goldwell was of the opinion that, considering the state to which their country was now reduced, it could have been even harsher.

13
Whit Sunday 1549

Thomas Cranmer, Archbishop of Canterbury, who was now sixty, had been moving steadily in the direction of extreme Protestantism and had privately accepted the doctrine of Justification by faith alone with all its implications; but as long as Henry VIII was alive he had outwardly conformed to the King's six-point belief in transubstantiation, the sufficiency of communion in one kind, the efficacy of chantry masses for souls in Purgatory, the necessity of confession, the celibacy of the clergy and the perpetual obligation of the religious vow of chastity.

As soon as Henry was dead, however, Cranmer felt free to follow the logic of his new insights, but, as Luther once had been, so was he now caught intellectually in the dilemma that, if faith is everything, there is no necessity for the sacraments and yet the New Testament records that Christ instituted them. As, consequently, it was impossible to abandon the sacraments, it was necessary to devalue them—to substitute for the Sacrifice of the Mass and the veritable Body and Blood of the Crucified a mere memorial meal in which bread and wine were no more than symbols to facilitate subjective meditation and to exhibit Baptism not as the washing away of sin and incorporation into Christ by the power of Calvary but as an interesting rite indicating that faith alone had already established sinlessness in the recipients of it.

The Archbishop, in preparing to enact these changes and rescind Henry VIII's legislation, was opposed by Stephen Gardiner, Bishop of Winchester. That experienced statesman and man of the world who was also a priest, a lawyer and a humanist, objected that both he and Cranmer had accepted the Henrician settlement, that, as members of the Council of Regency, they had sworn to continue it until Edward VI came of age and that Cranmer's repudiation of it now would 'teach the people, by the example of the Archbishop of Canterbury, that in England religion is nothing more than a consent given according to the necessities of the time to be revoked or changed according as the occasion arises.' In addition Gardiner pointed out that to be now required to say that 'whoever denies the doctrine that only faith justifieth is to be reputed not a true Christian man' was a slander on the late King who had not only denied the doctrine but had ordered the denial to be taught as part of the Christian religion.

Cranmer, however, had the firm support of the Protector Somerset who, in correspondence with Calvin, had gone further even than the Archbishop and had actually embraced the creed of predestination which, in relieving him of all responsibility for his actions, he found peculiarly acceptable.

The result of the clash was predictable. As Gardiner palpably could not be answered, he must be silenced. He was sent to close imprisonment in the Tower to await his trial—which was delayed for two years—for being 'a person much grudging, speaking and repugning against godly reformation of abuses in religion'. The new religious instructions were then issued and King's Commissioners appointed to make a new visitation of England. They were to see that all altars, crucifixes, religious pictures, stained-glass windows and statues of saints were destroyed 'so that there remain no memory of the same in churches or houses'. The use of holy water; the blessing of candles on the Purification, of ashes on Ash Wednesday and palms on Palm Sunday; and the veneration of the Cross on Good Friday were to be abolished. The vestments traditionally worn by the priest at Mass, emphasising the Sacrifice, were to be done away with in favour of a surplice, and a wooden table substituted for the old altar was to be set in the chancel further to emphasise that there was now only a memorial meal. The usual Sunday procession in church when the congregation recited the Litany of Our Lady was to be discontinued and in its place was to be taught a new Litany in English, in which the petition 'From the tyranny of the Bishop of Rome and his detestable enormities, good Lord deliver us' had pride of place.

Meanwhile Cranmer, with Gardiner silenced, set to work to fashion a new system of public worship to enshrine the new beliefs. The Missal, the Breviary and the Pontifical were abolished and in their place a single Prayer Book, based on a German Lutheran compilation and inspired by the 'by faith alone' theology, was prepared and enacted by Parliament to be exclusively used from Whit Sunday, 1549. Folio copies were printed for all incumbents, though the laity were to have no access to the book.[1]

The effect of the new measures was to bring home for the first time to the ordinary people of England that there had been a change in religion. Henry VIII's repudiation of the Pope, because it had been accompanied by the retention of the other beliefs and the forms of Catholicism, had seemed little more than an academic alteration. In practical terms, it meant that the people, instead of paying their accustomed dues to Rome, now paid heavier dues, which were collected more severely and swiftly, to the new Supreme Head. The dissolution of the monasteries had, indeed, made a profound difference to the normal life of the countryside, but its effects had been mainly social and economic. The ordinary practice of religion had continued uninterruptedly.

Certainly the social consequences were considerable. The monastic lands had been granted chiefly to courtiers who had no connection with the particular locality and, even when the

---

[1] The first Prayer Book for the laity was not issued till forty years later.

property continued to be managed by the same bailiffs who had served the monks, there was the difference that they now did all they could to increase the revenues of their new lay masters lest they themselves should be dismissed. Additionally, the new owners were prone to revive ancient and forgotten claims in order to deprive tenants of their customary privileges and illegally to enclose common pasture land for their own use.

With the presence of these new conditions there was the absence of the old charitable activities of the monks—the daily doles to poor tenants and neighbours, the distribution of gifts and money at 'month's minds', the unending hospitality of 'the inns of God where no man paid'—to alleviate the harshness of existence. Nor had there been any great absorption of the tens of thousands of unemployed created by the dissolution, not only the monks and nuns but the cooks, bakers, barbers, porters, laundresses, personal servants of the superiors and old servants kept on for charity.

These economic conditions, worsened by two devaluations of the currency, led to countrywide unrest and sporadic riots for which Roger Ascham, the Protestant tutor employed by the Protector for the education of Princess Elizabeth, laid the blame firmly on 'those who everywhere in England got the farms of the monasteries and are striving to increase their property by immoderate rents. Hence the exaggerated price of things. These men plunder the whole realm. Hence so many families dispersed, so many houses ruined. Hence the honour and strength of England, the noble yeomanry, are broken and destroyed.'

But amid the social and secular grievances there had still remained the consolations of religion to what had once been the most religious nation in Christendom.[2] Now even these were to

---

[2] According to foreign observers, the English in the first part of the sixteenth century were exceptional for their attendance at Mass—and not only on Sundays—and their devotion to Our Lady, shown in the public recitation of her Office. They understood the faith they practised and the circulation of devotional and instructional books among the population of three million may be gauged by the fact that, in the holocaust of Catholic piety and learning which Cranmer initiated, a quarter of a million liturgical books alone were destroyed.

be taken away and strange new services in English held in unfamiliarly plain and whitewashed churches were to be substituted for the rites and ceremonies of a thousand years. Emotionally, illogically—and to Cranmer and Somerset, incomprehensibly—it was this that pushed the men of the West into armed protest, remembering how thirteen years earlier the men of the North had, more perceptively, seen in the dissolution of the monasteries a reason for revolt and had marched in the Pilgrimage of Grace under the banner of the Five Wounds of Christ.

One of the King's Commissioners for Cornwall was William Body, a former servant and spy of Thomas Cromwell, who had already been in trouble for persuading the feckless Archdeacon of Cornwall, an illegitimate son of Cardinal Wolsey, to sell him the spiritual and temporal rights of the archdeaconry for a term of thirty-five years. Considerable bitterness had been engendered by the subsequent lawsuits and Body, a blustering bully, was unpopular in the West even among the gentry who shared his religious convictions. When he arrived at Helston to enforce the new measures, he was greeted by a threatening crowd of about a thousand who had gathered from the surrounding countryside —priests, sailors, fishermen, husbandmen, armed with swords, staves, sticks and bows and arrows. The result was, as reported by the French Ambassador, that 'people in the county of Cornwall killed the Commissioner who had gone there to remove images because he had broken and cut down the crucifix of a church which the people insisted should be left.'

The ringleaders in the protest were eventually arrested and nine of them were hanged, drawn and quartered in Launceston as a discouragement to the dissatisfied. None the less, dissatisfaction continued and at Bodmin, on Whit Sunday, June 9, a great host assembled under the command of Humphrey Arundell, of St. Michael's Mount, and John Bury, a former retainer of that Marquis of Exeter, Cardinal Pole's cousin, who was executed at the same time as Pole's elder brother, Montagu. The company determined to march, under the old banner of the Five Wounds, to lay their objections before the young King who, they thought, was being misled by his advisers.

On the same day, in the little village of Sampford Courtenay at the edge of Dartmoor, the inhabitants awaited the first use of Cranmer's Prayer Book. They had no doubt that their parish priest, Father William Harper, did not approve of it, but he had explained to them: 'In obedience to the law, I must say the new service.'

William Harper was now nearly seventy and three years ago he had been presented to the living of Sampford Courtenay (which, on the Marquis of Exeter's execution, had fallen to the Crown) by Queen Katherine Parr whom he had served in the capacity of Clerk to the Queen's Closet. When, after Henry VIII's death, she had married Seymour, Harper, who had never been happy in her service—for his duties involved among other things accompanying her on her journeys and saying Mass for her, though he knew her secret hatred of the Faith—grasped the opportunity to lose himself in the depths of the country by retiring to the parish which, as long as he was at court, was a sinecure served by a curate. In the event, he was not granted the obscurity he craved.

After the Whit Sunday service was over, the villagers swarmed into the crooked street leading to the church, stridently complaining and planning to take measures against repetition. Before the Whit Monday Mass, they gathered in force outside the church and when Father Harper appeared, a tailor and a labourer acted as spokesmen of the rest and demanded which service he intended to use. Again he replied: 'In obedience to the law, the new service.'

'That you will not,' said Thomas Underhill, the tailor. 'We will have our religion as it was appointed by King Henry until the

143

King's Majesty that now is reaches the age of twenty-four years, for so his father appointed it.'

And so, acording to the chronicler, 'whether it was with his will or against his will he yielded to their will and forthwith re-vested in his old popish attire and said Mass and all such services as in past times accustomed.'

The news spread like wildfire. The local Justices hurried to Sampford Courtenay to keep the King's peace, but the villagers, 'so addicted and wholly bent on their follies that they fully resolved themselves wilfully to maintain what naughtily they had begun', banded themselves together and gathered on the main road to join the Cornish men who were marching to Crediton. To Crediton also flocked sympathisers from all the district round, for the news of the defiance at Sampford Courtenay was as 'a cloud carried with a violent wind and a thunderclap sounding through the whole country; and the common people so well liked it that they clapped their hands with joy and agreed to have the same in every parish.'

The demands of 'the Commons of Devonshire and Cornwall' which they now framed and sent to London were that the Mass should be restored 'as was before' and that the Blessed Sacrament should be again reserved in a pyx over the altar. But, they said, 'we will not receive the new service because it is but like a Christmas game, but we will have our old service of Mattins, Mass, Evensong and Procession (the Litany of Our Lady) in Latin and we will have every preacher in his sermon and every priest at his Mass pray by name for the souls in Purgatory as our forefathers did'. Baptism should be available 'as well on week-days as on holy days'. The blessings of simple things should be restored, palms and ashes should be distributed at the accustomed times, with 'all the ancient old ceremonies used heretofore by our mother, the holy Church'. There should be at least two abbeys restored in each county and 'because the Lord Cardinal

Pole is of the king's blood, he should not only have his pardon but also be sent for to Rome and promoted to be of the King's Council'. This last clause was insisted on by John Bury who was anxious that there should be someone in authority to see that Government promises, if they were given, should be kept.

Cranmer was incensed not only by the articles themselves but, even more, by the fact that ignorant peasants, 'Hob, Will and Dick', should presume to question his theology. He settled down to write them a very long letter, beginning: 'O, ignorant men of Devonshire and Cornwall, as soon as ever I heard your articles I thought you were deceived by some crafty papists to make you ask you wist not what. How many of you, I pray you, do know certainly the holy decrees of the Fathers and what is in them contained? The holy decrees, as they call them, be nothing else but the laws and ordinances of the Bishop of Rome whereof the most part be made for his own advancement, glory and lucre.'

They prefer Latin to English? 'Had you rather be like pies or parrots that be taught to speak and yet not understand one word of what they say than be true Christians who pray to God in faith? Be you such enemies to your own country that you will not suffer us to laud God in our own tongue?'

Reservation of the Blessed Sacrament? 'Is this the Catholic faith that the Sacrament shall be hanged over the altar and worshipped? Although Pope Honorius III decreed the worshipping of the Sacrament he made no mention of hanging it over the high altar and in Italy until this day it is not so used.'

Like a 'Christmas game'? 'You declare what spirit leadeth them that persuaded you that the word of God is but like a Christian game. It is more like a game and a foolish play to hear the priest speak aloud to the people in Latin. In the English service there is nothing else but the eternal Word of God. If it be to you but a Christmas game, I think you not so much to be blamed as the papistical priests who have abused your sincerity.'

Purgatory? 'To appeal to learning with you who are ignorant were but folly. The Scripture maketh mention of two places where the dead be received after this life, of Heaven and of Hell. It is certain that Purgatory is feigned for lucre and not grounded upon God's Word.'

Blessings? 'You will eat often of the unsavoury and poisoned bread of the Bishop of Rome and drink of his stinking puddles, which he nameth holy bread and holy water! O superstition and idolatory! how they prevail among you!'

So, for page after page, the invective continued till it ended with a warning: 'That most godly prince of famous memory, King Henry VIII, pitying to see his subjects brought up in darkness and ignorance of God by the erroneous doctrine and traditions of the Bishop of Rome brought you out of your said ignorance and darkness. And our most dread Sovereign Lord that now is hath with no less care and diligence studied to perform his father's purpose. Yet you, like men that wilfully shut their eyes, refuse to receive the light. This I assure you of, that if all the whole world should pray for you till Doomsday, their prayers should no more avail for you than they would avail the devils in Hell, if they prayed for them, unless you be penitent and sorry for your disobedience.'

The Government as a whole was less concerned with the Archbishop's theological niceties than with practical measures for putting down a rebellion. The rebels, about 5,000 strong, had occupied Crediton and were besieging Exeter and the local magnate, Sir Peter Carew, failing to stop them, rode quickly to London to ask for help. The news of the rising, however, had outdistanced him and at Chard, just over the Somersetshire border, he met Lord Russell, the High Steward of the Duchy of Cornwall and one of the best soldiers in England, who had been sent down with a small force to deal with the situation.

Russell,[3] now sixty, was, as Lord Privy Seal, a member of the Council and, so, personally involved in the fate of the Govern-

[3] For Russell's earlier career see *A Matter of Martyrdom*, chapter 3.

ment. He was also the owner of much property in the district and, among other ecclesiastical spoils, had acquired Tavistock Abbey and its extensive lands as well as thirty manors in Somerset, Devon and Cornwall. But at the moment he thought primarily as a soldier. And as a soldier he realised that not only was his force outnumbered—he had only about two thousand men—but that it could probably not be relied on to fight fellow-countrymen. Moreover he could hope for no recruits in the district where popular sympathy was entirely on the side of the rebels. For an effective army he must await the dispatch from London of foreign mercenaries, especially Germans whose Protestant enthusiasm could be depended on—although Italians and Spaniards of the type who sold their swords were, even if Catholic, hardly likely to be troubled by religious scruples.[4] It was the first time for over three hundred years—since the reign of King John—that foreign troops had been employed on English soil against Englishmen. It was unfortunate, Russell thought, for it would hardly make for popularity, but it could not be helped.

Meanwhile, following the precedent set by the Pilgrimage of Grace, he parleyed to gain time, making promises which no one in authority intended to keep. Gradually the necessary reinforcements arrived—a thousand German foot whose ferocity was exceeded only by the Switzers who boasted of 'irrigating and inundating the earth with human blood'; 150 Italian 'harquebutters'[5] under a Genoese adventurer, Paolo Spinola and 450 Spanish and Italian cavalry under Jacques Jermigny and Pietro Sanga. Ordnance also was on its way from the capital under the Knight Marshal. In addition, a thousand-strong force under Lord Grey

[4] Oddly enough, they were. When it was all over, the English Ambassador to the Emperor recorded: 'Many Spaniards and Italians went to the Bishop of Rome's Nuncio to be absolved for that they had served the King of England in his wars.'
[5] The harquebut (or hackbut) was a hand-gun, the sixteenth-century predecessor of the musket. The derivation of the word is from the German Hakenbühse, 'hook-gun'. The weapon had been brought to a high degree of efficiency in the wars on the Continent.

de Wilton, who had just put down small risings in Oxfordshire and Buckinghamshire and hanged a number of priests from the steeples of their own churches as warning exhibits, joined Russell while Sir William Herbert brought him two thousand archers from Wales.

With such forces, whose numbers alone were now more than double those of the rebels, Russell felt it safe to advance. Not far from Exeter, he came upon about two thousand of the insurgents who had thrown up entrenchments of earth to try to block his way. The defenders were easily overcome and, according to an observer with the Royal forces, 'were slain like beasts'.

As Russell's men were preparing to rest after their labours, Spinola approached him. 'My Lord,' he said, (according to the Spanish Chronicler), 'my company of seasoned men is not tired, though the enemy will think that we, like your levies, require rest; so I suggest that we should feign to lead their spies to believe that we are going to sleep, and, instead, if Your Lordship wishes, we can be with them at daybreak, take them unawares and easily defeat them.'

Russell agreed and in the morning the rebels were again forced back, leaving behind them many dead, dying and prisoners.

They fell back on Clyst St. Mary. Russell gave orders for the village to be set on fire. The timbered houses with their thatched roofs were soon a mass of flame. 'Cruel and bloody was that day,' an eye-witness recorded, 'for some were slain, some burnt in the houses, some were taken prisoners and many, trying to escape over the water were drowned, so that there were dead that day by one or another about a thousand men.'

Nevertheless next day, the rebels, of whom Lord Grey reluctantly admitted that 'never in all the wars he had been in had he known such stoutness', determined to fight to the end. They made a surprise attack. It was easily repulsed. In revenge for its temerity, Russell ordered his men to kill all their prisoners. At first the mercenaries demurred because such a course deprived them of their ransom, but discipline prevailed and before night-

148

fall cries for mercy and screams of those being ingeniously butchered rang through the Devon lanes and fields as each soldier, regarding neither age nor youth, murdered his victims.

Next day, the remainder of the rebels, surrounded on Clyst Heath, were called on to yield. They preferred to fight to the death. 'Valiantly and stoutly they stood to their tackle and would not give over as long as life and limb lasted, yet in the end they were all overthrown and few or none left alive.'[6]

When the news reached London, 'the Archbishop of Canterbury made a collation in Paul's choir for the victory that the Lord Russell, Lord Privy Seal, had against the rebels in Devonshire'. In his sermon before the Lord Mayor and Aldermen, Cranmer admonished his auditors that 'the plague of sedition and division among ourselves, the like of which has not been heard of since the passion of Christ, is come upon us by the instigation of the Devil, in that we have not been diligent hearers of God's Word by his true preachers but have been led away by popish priests.'

In Devonshire, Russell was at pains to emphasise the same point and adopted Grey's device of hanging priests from their own steeples. An eye-witness described his method. Russell's personal servant, Bernard Duffield, 'caused a gallows to be set on top of the tower of the parish church and when all things were ready the vicar was by a rope about his middle drawn up and there in chains hanged in his popish apparel and a holy water bucket, a sprinkle, a sacring bell, a rosary and such other popish trash hanged about him; and there he with the same about him remained a long time before he died.'

Lest such warnings and countless executions of laymen were

------

[6] 'Years after—close on three centuries—the virgin soil of the once desolate heath was turned by the plough, disclosing a vast number of bones, which not only bore witness of the terrible carnage on the spot but, by the enormous size of many, indicated that the men were of no mean stature and might well have proved formidable opponents of the King's forces.'—F. Rose-Troup: *The Western Rebellion of 1549.*

not sufficient to prevent a recrudescence of rebellion, Russell
gave over the whole countryside 'to the spoil of the soldiers who
were not slothful to glean what they could find'.

14

Princess Mary's Mass

The leaders of the Western men, Humphrey Arundell, John Bury and eight others were sent to London for further examination. The Privy Council was anxious to 'pick out' matter incriminating Princess Mary and Cardinal Pole. In this the examiners were unsuccessful and the rebels, at the end of September, were sent to the Tower to await trial and execution at the year's end.

Early in October they were most unexpectedly joined in the Tower by the Lord Protector Somerset.

The architect of Somerset's sudden fall was his rival for the Protectorship, John Dudley, Earl of Warwick who had just put down, with even greater cruelty than Russell, a rising in Norfolk under Robert Kett which had broken out just after that in Devon and Cornwall but which, unlike the western rebellion, was concerned almost exclusively with social and economic grievances.

John Dudley was the son of the hated lawyer, Edmund Dudley, whom Henry VII had employed in mulcting his subjects and who had been executed by Henry VIII to the general satisfaction as soon as he came to the throne. John had been adopted and brought up by Sir Henry Guildford, whose daughter Jane he eventually married. He was taken into favour by Henry VIII and, as a result of his military ability, had been made successively Governor of Calais, Warden of the Scottish Marches, Lord High Admiral and, after its recent capture, Governor of Boulogne. He was a Knight of the Garter, a Privy Councillor and was created, as a reward for his services, Viscount Lisle and Earl of Warwick. But his ambition was limitless. Always he had intended to supplant Somerset, whom he loathed under the cover of apparent and excessive friendship, and it was he who had been foremost in urging the Protector to execute his brother, calculating that fratricide would inevitably lessen his popularity with the people.

Dudley himself, tall, dark and overflowing with vitality even now in his late forties, was endowed with all the charm that Somerset so conspicuously lacked and had always managed to carry most men and situations before him. The aftermath of the rebellions, with his own prestige enhanced and Somerset's reputation brought by the misery of the country to its lowest ebb, seemed to him the time to strike. The Protector was arrested and imprisoned and Cranmer was entrusted with the task of turning Edward against his uncle, without which no lasting progress could be made.

When the Duchess of Somerset requested an audience, she was received by the King, supported by Dudley and Cranmer. She threw herself on her knees and implored Edward at least to spare her husband's life.

Edward, completely taken aback, asked where the Protector was.

'A prisoner in the Tower,' she said, surprised that the boy knew nothing of it, 'and if Your Grace does not pardon him, the Council will kill him.'

'Jesu!' said Edward, 'they told me the Duke was ill. Why have they taken him prisoner?'

As no one answered, Edward turned to the Archbishop: 'Godfather, what has become of my uncle, the Duke?'

'He is a prisoner in the Tower,' said Cranmer.

'Why? What evil has he done that he should be arrested?'

'May it please Your Majesty,' said Cranmer smoothly, 'if God had not helped us, the country would have been ruined and we feared that he might kill you.'

This shattering lie was too much even for a boy of twelve. Edward was silent for a moment before he retorted: 'The Duke never did me any harm.'

Cranmer said, in his most convincing archiepiscopal tones: 'Your Majesty dooes not know everything. The Lords of the Council know what they are doing.'

He hoped that Dudley would say something, but Dudley was careful to observe the silence he had kept all through the interview.

The evidence necessary to dispose of Somerset was provided by his confidential secretary, William Cecil. This small, foxy man of twenty-nine was the son of Henry VIII's Groom of the Wardrobe, one of his favourites who had managed to acquire reasonable riches from grants of monastery land. William Cecil had been sent to Cambridge where he had stayed for six years without taking his degree but working so hard that, according to his biographer 'he hired a bell-ringer to call him up at four of the clock every morning; with which early rising and late watchings and continual sittings, there fell abundance of humours into his legs which was thought one of the original causes of his gout.'

While he was at Cambridge, Cecil married, much to his father's annoyance, the sister of his best friend, John Cheke, a brilliant scholar whose widowed mother kept a wine-shop in the town. The girl died in child-birth within a year and Cecil became a law-student in Gray's Inn. Two years later, John Cheke was appointed tutor to Prince Edward, whose education was under the general supervision of Sir Anthony Cooke. Cecil then married one of Cooke's sisters and thus, through two brothers-in-law, obtained a double entrée into the royal household. When Edward became

King, Somerset took Cecil, who shared his religious views, into his service and appointed him his Master of Requests. In this capacity everything which did not appertain to the official Secretary of State went through Cecil's hands and the position gave him sufficient power to have Dudley himself as his suitor.

To the acquisition of many important secrets, Cecil added a continual acquisition of property and at the age of twenty-nine had become wealthy enough to maintain thirty-six servitors wearing his badge and livery. Among his maxims were: 'Beware of being surety for thy best friends, for he that payeth another man's debts seeketh his own decay'; 'Let thy hospitality be moderate; spend not more than three parts of thy revenue and not a third part of that in thy house' and 'Be sure to keep some great man thy friend but trouble him not with trifles; compliment him often with many but small gifts'. He was also averse to travel: 'Suffer not thy sons to cross the Alps, for they shall learn nothing there but pride, blasphemy and atheism.'

Characteristically, as soon as he saw his master, the Protector, in difficulties, Cecil discreetly approached Dudley and, from his deep knowledge of Somerset's affairs, supplied him with a list of fifteen questions to be put to the prisoner, all of them of a leading character and calculated to compromise him.

The result was splendidly successful. Somerset was eventually executed; Dudley was created Duke of Northumberland and Cecil was rewarded with a knighthood, the manor and rectory of Wimbledon, the manor of Berchamstow and Deping in Lincolnshire, the manor and hall of Thetford, the reversion of the manor of Wrangdike in Rutland, the manor of Liddington and a moiety of the rectory of Godstow. He was also made Secretary of State to the new Protector.

Among those whom the substitution of Northumberland for Somerset affected most adversely was the Princess Mary. As soon as the religious changes had begun, she had obtained permission to retire from court and to live in one of her own houses —Newhall in Essex, Kenninghall in Norfolk and Hunsdon in Hertfordshire—which her father had left her. Here she could quietly practise her Faith, making her household still, as it had always been, a refuge for Catholics. Here Mass was, and would continue to be, offered.

Her brother, though himself being relentlessly educated into extreme Protestantism, had assured her, whom because of her twenty-two years seniority he looked on almost as a mother: 'If you are troubled or molested, it is against my will and I will see you contented.'

That Edward meant it, Mary had no doubt. But she also realised his complete powerlessness and the fact that the men around him would exert all the pressure they could to estrange him from her. Charles V's ambassador wrote to his master: 'It is quite certain that the King will only say what he is told to say. There is none about him, or among the gentlemen of the Bedchamber, except those well-known as partisans of the new doctrines.'

As the time approached for the enactment of the abolition of the Mass and the enforcement of the new Prayer Book, Mary, conscious of her complete isolation and fearful that the Act would be applied to her, wrote to the Emperor, saying that he was, after God and while her brother was so young, her only refuge. She had never been in such need of help as now when all these changes in religion were occurring. What support can she count on if the Council try to compel her by violence? Can Charles somehow provide that she shall live in the ancient Faith? If not, as she has sworn, she will die in it.

Charles, through his ambassador, sent her a verbal message that he loved her well, not only as his cousin but also for her constancy in religion. He did not write to her, for fear of making things worse for her, but he would none the less look after her. At the same time he ordered the ambassador to go to Somerset and ask for a written and permanent permission for Mary to use what service she chose, in spite of any innovations. He was to point out that it was impossible for the Council to treat the Princess as others were treated, since she was the King's sister and the heir to the Throne.

Somerset refused a written assurance but agreed: 'She shall do as she thinks best till the King comes of age and I shall favour her in anything that does not prejudice the King.'

When, however, the matter was brought up at a meeting of the Council, Dudley urged that Somerset had no power to give the Princess 'licence to attend Mass and have access to her sacrificing knaves'. Mass, he said, was either of God or of the Devil. If it was of the former, then all ought to have it, if of latter, 'should not the voice of this fury be equally proscribed to all?' The Council agreed. A fortnight after the fatal Whitsunday they sent Mary an order to replace Mass by the new Prayer Book service and to send to them her chaplain who, they heard, had been temerarious enough still to say Mass. For good measure, they accused her of encouraging the Western rebels through one of her chaplains at Sampford Courtenay, who had helped to foment the riots.

On receiving the letter, Mary ordered her chaplain at Kenninghall to sing three Masses instead of two and to use greater solemnity in them than ever before. To Somerset she wrote that he and all the Council had sworn to maintain her father's settlement of religion 'and *that* I have obeyed and will do till my brother have sufficient years to judge the matter for himself'. She refused to send her chaplain to London and 'as for Devonshire, no indifferent person can lay their doings to my charge'. No chaplain of hers was there and 'it was your new alteration and unlawful liberties that were rather the occasion of these assemblages than my doings'.

When the Imperial ambassador added his protests to hers: 'I see you are trying to deprive the Lady Mary of Mass', Somerset replied: 'We must hold by the King and enforce his laws, but if she does not wish to conform, let her do as she pleases quietly and without scandal.'

Somerset's diplomatic *modus vivendi* was however immediately abandoned as soon as Northumberland replaced him. The ambassador's mention of Mary's conscience was met by a brusque: 'You talk much of the Lady Mary's conscience. You should consider that the King's conscience will receive a stain if he allow her to live in error'. Two of her chaplains were arrested and sent to the Tower and she herself received a formal summons to come to London and appear before the King and Council.

She came in solemn state, 'with fifty knights and gentlemen in velvet coats afore her' says the Chronicler, 'and after her four score gentlemen and ladies, everyone having a pair of beads (rosaries) of black'. The streets of London were thronged to see her, some having walked 'six miles through the fields' and she was cheered all the way down Fleet Street and along the Strand to the gates of the palace of Whitehall. Here she was received with only very ordinary honours by the King's Comptroller.

As she faced Edward and the Council, Northumberland pointed out that no promise had been given about the continued celebration of her Mass.

This Mary denied and quoted her brother's letter to her saying 'for the good affection and brotherly love which we bear towards you we have thought good in respect of your weakness to dispense both you and your chaplains and priests for the hearing and saying any other service than that in the new Prayer Book'.

Edward admitted the letter, but a Councillor quickly intervened: 'Although Your Grace had exemption from the said ordinances, it was not for always.'

'I had understood so,' the Princess answered. 'It was only till the King my brother came of age.'

She then complained to Edward that she had received hectoring letters from the Council.

'I knew nothing of them,' he said.

'In that case,' retorted Mary, 'Your Majesty did not draw up the new ordinances of religion.'

'Your Grace will cause trouble by this obstinacy,' said another Councillor.

'I have always prayed for the King's prosperity and peace. As your Lordships have already praised His Majesty's great knowledge and understanding, then I will pray God that his virtues may increase.' She turned to her brother and said: 'Riper age and experience will teach Your Majesty much more yet.'

It was, perhaps, an unfortunate remark. Suddenly the atmosphere became one of the nursery where a small boy was made to smart under the tongue of an elder sister.

'You also may have something to learn,' he said. 'None are too old for that.'

A Councillor, breaking the family conversation, informed Mary that, by her father's will, she was subject to them.

'I have carefully read the will,' she replied, 'and I am bound but on the point of my marriage.' And, if it came to the will, how had they observed it? 'Your Lordships have said no masses for the King, my father's, soul as he commanded.'

'That would be harmful to the King's Majesty and state,' came the answer.

'I know the King my father never ordered aught harmful to his present Majesty, because of his love for him. He cared more for the good of his kingdom than all his Council put together,' said Mary.

This was too much for Northumberland who had been watching Edward's reactions. 'How now, my Lady,' he said loudly, 'it seems that Your Grace is trying to show us in a hateful light to the King our master without any cause whatsoever.'

'I have not come hither to do so,' she replied, 'but you press me so hard I cannot dissemble.' She turned again to Edward: 'I hoped,' she said, 'that because I am Your Majesty's unworthy sister you would have allowed me to continue in the old religion.

There are but two things—soul and body. My soul I offer to God and my body to Your Majesty's service. I would rather that you took away my life than the old religion in which I desire to live and die.'

'I desire no such sacrifice,' said Edward.

She felt suddenly tired and asked his permission to withdraw. 'I beseech you to give no credit to those who wish you to believe evil of me,' she said, looking at Northumberland. 'I shall always remain your humble and obedient sister.'

'I do not doubt that,' said her brother. 'But I cannot longer suffer your Mass.'

'I will not change my faith,' said Mary, 'nor dissemble my opinion of contrary doings.'

'I am not constraining your faith,' said Edward illogically. 'I only wish you to think of yourself not as one who rules but as a subject who obeys.'

There was a silence and then he blurted out, hoping she would see his practical dilemma: 'Your example might breed too much inconvenience.'

When she had gone, Edward, according to his custom, entered the matter in his diary: 'March 18: The Lady Mary, my sister, came to me at Westminster where she was called with my Council into the Chamber where was declared how long I had suffered her Mass against my will, in hope of her reconciliation. She answered that her soul was God's and her Faith she would not change.'

On second thoughts, he decided to be as truthful as she had been. He struck out the words 'against my will'.

Next day the Imperial Ambassador asked to be received by the Council and informed them that, if the Princess Mary were not allowed her Mass, the Emperor would declare war.

Northumberland and his colleagues, who realised that, in the present state of the country, the conquest of England would probably be a matter of weeks, asked Cranmer whether, in these changed circumstances, he could recommend to the King's conscience that perhaps, after all, the Princess might be allowed her Mass. Considering everything, the Archbishop thought that it might be 'winked at'. A Council was hurriedly called 'as though the realm had been already upon the sacking' and the King was informed, after the Emperor's demands had been read to him, that he must agree to Charles's request.

'I cannot do it at your advice,' said Edward, 'nor at any king's or emperor's.' He must be assured that the Bible would allow it.

Cranmer, prepared for this, started to discourse on how 'there were good kings in the Old Testament that suffered ill alterations and yet were good kings', but his godson 'roundly' interrupted him with: 'As good examples have God to allow them, so are evil examples set out to warn us. Abraham lay with Agar his maid; David took Uriah's wife to him and to hide his adultery committed a murder. Did they this that we should think it lawful to do it or does Scripture make mention of it that none should do as they did? My lord, if you will have me grant you this suit, you must show me by Scripture that I may do it.'

No one could think of any good examples from Scripture and when Cranmer, who, in his coronation address had bidden Edward take up his sword against the power of the Pope in all his dominions, suggested that the danger itself was so great as to warrant compromise, the King said fiercely: 'I require you to fear God with me and rather to disdain any peril than to set aside God's will to please an Emperor.'

There was silence and Edward continued: 'The Emperor is a man liker to die any day than to do us harm. I know God is able to defend me against as many Emperors as ever the world had. He that preserved David will preserve me from harm. I would give my life and all that I have rather than to agree certainly to what I know to be against the truth.'

The boy could not understand why the Councillors could not grasp so simple a point. If there was anything that they were all agreed on and that the whole of their policy was based on, it was that Mass was the ultimate evil which must be rooted out of the realm. And now they wanted him to go back on his word and make terms with that evil.[1]

'I must do as God giveth me in commandment,' he said. 'God would chastise me for breaking His will.'

But it was useless. Someone mentioned the adverse effect on trade, even if the Emperor refrained from war. Another emphasised the danger to Edward's Most Sacred person. A third said that Edward's life was not his own to give and that he was the guardian, not the owner, of the realm.

Here the King suddenly broke down. 'I will shed my tears for both,' he said, and sobbed. 'Be content . . . be content . . . let me alone.'

Cranmer eventually devised a formula which was, even for his skill, a masterpiece of prevarication: 'Although to give licence to sin is sin, yet, if all possible haste is observed, to suffer and wink at it for a time is to be borne.'

So Princess Mary kept her Mass.

[1] Sir Frederick Madden in his introductory essay in *Privy Purse Expenses of Princess Mary* puts it: 'It would appear that the Bishops had some difficulty in making the simple-minded King understand their logic.'

15

The Death of Pope Paul III

The unaccustomed celerity with which Charles V had interfered in English affairs was a clear indication of the way in which his mind was now moving. Since Mülhberg, his thoughts had become increasingly dynastic and the inclusion of England in the immensity of his realms had become to him a practical consideration. He had not altogether abandoned the idea of marrying Princess Mary himself, but a better plan, slowly maturing, seemed to be that she should become the wife of his only legitimate son, Philip.[1]

At the time of the outbreak of the rebellion in England, Charles was in Brussels awaiting Philip, so that he might present him to the people of the Netherlands as their future ruler. Philip was twenty-two, a widower with one son, Don Carlos, and he had spent all his life in Spain. If Charles always remained more a Fleming than a Spaniard—he never learnt to speak Spanish—Philip was always emphatically 'Philip of Spain'. When first his journey to Brussels had been announced, the Cortés had immediately sent a protesting letter to his father, begging him not to summon his son away from Spain, of which he was Regent in Charles's continual absences. But the Emperor was determined that Philip should now know at first hand something of the other

---

[1] His celebrated bastard, Don John of Austria, was at this time only one year old.

nations whom one day he would be called on to rule and his son, after a leisurely progress through Italy, eventually arrived at a Brussels *en fête* to receive him, with triumphal arches erected in the streets to welcome 'Philip, Hope of the Century' and 'Philip, future Heir of the World'. The magnificence and liberality of the entertainments which the Emperor provided, overcoming for this occasion his habitual parsimony, recalled the almost-forgotten splendours of the old Burgundian court and they were repeated as the handsome, intelligent, reserved young man went on to Louvain to be sworn as Duke of Brabant and to Ghent as Count of Flanders.

Charles had prepared for his son a political testament, of which the first words summed up the Emperor's own experience with devastating clarity: 'Seeing that all human affairs are beset with doubt, I can give you no general rules save to trust in Almighty God.'

There were, however, certain particular instructions. 'After all our trouble and labour in bringing back the German heretics, I have come to the conclusion that an Ecumenical Council is the only way. Even the German estates have agreed to submit to it. Have a care, therefore, that the Council continues in all reverence to the Holy See; but proceed cautiously against the abuses of the Vatican when they affect your own lands. You yourself know how unreliable Pope Paul III is in all his treaties, how sadly he lacks all zeal for Christendom and how ill he has acted in this affair of the Council.[2] Nevertheless, honour his position. The Pope is old; therefore take careful heed of the instructions which I have given my ambassador in Rome in case of an election.'

He then turned to the eternal enemy, France. Francis I had died two months after Henry VIII and had been succeeded by his thirty-year-old son, Henry II. 'France has never kept faith,' wrote Charles, 'and has always sought to do me hurt. But act cautiously and try to keep the peace for the weal of Christendom

[2] Charles means by transferring it from Trent to Bologna.

163

and your own subjects. But the young King seems about to follow in his father's footsteps. Never yield to French demands, not so much as an inch. They will take an ell. At the present time they have emphatically refused to give back to the Duke of Savoy the lands they have unjustly seized from him. I have always supported the Duke in his claim. But if you give troops to the Duke to regain his land, do it with the utmost caution. Only if the French and the English are fully engaged, and if you can get the help of the Swiss, will it be safe for you to send troops to Savoy. At the moment the troubles in Germany and the pacific policy of the regency in England make this impossible.'

After analysing the situation in other parts of Europe, the Emperor urgently entreated his son to look for a new wife. 'You cannot be everywhere,' he wrote, 'so you must find good viceroys and such as will not overstep their instructions. The best way is to hold your kingdoms together by making use of your own children. For this you will have to have more children and must contract a new marriage.'

While Philip, on his way to the Netherlands, was in Italy the Pope sent a special mission to ask him to intercede with his father for the restitution to the Holy See of Piacenza, which was now held for the Emperor by Gonzaga, Pierluigi's murderer. The death of his son had had, when the first shock and bitterness was past, an unexpected effect on the Pope. Paul was now eighty-three and, though still in lively health, could in the nature of things not expect to live long. Always he had had sufficient self-knowledge to recognise that nepotism was his besetting sin. 'If it had not had the mastery over me,' he said truly enough, 'I should have been without great offence.' Might not the murder of Pierluigi be construed both as an appropriate punishment and as a call for amendment? He would make what restitution he could and demand the return of Piacenza and Parma not to his Farnese family but to the See of Peter.

This eccentric decision startled his grandsons, Ottavio, Duke of Parma, and his brother, Alessandro, Cardinal Farnese, into shocked but discreet activity. They assumed that senility rather than sanctity was at the root of their grandfather's inexplicable action and at first tried gently to dissuade him. He listened to them but remained adamant. Their objections grew fiercer and less courteous. He sent to the Governor of Parma, Camillo Orsini, peremptory instructions to hold the city for the Church and for her alone. He was to deliver it into no other hands.

Ottavio, realising that this was directed as much against him as against the Emperor, wrote to his grandfather that, unless Parma were delivered to him, he was prepared to make common cause with the Imperialists and call in the aid of Gonzaga, his father Pierluigi's murderer.

The Pope, at first incredulous that his favourite grandson should so betray him, was stricken to the heart. He declared that no event in his life, not even the death of his son, had given him so much pain as the treachery of the grandson for whom, by his past nepotism, he had imperilled his soul. His one consolation was that Ottavio's younger brother, Alessandro the Cardinal, was still loyal to him and to the Church.

In this he was wrong. On All Saints Day, November 1, 1549, he discovered that Alessandro whom he had trained and implicitly trusted and into whose hands he had committed the whole conduct of his affairs was at one with Ottavio. Rather than relinquish Parma to the Holy See, to which it by right belonged, both Duke and Cardinal were prepared to deliver it to the Emperor, provided only that the Farnese could still hold it as a fief from him.

The third of November was the fifteenth anniversary of the Pope's coronation. Paul spent the following day resting after the arduous ceremonial. On November 5 he ordered Cardinal Farnese to attend him in his private villa on the Quirinal. He did not wish what he had to say to him to be overheard at the Vatican. The interview ended with the old man tearing Alessandro's red hat from his head and stamping it on the ground.

Five days later Paul was dead. The doctors who carried out the autopsy reported that 'internally he was found in the most healthy state and as one likely to live for some years; but there were three drops of coagulated blood in his heart, judged to have been caused by the movements of anger'.

At his last hour, during a brief rally, the Pope dictated a message ordering Camillo Orsini to deliver Parma to Ottavio as soon as the tidings of his death arrived. Orsini, troubled by the two contradictory demands, sent his son to Rome to ask Pole, who, it was generally assumed, would be the next Pope, what he should do. Pole replied that he could not interfere publicly in a matter of state but that, as a private Cardinal, he recommended Orsini 'to keep the royal road', which was to refer the matter to the College of Cardinals and to abide by their decision.

Orsini, 'being very devoted to the Cardinal of England' took his advice to the extent of consulting the Sacred College but still refused to deliver Parma to Ottavio even though they sanctioned it. He was suspicious of the circumstances under which the last letter was written.

Alessandro ordered the gates of Rome to be closed and the Conclave for the election of a new Pope was settled for November 29, the day after the body of Paul III was placed in a temporary tomb behind the organ in St. Peter's to await a more splendid sepulture when the new building was more advanced.[3]

[3] His monument is now in the apse to the right of St. Peter's Chair.

16

The Conclave

The rebuilding of St. Peter's was proceeding at a snail's pace. For forty years, six successive architects, from Bramante, 'the Destroyer' to the younger Sangallo, had produced contradictory plans which had introduced almost total confusion into the conception of the great church. At last Paul III, convinced that only Michelangelo could successfully bring the work to completion, had managed to induce him at the age of seventy-two to accept the responsibility of being Chief Architect of St. Peter's. The artist had made two conditions—that he should receive no payment, because he undertook the work only for the love of God, and that he should have full powers and freedom to create as his own vision dictated. His long experience had taught him that he would be hindered at every step by the envious and the jealous, the pedantic and the self-opinionated, the spiteful and the critical, the official and the officious and he had asked for a written confirmation of the Pope's verbal promise of complete independence.

One of Paul's last actions, less than a month before his death, had been to climb the ladder to the platform in the Pauline Chapel so that he could examine minutely the detail of the now-finished *Crucifixion of St. Peter* and Michelangelo had taken advantage of their conversation to remind the Pope of his architectural

167

request. Paul had thereupon issued a *motu proprio* to the effect that Michelangelo's model for the new St. Peter's[1] was to be strictly adhered to for all time and that he was to continue for his lifetime as the architect of the Basilica of the Prince of the Apostles.

Yet many wondered whether even Michelangelo would be able to bring the matter to completion. An English visitor that year wrote: 'The new building, if it were finished, would be the goodliest thing in the world. Nevertheless, it has been so many years a-doing and is yet so imperfect that most men stand in doubt whether ever it shall be finished.'

It was in the chapel in the old St. Peter's named after Pope Sixtus IV—he who had built the Sistine Chapel in the Vatican and had now been dead forty-five years—that High Mass was sung with great solemnity before the cardinals entered the Vatican to elect a new Pope. There were in Rome when Paul III died twenty-nine of the fifty-four[2] cardinals and within the next fortnight twelve more arrived, though none of the French had yet even started on their journey.

Their official appearance at St. Peter's was marked by the usual ceremonial pageantry which the Roman populace loved. In conformity with custom, whenever a cardinal crossed the Ponte Sant' Angelo, 'there was a piece of ordnance shot off for an honour'. By the number of shots at any one time, the crowd round St. Peter's knew how many Eminences to expect. When the approaching prelates were seen at the further end of the Borgo, 'a fair street, straight and level and more than a quarter of a mile long' running from the Castel Sant' Angelo to the Vatican, the Swiss Guard turned out 'all in white harness and there alongst before the gate made a lane, half on one side and half

---

[1] A model, finished within fourteen days, gave Paul III an idea of the new plan. Although the final model of the incomparable dome was not made till thirteen years later and the dome itself was not built in Michelangelo's lifetime, Paul was able to see and grasp the essential design.

[2] Only forty-seven, because of illness and other reasons, actually took part in the final voting.

on the other, with their two drums and a fife before them; and as the cardinals approached the drums and fife began to play and so continued till the cardinals were well entered amongst them. Then the trumpets blew up till the cardinals were about at the gate and as they entered the shawms began to play and ceased not till they were alighted from their mules and mounted up the stairs.'

Inside the Vatican all the necessary preparations were made. The wooden 'cells' for the cardinals were erected in the Sistine Chapel, the Pauline Chapel and the long Sala Regia which connected the two and in addition four other halls were set aside for private and for public consistories, while special provision was made for any who should fall sick. Two days before the opening of the conclave the cells were chosen by lot and those which were to be occupied by the 42 cardinals created by Paul III were hung with violet and the remaining twelve, six for those of Leo X's creation, six of Clement VII's, with green. Each cardinal was allowed to have with him two 'conclavists'—Pole naturally took Alvise Priuli and Thomas Goldwell—and, if the cells were hardly commodious, they were not expected to be occupied for long. By the election decree of Gregory X, two centuries earlier, a conclave could not last for more than ten days and the election of Paul III had occupied only one. No one foresaw that this, the longest conclave in history, would drag on for ten weeks.

On the evening of St. Andrew's Day, November 30, the doors were solemnly barred within and without by six bolts and the forty-one cardinals were cut off from the world; but their enclosure was in fact maintained with so little strictness that its laxity became a scandal. To the eye of a realist, however, this was less serious than it seemed if only because the election was politically construed as the latest incident in the unresting struggle between the Emperor and the French, in which the protagonists were outside rather than inside the Vatican. The cardinals within might be seeking the guidance of the Holy Spirit. Without, the Imperial envoy, the inevitable Mendoza, and the French envoy, Claude d'Urfé, who in his energy and unscrupulousness was a not unworthy opponent, were intent on gaining political advantage for their respective masters. They could each count on almost the same number of votes for the cardinals were almost evenly divided in their secular allegiances and almost equally liable to pressure, if not to actual bribery. In the opinion of one of their number there were only three who obeyed their consciences alone—Cervini, Caraffa and Pole. And as they were all dedicated to reformation of the Church, the possible election of any one of them filled the majority, who had no particular desire to be reformed, with something like apprehension.

The Emperor's choice had in fact fallen on Pole. Charles's main concern was that the next Pope should be one who would recall the Ecumenical Council to Trent and for this reason he vehemently opposed the austere Cervini (now the Librarian of the Vatican) on the grounds that it had been he who had been mainly responsible for the removal of the Council from Trent to Bologna. The Emperor also favoured anyone who was prepared to see Piacenza and Parma returned to the Farnese—and so, in the present circumstances, to the Empire. A third consideration was that, for the sake of his Protestant subjects, the Pope should be one of reforming tendencies. But the Emperor's overriding reason was dynastic and one which was realised by no one but his son, Philip. If Pole became Pope, he could not marry Princess Mary.

Pole, though as a diplomat he was perfectly aware of the general situation, had no inkling of this. Even if he had had, it would not have affected his attitude which was well understood by everyone. More than ever now, he saw God making use of the strange unpredictable course of human history, using unexpected people and unpleasing circumstances, to carry out His will. After so long a schooling, Reginald's unworldliness had become absolute. He refused even to solicit a single vote.

'At the bankers' shops,' wrote the Venetian Ambassador, 'the odds are greater than before in favour of the Rt. Rev. of England whose election, should it take place, may be believed to proceed from God; for although urged by many cardinals to assist himself on this, so great an occasion, he answered them that he would never utter a single word, even if his silence were to cost him a thousand lives; not choosing to deviate from his ancient maxim which enjoined him to follow the Lord God and to desire nothing but His will.'

The French had not, like the Emperor, a positive policy. Their mainspring was disagreement with his and their opposition to Pole was automatic. Additionally, the idea of an English Pope was naturally anathema to England's traditional enemy. But they had no particular preference and they accepted, without any noticeable enthusiasm, the choice made by the Cardinal d'Este, who was their leader in the absence of the French delegation. He chose Caraffa as one who was as earnest as Pole in the cause of reform and of more unimpeachable orthodoxy. Also, as an Italian, he might be expected to attract the votes of undecided Italian cardinals who, though less vehemently than the French, disliked the idea of an English Pope.

At the first ballot, Pole received twenty-one votes and Caraffa ten, the remainder being distributed among four other cardinals. As the two-thirds majority required was twenty-eight, it seemed reasonable to expect that at the second ballot a transference of votes would give Pole the required number. He received only twenty-four, but it was enough to terrify the French who managed to get word to D'Urfé that the Cardinal of England was bound to secure election unless the envoy could think of some way of preventing it.

D'Urfé thereupon went to the door of the conclave and, through the Master of Ceremonies, informed the assembly that the French cardinals had already arrived in Corsica and that, should the electors not wait for them at least till the end of the week, the French king would refuse to acknowledge the election. For good measure, d'Urfé threatened a schism. It was a lie, of course. The French cardinals had not even started.

Shortly afterwards, according to the Venetian Ambassador, Mendoza 'arrived in a passion and he, in like manner, sent to their lordships and protested to them mildly and lovingly that they must observe their due rules and regulations and not wait for anything else; whereupon at the bankers' shops at the second hour of the night England was at 80'.

Meanwhile, within the Vatican, the Imperialists decided that immediately, without formal voting, they would acclaim Pole Pope by a general rendering of 'adoration'. The French countered by argumentatively delaying that quite legitimate course of action till well after midnight, by which time Pole had sent his chaplain to Cardinal Farnese, the leader of the Imperialists, with the message that though he was prepared, if necessary, to approach the Papal throne by the door, he was not prepared to use the window. Nevertheless Farnese persisted.

Pole left his own account of it: 'When the two Cardinals came to my cell to proffer 'adoration' I thought of the two disciples whom our Lord sent to fetch the ass on which He meant to ride into the Holy City. So I listened to them and would not have denied them but for the night-time and its darkness. Was I right or not? I made no disputation, save that I could have no part in anything which night and darkness might render suspect. Then came other two with the same authority to show that they were not asking anything of me not customary or unlawful but something sanctioned and just. Yet I prayed them to wait and leave the issue to be proved by daylight.'

After the events of the daylight of December 5, he added: 'As it happened, the Lord did not require this particular ass.'

Yet that morning it had seemed so certain. Most of the cardinals, before proceeding to vote, had ordered their cells to be emptied, as they did not wish to be plundered by the rush of people after the election. The Papal vestments had been laid out for Pole and he had actually composed an address of thanks. Outside, great crowds of people and the five thousand troops who were keeping order in the city were waiting—the soldiers with colours flying—to greet the new Pope.

The French party had decided to fight to the last. They had assembled in the Sistine Chapel—the Imperialists occupied the Pauline—and Caraffa had heartened them by delivering a fierce invective in his best oratorical manner accusing Pole of unsoundness on the doctrine of Justification as evidenced by his feigned illness to escape the crucial debate at Trent.

When the vote was taken, Pole was found to have twenty-three, whereupon two cardinals who had hitherto been neutral rose to their feet and announced that they would support the Cardinal of England. Pole now needed only one more vote, for if he could obtain twenty-six, he was, because of an agreement made in the night, certain of at least twenty-seven and he could, if necessary, give the twenty-eighth himself.[3] But no vote was added. When the Cardinal-Dean in charge of the proceedings asked if anyone else would come over to Pole's side, deep silence was the only answer and no one moved.

A week later four French cardinals arrived, led by the twenty-three-year-old Charles Cardinal Guise, the confidant of the French king. This young man, whose expression of sad cynicism made him look older than his years, was the brains of the Guise family which was rapidly gaining disproportionate power in France. They were a peculiarly ecclesiastical house and held three cardinalates and eighteen archbishoprics and bishoprics. Charles himself was an eloquent speaker, a subtle intriguer, a good administrator and a facile theologian, but he was a physical coward and

[3] Whether, considering his attitude, he would have done is doubtful, but it would have been in order as a cardinal's vote in his own favour was not made invalid till 1621.

173

unpopular on that account alone. He had other drawbacks. 'He is not well beloved,' one observer wrote, 'for he is insincere and has a nature both artful and avaricious, equally in his own affairs and in those of his King.' But not even his worst enemy gainsaid his ability and his arrival marked a new stage in the history of the conclave.

Guise's candidate for the Papacy was his uncle, John Cardinal of Lorraine,[4] one of the oldest of the cardinals of Leo X's creation, though he was prepared, if necessary, to continue with Caraffa. In any case Pole's candidature was now hopeless, even though the betting odds remained at 40 'nor is any other person whatever mentioned', and the Imperialist party swore 'that they would die with Pole on their lips'. Every morning they gave him their twenty-three votes. Caraffa, with equal regularity, got twenty-two. There were sixty of these fruitless ballots. The deadlock seemed complete.

The conclave occasionally diverted itself by proposing various candidates strictly for honorific reasons. On one occasion the Imperialists gave fifteen votes to the Cardinal-Infante of Portugal for no other reason than his birth, whereupon next day the French outdid them by giving twenty to Guise. 'Behold,' wrote Angelo Masserelli who, as secretary to the Council of Trent had become almost impervious to ecclesiastical eccentricities, 'at what times we have arrived! After we have vainly employed twenty days in electing a Pope and the whole of Christendom is daily clamouring for one, behold the zeal which the cardinals display for the common weal by bestowing twenty votes on a young man of twenty-three, not with the intention, as they themselves admit, of making him Pope but out of consideration of the favour he enjoys with the King of France.'

[4] Lorraine died a few months later and Guise succeeded him in his title. Charles thus became Cardinal of Lorraine (by which title he is usually known in history) while his younger brother Louis succeeded him as Cardinal Guise.

That same day the 'young man of twenty-three' decided to remonstrate directly with Pole. Under Caraffa's guidance, Guise accused the Cardinal of England of not possessing the necessary qualities for the Papacy. He repeated Caraffa's innuendo about Pole's illness at Trent and his accusation of near-heresy in the matter of Justification, and called on him therefore to withdraw his candidature. Pole, who had remained silent in face of Caraffa's attack, decided that a reply was in this case necessary and answered calmly that his absence was due to health alone and that, though he would take no steps to be chosen Pope, yet neither would he prevent the cardinals bestowing their votes on him if they were so inclined. He then retired to his cell and continued writing a careful essay on 'The Duties of a Pope' with which he occupied his time in preference to joining in the general gossip.

The atmosphere of the conclave went from bad to worse. Even the physical conditions were so unhealthy, with the fumes of the candles and the torches and the stench of the lavatories, that the leading physician in Rome feared a plague. Cervini became so ill that he had to leave the conclave and another of the cardinals died.

Other conditions were even more distressing. The more worldly cardinals insisted on enlarging their cells and taking over those that were empty for the accommodations of their barbers and cooks. The rules for the limitation of meals were totally disregarded. There were feasts that would have satisfied Lucullus—the description is Masserelli's—and the eminent gourmands issued invitations to one another or sent elaborate dishes to their friends.

The very word 'conclave'—an assembly behind locked doors—assumed an ironic air. Openings were made in the walls; windows were opened; the rule of limiting to two the number of each cardinal's 'conclavists' was shamelessly broken and so many servants and political spies were introduced that, instead of the hundred-and-fifty or so people officially there there were nearer four hundred. Letters were easily delivered to the outside world—the servant of one cardinal had so many missives from other cardinals stuffed in his boots that he forgot to deliver his master's message—and a preponderance of Eminences, through their servants, managed to place bets with the bankers and even, in some cases, to go partners with them in so lucrative a business. After Pole's refusal of 'adoration', even Priuli and Goldwell were suspected. 'His conclavists,' it was said, 'must be in partnership with the bankers in the wagers which have caused many tens of thousands of crowns to change hands.'

In matters of major political importance, actual interviews with the cardinals were arranged and d'Urfé was able to inform the French king that by climbing with the aid of ladders over the roofs he had been able to hold a long conversation with Guise.

Meanwhile outside disorder and impatience increased. The irritated citizens perpetually stormed in front of the Vatican shouting their demands for a new Pope. Monks and secular priests processed daily, interceding with Heaven. Innumerable satirical poems and drawings flooded the city, castigating the cardinals for their slavish adulation of secular princes. And in Germany the Lutherans jeered at a church divided between those who expected the Holy Ghost from France and those who anticipated His advent from the Empire.

As Christmas approached the cardinals discovered a new topic for debate. The year 1550 was a Jubilee year to be inaugurated, as always, by the opening of the Golden Door by the Pope on Christmas Eve. Already the first pilgrims were arriving in Rome and the shopkeepers were insistent that no ecclesiastical technicalities should impede the profitable flow. Whether or not a Holy Year could be inaugurated without a Pope and the customary ceremonies became the subject of an ingenious debate within the Vatican; but in the city, when Christmas Eve came and nothing had been done, protests mounted dangerously. Protocol had to give way to practicality and on December 29 it was solemnly announced that the Holy Year had already begun and that the

Golden Door would be opened as soon as there was a Pope to open it.

There seemed no immediate prospect of this taking place. The year 1549 closed with 40 to 1 odds against there being a Pope in January and 10 to 1 against there being one even in February. But the conclave itself was becoming sufficiently restless for some attention to be paid to the suggestion that the leaders of the opposing parties, Farnese and Guise, should be shut up together without food until they reached agreement.

On January 19, Farnese went so far as to approach Guise with the suggestion that they should begin to look for a new and acceptable candidate by eliminating Caraffa and three others whom the Imperialists, under the Emperor's orders, would in no case vote for. Guise replied by demanding an equivalent repudiation, saying that the French 'would never in all eternity vote for Pole' or three others whom his King had interdicted. Neither would agree to this and the situation was further exacerbated a few days later by Guise refusing to speak to Farnese at all because—so Guise said—Farnese had promised to vote for the Cardinal of Lorraine and then had not done so, which was not the act of a gentleman.

At the end of January, however, an unexpected complication occurred. There was a rift among the Farnese. Of the four brothers who were Paul III's grandsons, Alessandro—Cardinal Farnese—continued to act, as he had always done, in concert with Ottavio, Duke of Parma. Their two younger brothers, Orazio, Duke of Castro and Commander of the Papal troops and Ranuccio, Cardinal-Archbishop of Naples, also tended to agree with each other. Orazio, at the moment, was hoping to become the son-in-law of the French King; and, on January 29, Ranuccio startled the conclave by deserting the Imperialists and voting for the French candidate. It took four days and at least one sleepless night for Cardinal Farnese to win his brother back to the Imperial side and by February 3 he had decided that the conclave must end as quickly as possible. If party discipline,

177

which hitherto had been so effective, could so suddenly crumble and the culprit be his own brother, anything might happen. Delay now was actually dangerous. As Guise by this time had also realistically abandoned any hope of success for a French candidate, the leaders decided to co-operate in choosing one who, if not particularly desired by either side, was relatively inoffensive to both.

Their choice eventually fell on del Monte. At first there were objections to him on both sides. Farnese pointed out that he was on the Emperor's list of the prohibited; Guise objected to a sodomite as Pope. But after del Monte had privately promised Farnese that, if he became Pope, he would restore Parma and Piacenza to Ottavio and the Cardinal d'Este had assured Guise that the 'ape-boy' Innocent was really del Monte's son and not his catamite, both decided to recommend him and on February 8 del Monte was unanimously elected to the Papal Throne as Julius III.

The event was so unexpected that even on that day the foreign ambassadors had informed their masters that no one was anticipating an election and that most people had even given up talking about it. The Roman citizens rejoiced more at the fact that they had again a Pope than that he was del Monte, for whom they had no particular enthusiasm and who, many thought, was an odd choice for the Holy Ghost to have made.

One effect of del Monte's accession was to bring Pole and Caraffa together again. As soon as they heard that he intended to raise Innocent—who was now seventeen and more insufferable than ever—to the Cardinalate, they both rushed to remonstrate. Pole reminded the new Pope of the canonical decrees, by which Innocent was too young, and of the gravity of the times. Such an action would do more to prejudice the Papacy in the eyes of the Protestants than anything that could be imagined and no one would any longer believe that there was any serious intention to reform the Church. Till three in the morning Pole stayed with Julius, arguing and imploring, but was unable to move him.

Caraffa, passionate and even more indignant, was less diplomatic. As an older man, he saw no reason to mince his words. He told the new Pope that the shame which would result from so unfortunate a step would never be outlived. He expatiated on the probable—nay, certain—ribald talk among the people, which was something that should be avoided by any Prince and especially by the successor of the Prince of the Apostles. He, like Pole, insisted that it made a mockery of the reform as well as giving to the secular rulers an occasion to despise the Papal Court. He described Innocent as, however dear he might have become to del Monte, 'a vicious and fatherless young man'.

But the more vehement were the Cardinals, the more stubborn the Pope became. He was, though he tried to conceal it, still entirely besotted and what Innocent wanted Innocent must have. At Julius III's first consistory, which Pole and Caraffa, knowing what it would hold, pointedly refused to attend, the keeper of the ape was raised to the purple.

17

Doubts

'That comedy, not to say tragedy!' So Pole eventually described the conclave, courteously refraining from categorising the disparate elements. For himself tragedy predominated. It was not simply that the change in the Papacy affected his outward circumstances, but that he started ceaselessly to question his motives in refusing the Chair. The very praise he received on this account served only to deepen his self-suspicion.

Men began to apply to him a version of the pun—'Not angles but angels'—which St. Gregory had made nearly a thousand years before. 'Your Serenity should know,' wrote the Venetian Ambassador in Rome to the Doge, Priuli's brother, 'that his Rt. Rev. Lordship of England is styled "angelical" rather than "anglican".' The new Pope, despite recognised areas of disagreement, continued to insist that he was indebted to the Cardinal of England for the Papal throne. When on the day of his election the Cardinals had rendered the customary homage, he had forestalled Pole by rising and, with tears in his eyes, embracing him as the one to whom he owed the pontificate; and subsequently when he was in any great difficulty Julius III was accustomed to say: 'God sends me this affliction for failing to give my vote in conclave to that holy man, Cardinal Pole.'

But for Reginald the praise was bitter and what was generally acclaimed as his integrity, he was more inclined to consider as his pusillanimity. In conversation with Priuli, he returned to the subject again and again. Had he in fact failed in his duty by refusing that night the 'adoration' of the Cardinals? It was true that he would not have accepted the Papacy unless God made His will clear. But how was this to be known? By the result of the election, certainly, but was it tied to any particular manner of election? Was he not, by the 'adoration', even more certainly and lawfully elected than was del Monte by the subsequent tedious intrigue that had resulted in a unanimous vote?

But, suggested Priuli, trying to reassure him, it was surely more proper, since the final result included the French.

'No, Alvise,' Pole replied, 'according to the rules of the conclave, the vote is to be taken within ten days from those who are in attendance. Guise did not arrive till the thirty-second day after Pope Paul died. Had he given the matter the importance it deserved, he and all the French cardinals could have been there on the day the conclave opened. And as it was, had I received the twenty-eight votes that morning, I should not have questioned the result because the French were absent. No, Alvise, let me face it. You and Thomas and too many others praise me for my faith in leaving all in God's hands when you would do better to blame me for my cowardice and indolence.'

'No, Reynold, no.'

Pole gave the curt nod with which in moments of extreme stress he declined and dismissed argument. 'It is so. It seems to me in my conscience that though, certainly, I wished to do God's will, I wished with even more vehemence to avoid the Triple Crown.'

Priuli did not ask why. He knew why. In trying to control the complicated political and financial machine which the Papacy now was Reginald would have been lost. To administer the Patrimony was one thing; to rule Christendom as Christendom had to be ruled was quite another. For this, as the world had it, Pole was certainly unfitted. Yet, as Priuli and other friends saw it, the mere fact that a pre-eminently good man was sitting in Peter's Chair, a man dedicated, as everyone knew, to the reform of the Church might—must—have outweighed any practical shortcomings. It would have raised the Papacy in men's estimation to forgotten heights and could have even turned their minds from the futilities of politics to the commandments of God.[1]

Pole himself naturally could not see it so. To him his avoidance of the pontificate seemed increasingly to have been nothing but another instance of his temperamental preference of withdrawing from the great world to find satisfaction and comfort in a small chosen circle. Had it this time betrayed him into making 'il gran refuito'—that 'great refusal' of the Papacy for which Dante had put Pope Celestine V, who renounced his election, on the borders of Hell? Was he, like Celestine, to be one of the whirling, unstable millions, who, serving neither God nor the Devil with conviction, were rejected even by Hell, those Laodiceans on whom God's judgement, as recorded in the Apocalypse, was: 'Because you are neither hot nor cold I will spue you out of my mouth'? Here lay Pole's secret fear, which he did not admit even to Priuli. All he said was; 'When I called myself God's ass that night, I meant it in every sense. He does not want me for any great service. I am no more than an ordinary beast of burden, meant for lowly tasks. . . .'

Yet even as he said it, he knew it was not true. He remembered Cervini's reproach that he, being who he was, should presume to enjoy 'the largesse of obscurity'.

What Pole did not allow for in self-defence was a persistence of that family trait of disdain and indifference which, though he was unaware of it, he could not escape. As his grandfather, the Duke of Clarence had, lordlily, not troubled to notice, until it was too late, the snares in which his bastard brother was preparing to entangle him; as his mother had ignored, until it was too late, the plain evidence that Henry VIII was preparing to destroy

---

[1] One of Pole's biographers has epigrammatised it: 'He might not have been a good *Pope*, but he would clearly have been a *good* Pope.'

the family, so had he too stood nonchalantly above the battle. It was, he hoped, impartial devotion to God. It did not occur to him that it might be only the Plantagenet way. They would not, any of them, descend to the day-to-day intrigues applauded as practicality. They could, had they wished, easily have mastered Macchiavelli. But they would not so defile themselves.

If Pole repudiated as undeserved the praise men gave him, he was troubled by calumnies even more unfounded. The fact that they were false suggested that his reputation was still the object of attack by those cardinals who had feared his election 'because' (as one of them was honest enough to put it) 'in that case the whole of this Court would have had to lead a new life'—a prospect which inspired something akin to terror.

Life ordinarily strikes a rough balance, offsetting a man's virtues by his vices, cancelling out praise with blame. Only when detraction has to be based on falsehood does goodness begin to appear dangerously disproportionate, even suggesting sanctity. *L'homme moyen sensuel* is not worth the Devil's attention. Pole in his humility could honestly discount and deny praise. He could not escape the tribute of blame.

He was nevertheless surprised at its venomous fatuity. Because, during his administration of the Patrimony (of which the new Pope relieved him three months after the election), there had been hardly any executions, Pole was accused of indolence and dereliction of duty. So charity and clemency could be construed. The intellectual curiosity of the Viterbo Society was seen as the encouragement of heresy. And because the Cardinal of England had arranged for the orphan daughter of a poor Englishwoman who had recently died in Rome to be placed in a convent, he was credited with the child's paternity. This was considered proved beyond doubt by his addition of 100 ducats to the small sum left by the mother to be invested for a modest dowry when the girl grew up.

This last *canard*, which conveniently emphasised his hypocrisy, Priuli urged him to refute in an open letter. Thomas Goldwell

183

also advised him, for the sake of the Reform, to defend his reputation in this particular. But when Pole consulted Caraffa, (to whom, since their reconciliation, he showed what Priuli and Goldwell considered disproportionate deference) the old Theatine counselled him to remain silent. The reason he advanced for this—that, however just and cogent his defence it must convict him of having been suspected of the offence—struck Pole as sufficiently curious to make him to seek the opinion of the Pope.

Julius supported Caraffa and adduced a reason which, in the circumstances, was still more curious. Pole was to remain silent not for the sake of his own honour, which could defend itself, but for the sake of the honour of the order of Cardinals and their College which might incur some mark of infamy if it were known that such an accusation had been made.

This protection of the Cardinals' reputations in general suggested, were it genuine, a certain detachment from current opinion. An Englishman visiting Rome at the time wrote of episcopal connections with the Via Julia—the splendid, half-mile-long street which had been planned by and named after Pope Julius II, to whom del Monte had been Chamberlain and in whose honour he had chosen to be known as Julius III: 'The street, fair builded on both sides, is inhabited by none others than courtesans, some worth ten, some worth twenty thousand crowns, more or less, as their reputation is. And many times you shall see a courtesan ride into the country with ten or twelve horses waiting on her. By report Rome is not without 40,000 harlots, maintained for the most part by the clergy and their followers; so that the Romans themselves suffer their wives to go seldom abroad and some of them scarcely to look out of a lattice window, whereof their proverb saith: "In Roma vale piu la putana che la moglie Romana", that is to say,

> The harlot hath a better life
> Than she that is a Roman's wife.'

And Julius III was now about to add to the modern glories

of the Eternal City a Villa Julia, where, on the Pincian, he and Innocent could enjoy, in surroundings reminiscent of Imperial Rome, the succession of banquets, plays, concerts and more questionable entertainments which was to characterise the new pontificate and gain for Julius III the nickname of 'the Heliogabalus[2] of the Church'.

The construction of the 'Vigna di Papa Giulio' was, from the moment of his accession, the Pope's main concern. Thirty-six thousand trees and shrubs of every variety were purchased for the making of the surrounding gardens, with their rare flowers, their aviaries and fish-ponds and fountains. At the centre of the great horse-shoe-shaped courtyard of the Villa itself, with its sunken nymphaeum, was a magnificent basin, constructed out of a single piece of porphyry, which had once graced the Golden House of the Emperor Nero. Everywhere, in the Villa and in the gardens, was such a profusion of classical statues, Pan, Bacchus, Apollo and Ganymede predominating, that in transport they filled a hundred and sixty barges.

Julius himself liked to use the river to visit his retreat and Rome became accustomed to watching his water-progress in a magnificent barge decked with flowers and accompanied by musicians. A small harbour was constructed for his landing, whence a pergola covered with vines, jasmine and roses ran to the Via Flaminia, bordering the Villa, at whose gate was a fountain, with a head of Apollo dispensing the water and, sculpted above, the two laurel wreaths of the del Monte arms.

The highest praise that connoisseurs could pay was to compare Julius's work with the still-legendary gardens of Nero and to say that Nero's spirit, if it still walked, must at least be appeasedly at rest. For the Pincian Hill was, pre-eminently, the domain of Nero. At its foot he had been buried after his suicide there and for a thousand years his tomb was a place of ill omen. Men believed

---

[2] Quite apart from the difference in their ages, the comparison is manifestly unfair in one particular at least. Heliogabalus had the reputation of 'never using the same robe, the same shoes or the same boy twice'.

that his terrible ghost haunted the Hill, attended by thousands of demon-crows who flew to do evil at his bidding. Even the destruction of the tomb, in 1099, and its replacement by a church dedicated to Our Lady did not altogether dispel the fear and superstition, and when Caraffa founded the Theatines it was of deliberate purpose that they first went to live in the wilderness of the Pincian, that they might by prayer and mortification exorcise the region, rather as St. Benedict had made his cell hard by Nero's villa at Subiaco.

Caraffa refused all invitations to visit the Villa Julia. Pole found its construction an additional reason to doubt whether he had been right in refusing the Papacy.

But, whatever his inward uncertainty, Pole because it was ingrained in his nature, observed scrupulously the outward courtesies. He even wrote to Innocent to congratulate him on his cardinalate, choosing his words with even more than his usual care.

'Were it not for the hope I entertain,' the letter ran, 'that the affection which has moved our lord the Pope to promote your rt. rev. lordship to the cardinalate will also induce His Holiness to use all care to protect you from the perils that are wont to accompany high offices at such an age, I should not dare to congratulate you on your elevation, as I do, relying chiefly on this hope. At the same time I pray God that He will give you the grace to acknowledge this care on the Pope's part as a far greater benefit than any dignity or advantage you have received or may anticipate from him. You must know that you have no other means of showing your gratitude than by trying, with God's grace, to so act as to justify more and more the opinion and hope of you entertained by His Holiness. To this I exhort you with the utmost earnestness, offering you my services, as I am bound to do.'

Pole thought it unlikely that it would have any effect on Innocent or that he would even read it. But Julius might understand.

It was in another letter that Pole came nearer to baring his heart. Contarini's nephew, Placid, had written to him from a Benedictine monastery in Padua asking for spiritual advice. The young man, who had been happy as a simple monk, had been appointed Cellarer and because of his new duties found it impossible to lead the life of prayer, praise, study and contemplation to which he had become accustomed and which he regarded as his true vocation. What was God's will for him?

The answer in this case presented no difficulties. The Rule of St. Benedict made it quite clear that, for a monk, whatever his superiors ordered him to do was to be understood as God's will. Yet Pole realised that this admirable simplicity, however certainly Dom Placid might have given it the assent of his will and intellect, had left his emotions unresolved. He tried to elucidate it for him. The most menial duty, the Cardinal wrote, as long as it was undertaken in the right spirit could be a way of serving God. 'You monks are not called on to serve Christ with voice and words, but in your lives and actions; by these you will truly show whether you have the spirit of the Apostles.' The Apostles, it was true, left their menial work, but only because they were called to preach the Word of God; they left 'the serving of tables' not for a life of contemplation but for a dangerous and laborious strife in the world.

'Pray for me,' the letter ended, 'that I, who give you this advice, may be able to follow it myself. To tell you the truth, I am often perturbed by the same conflict.' The world in which Pole, 'the ass', was called on to labour was growing daily more distasteful, the attraction of the religious life more intense. Yet to the latter he dared not respond lest it should be nothing but a mask for his desire to withdraw from the world and, so, another betrayal of the menial work to which God had called him.

The Ecumenical Council had been summoned to reassemble at Trent but had once more to be suspended because the usual hostilities had broken out between France and the Empire. 'It so happens,' Pole noted, 'that the day on which it was decided to suspend the Council was Good Friday. It seemed to me that as if

I saw the dead body of Christ, of which the Council, representing the whole Church, His Mystical Body, is the image. Only a short time before, the Council had evoked the brightest hopes of reform; now it seemed scourged with rods and dead, ready for the burial. Yet on that same day I was admonished to remember Christ's speedy return to life and all the other blessings which immediately followed His death and then I was induced to conceive new hope for the Council and reform.'[3]

Julius III, completely lacking Paul III's diplomatic ability, had compromised the Papacy by allying himself, first with one, then with the other, of the combatants, and had thereby lost any religious prestige he might have been able to employ in the interests of peace. When he asked Pole's advice as to how peace could best be restored, the Cardinal allowed himself an unaccustomed asperity. The endless wars between France and the Empire, he told the Pope, 'must be attributed to the wrath of God, Who uses them as a scourge for our sins, so that it is necessary to destroy the root by appeasing God and making peace, first of all, with Him: and thus we may hope subsequently for peace between the Sovereigns. The true way to do this is to bring about what for so many years has been so much desired by all good men, namely reform.'

For a moment it seemed that his words might have some effect, and for a week the Pope seriously considered degrading Innocent from the purple; but, as his reason was less any moral consideration than the chaos that the youth had produced after the infatuated pontiff had directed the nuncios in future to address all their correspondence to Innocent instead of to the Secretary of State or to Julius himself, no such step was taken. It was enough to provide him with empowered and efficient secretaries.

What finally alienated Pole was being made an Inquisitor-

[3] Pole, however, was dead when the Council was reconvened, ten years later.

General. Caraffa had suggested it and, as the Pope had endorsed it, Pole, the least inquisitorial-minded of men, saw no way of escape. He was under no illusions as to Caraffa's motive—obviously, in their new-mended friendship, it was to make certain of his orthodoxy—though their divergence was not, since the Trent definitions, doctrinal. Any disagreement was about the means, not the end. Pole refused to sanction torture.

Caraffa expostulated. One of the prisoners before the tribunal was an influential teacher who posed as an orthodox Catholic but who in fact did not believe in the divinity of Christ and was inculcating an inner circle of disciples with doctrines irreconcilable with any form of Christianity.

'In your opinion,' Caraffa asked, 'is it not necessary that by confessing his real belief he should discredit himself in the eyes of those he is deluding?'

'Yes,' Pole answered, 'but not by being tortured into saying it. For one thing, why should his followers believe what he says in his pain? I know that I would not. The body's weakness—'

'You have always been too prone to judge others by yourself, Reginald. There are natures—and his is one—which resist all other means of persuasion. Is his comfort more precious than the souls of those he leads to damnation?'

'No, but—'

Caraffa shot at him: 'What would you do if it were left in your hands?'

'I should remember,' said Pole, 'that the souls of corruptor and corrupted are equally dear to God and I should leave it to Him in prayer.'

Caraffa did not trust himself to answer. Pole, whose mind turned often to Flaminio, who had just died, continued calmly: 'Nothing could have seemed more obdurate than Marc-Antonio when he fell among the heretics; no one could have returned more firm in the Faith when love and reason had convinced him. Had you had your way with him, he would have hardened into despair.'

189

'It may be,' said Caraffa, 'but what would you say of those other friends of yours? How do you reckon with them, Your Eminence of England? Answer me that. How do you stand with Ochino and Vermigli?'

To this Pole could not reply. Peter Martyr Vermigli, now a fanatical Protestant, was in England as Regius Professor of Divinity at Oxford and Bernadine Ochino, the one-time Capuchin, who now openly denied the divinity of Christ, was in London with his wife, an ex-nun, advising Cranmer on the drawing up of a new and more extreme liturgy.

'If it so happens that you return to England,' said Caraffa, 'you will do me the courtesy to inform me of your edicts.'

But, as Pole saw it, there was now no chance of ever returning to England. The King was only fourteen and had a lifetime before him to turn his realm irrevocably Protestant.

Nor was Italy now, the country of Reginald's adoption, much more than a graveyard of hopes. Paul III, to whom he owed so much was gone and with him any hope of Reform. The Patrimony was no longer his to administer and Viterbo had become merely a place to visit. Contarini and Bembo and Vittoria and Flaminio were dead. For him, too, life seemed to have come to a stop.

After many days of discussion with Priuli, they decided to go together to the Benedictine monastery of Maguzzano on the shores of Lake Garda to test their vocation for the religious life.

18

The Problems of Thomas Cranmer

The Archbishop of Canterbury was beset by problems. With the fall of Somerset he had lost an ally who was genuinely at one with him in his ecclesiastical policy. Northumberland was essentially irreligious and believed in nothing but his own aggrandisement. As his secret plan was to subvert the succession and get the Crown into his own family, he decided to support the extreme Protestants, since, if their ideas were sufficiently widely disseminated, it would be the easier to debar the Princess Mary, with her unbending Catholicism, from the Throne. He played his part with such conviction that the new Bishop of Gloucester, John Hooper, a renegade Cistercian, described him as 'that most faithful and intrepid soldier of Christ, a most holy and fearless instrument of God's word,' adding: 'England cannot do without him.'

Cranmer, however, though not daring openly to defy Northumberland was less enthusiastic, and believed that the Duke had been 'seeking long time his destruction'. The Archbishop had indeed determined to make England irrevocably Protestant, but at the same time he nourished a wider ambition. He wished to hold a Council in opposition to Trent over which he would preside in London.

'Our adversaries,' he wrote to Calvin in Geneva, 'are now holding their Council at Trent for the establishing of errors, and shall we fail to summon a godly synod to refute errors and to purify and propagate our doctrines? They, I hear, are making decrees regarding Bread-worship; therefore we ought to leave no stone unturned not only to protect others against idolatry but also to come to some agreement among ourselves on the doctrine of the sacrament.'

Agreement, he knew, would be difficult enough in any case in view of the variety of Protestant beliefs and one of the problems that involved him personally was that his own rite of Holy Communion which he had composed for the Prayer Book was being 'twisted' by many Catholic priests who, in the saying of it, used gestures and silence to make it outwardly resemble 'the never-to-be-sufficiently-execrated Mass'. So despite all Cranmer's efforts there was retained 'the thrice impious and wicked trust of the simpler and more superstitious folk in the Mass'.

A new liturgy which would leave no loophole was obviously needed and to compose an adequate one only foreigners could be relied on. The native bishops were, for the most part, recalcitrant or incompetent. Tunstal of Durham was deprived of his see and kept under house-arrest, while Bonner of London, Heath of Worcester and Day of Chichester joined Gardiner in the Tower. They were replaced by fanatical Protestants. Deaths and retirements accounted for ten such new bishops, of whom seven were married ex-monks but, though they could be relied on to vote for any extremist measures, they were not intellectually qualified for theological formulations. The only tangible advantage of the change was to Northumberland. Every new bishop on his nomination was obliged to surrender some of the lands of his see and, though Cranmer tried to please, Sir William Cecil took it upon himself to admonish him for not alienating the church lands and revenues to the courtiers as fast as he might. Though Cecil was half Cranmer's age, the Archbishop, from long habit, recognised effective power when he met it. He answered mildly: 'I take your admonition most thankfully, as I have always been most glad to be admonished by my friends' and promised to do his best.

Liturgical and theological matters, however, were the province of the Archbishop alone and at his invitation Continental theologians of every variety poured into England. In addition to Vermigli and Ochino, the Alsatian Martin Bucer was given the Divinity Chair at Cambridge, from which he waged interminable theological war about *minutiae* with Vermigli at Oxford. Valérand Poullain, a Fleming who had succeeded Calvin at the Church of Strangers at Strasbourg arrived with the major part of his congregation, mainly French and Walloon weavers, who were settled in the grounds of Glastonbury Abbey. The Polish nobleman, John Laski, noted for his special vehemence against the Blessed Sacrament, stayed six months as Cranmer's personal guest and was then appointed as superintendent of French and German congregations in London and given the church of the Austin Friars as a 'temple'. Francis Dryander, a Spanish Lutheran; Emmanuele Tremelio, an Italian Jew; Paul Fagius, a German Zwinglian, detested by the Lutherans as 'a most pernicious talent' but invited especially by Cranmer 'since we are greatly in want of learned men'; the young John ab Ulmis, a Swiss devotee of Vermigli; Jan Utenhove, a Dutchman; Michael Florio, an Italian, and countless others were among the immigrants summoned to determine the new religion of the English people.

The foreigners were not impressed by the situation they found. Bucer, even after thirteen months in England, confessed: 'Affairs in this country are in a very feeble state. Things for the most part are carried on by means of ordinances which the majority obey very grudgingly.' The clergy, he found, remained obstinately unattached to the new religion: 'Only a very small number have as yet addicted themselves entirely to the kingdom of Christ.'

Vermigli echoed him. The Protestant ministers shrank from instructing their congregations in beliefs so controversial: 'Even our friends are so sparing of their sermons that during the whole of Lent they have not once preached to the people, not even on the day of the commemoration of Christ's death or of His resurrection.' Only Northumberland and his colleagues seemed really to approve of the new order of things. 'The ruling powers are virtuous and godly,' wrote John ab Ulmis, 'but the people have for a long time been contumacious.'

Cranmer grew increasingly disturbed at the situation which was playing into the hands of the Anabaptists who, Dryander complained, 'began openly to show themselves and trouble the Church'. The German Micronius was even more definite: 'There are Arians, Marcionites, Libertines, Davists and the like monstrosities in great numbers,' he wrote. 'We have need of help against sectaries and Epicureans and pseudo-evangelicals who are beginning to shake our churches with greater violence than ever.'

Cranmer's difficulty was to induce Northumberland to give him the necessary power to deal with the situation. He drew up a new code of ecclesiastical law which enacted the death penalty for all non-Anglicans and the reimposition of an inquisition to discover them; adultery was to be punished by banishment or life imprisonment and blasphemy by burning. Northumberland, however, rudely told him to stick to his clerical functions and refused Parliamentary facilities for enacting the code. The Archbishop, however, had some success against individual Anabaptists and burnt two of them, Joan Bocher and George van Paris, at Smithfield.

Cranmer, who, whatever his faults, could not be accused of a lack of respect for scholarship, was also disturbed by the decay of learning. A Reformed preacher, Bernard Gilpin, in a sermon before the King, did not scruple to point out: 'The decay of students is so great that there are scarce left of every thousand an hundred. There is entering into England more blind ignorance, superstition and infidelity than ever was under Romish bishops. Your realm (which I am sorry to speak) shall become more barbarous than Scythia.' The average number of degrees taken at Oxford had dropped from 127 to 33. The famous university libraries had all but vanished. In the Commissioners' Visitation of Oxford, thousands of books were destroyed. Cambridge suffered a slower but even more drastic denudation. Within a few years there were not more than 177 'cut and mangled' volumes left.

The great monastic collections had, of course, been dispersed or destroyed years before; and now the destruction of the chantries extinguished education at the popular level of the 'Song Schools' and the 'Reading Schools'—the elementary education of the time—as well as the Grammar Schools. The one, where the incumbent taught gratis 'the poor who asked it for the love of God' and the other which was usually attached to a college of priests, had been a feature of English life for the past two centuries. Now they were all swept away, though the King, by pressure of necessity was refounding a few of them.[1]

Side by side with the theological chaos, the breakdown of education and the grinding poverty and discontent of the people as a whole there was an increasing moral and spiritual squalor which Cranmer and all good Protestants deplored no less than did good Catholics.[2] An enthusiastic Lutheran wrote sadly: 'Those very persons who wish to be, so to speak, most evangelical,

[1] Edward VI's reputation as the 'Father' of the Grammar Schools is one of the more curious historical myths. Nearly two hundred Grammar Schools existed in England before his reign which were, for the most part, abolished or crippled during it and there was no Grammar School founded from the beginning of the reign till a century later which had not already existed as a chantry. As Professor R. H. Tawney has put it, 'the grammar schools that Edward VI founded are those which King Edward VI did not destroy'.

[2] 'Wherever we look, from the royal court and the circle of government down to the village and the parish,' writes Professor S. T. Bindoff, 'and whatever type of evidence we choose, we are confronted by the same black picture of irreligion, irreverence and immorality on a truly terrifying scale.'

imitate carnal licentiousness under the pretext of religion and liberty.'

Against this background, the Archbishop worked on his second Prayer Book striving to maintain at least a semblance of the traditional faith of Christendom against the pressure of the extremists. But as Northumberland was behind them, he realised that his chances were slender and he was insolently assured by Sir John Cheke, Cecil's brother-in-law and the most prominent English extremist, that the King himself, as his pupil, was prepared to coerce the moderates, if necessary.

The major change in the new Prayer Book, on which all were agreed, was to make plain to the simplest that there was no alteration in the bread and wine in Holy Communion. The words of administration were accordingly changed from 'The Body of our Lord Jesus Christ which was given for thee preserve thy body and soul to everlasting life' to 'Take and eat this in remembrance that Christ died for thee and feed on him in thy heart by faith with thanksgiving.'

Nothing could be more definite, but the change had implications which had not been fully considered. If the bread remained merely bread and the wine merely wine, why should anyone kneel to receive it, as had been natural in the case of the transubstantiated Body and Blood? Was not this bowing the knee to idols, 'Bread-worship' at its worst? Yet the new Prayer Book sanctioned it.

One of the most bitter opponents of such kneeling, which he described as 'the Table Gesture', was a Scottish Calvinist, John Knox, one of the Royal Chaplains whom Northumberland had imported as an irritant to Cranmer and whom he hoped would be made Bishop of Rochester to 'be a whetstone to sharp the Archbishop of Canterbury'.

In a sermon before the King just after the second Prayer Book had gone to the printers, Knox delivered a violent attack on this 'popish idolatry' and, by implication, on Cranmer. His tirade so terrified the fifteen-year-old Edward, who took his responsibilities as Supreme Head of the Church with dedicated seriousness, that he called for an alteration in the rubric about kneeling lest, through the new Prayer Book, he might become the agent of his subjects' damnation.

But Cranmer had reached the end of his tether. For once he remained adamant. He told the King and Council that they would be unwise to alter the book in deference to 'unquiet spirits who can like nothing but what is after their own fancy' and who would still find something to cavil at if the book were 'made every year anew'. In spite of a storm of opposition from native extremists led by Northumberland and his own imported foreigners, the Archbishop refused to allow communicants to stand or sit for the reception of the bread and wine and said they might as well 'lie down on the ground and eat their meat like Turks or Tartars'. They knelt not in adoration or idolatry, but in reverence and humility at the remembrance of Christ's death.

His protest was unavailing. The King was insistent and presided over a debate at Windsor in which Idolatry, Adoration, Reverence, Sincerity and Humility were terms much bandied about. The outcome was that, as it was now only five days before the new Book was enacted to be used, a special 'Black Rubric' was inserted pointing out that by kneeling 'it is not meant that any adoration is done or ought to be done'. Slips were hastily printed and stuck at random into all copies of the Prayer Book which had not yet left the printers' hands. The day was saved for the extremists, and Knox surpassed himself in his praise of the young king whose 'godliness passeth the measure given to other princes in their greatest perfection'. Edward celebrated the occasion by composing a poem on the right view of the Eucharist:

> Whoso eateth that lively food
> And hath a perfect faith,

Receiveth Christ's flesh and blood,
  For Christ Himself so saith.
Not with our teeth His flesh to tear,
  Nor take blood for our drink:
Too great absurdity it were
  So grossly for to think.

But Cranmer retired more and more into private life and busied himself with the affairs of his diocese.

Northumberland also temporarily absented himself from Court that Christmas of 1552 on the plea of ill-health. 'What should I wish any longer this life that seeth such frailty in it?' he wrote to Cecil from Chelsea. 'I have no great cause to tarry much longer here.' Cecil, who had nothing to learn from his master about diplomatic illness, thereupon fell sick at Wimbledon and found himself unable to attend meetings of the Council. The two invalids, thus freed from scrutiny, were able to pursue their plans and Cecil had the satisfaction of being rewarded by Northumberland, during his absence from affairs, by the office of Chancellor of the Order of the Garter and by the lease of Combe Park in Surrey.

The matter in hand was the exclusion of Princess Mary from the Throne. Speed was necessary for Edward, always sickly, had now obviously not much longer to live. When Mary had come up to London to visit him she found him in a high fever with congestion of the lungs and unable to speak to her. From that particular attack, Northumberland thought, he would probably recover, but the manner of Mary's coming was a warning that the court was obviously preparing itself for her reign. She rode from her London palace in Clerkenwell, up Fleet Street to Westminster accompanied, according to the chronicler, by 'a great number of lords and knights and all the great ladies. The Duchess of Suffolk, the Duchess of Northumberland, my lady Marquise of Northampton and lady Marquise of Winchester and the Countesses of Bedford, Shrewsbury and Arundel, my lady Clinton, my lady Browne and many more ladies and gentlemen.' It was an even more impressive display than her last appearance when she had come to defend her Mass.

Northumberland's plan was simple enough. Edward must make a new will debarring both Mary and Elizabeth from the Throne on the grounds that they might marry foreign Catholic princes and so bring England again under the Papal yoke. The crown was to go to their fifteen-year-old cousin, Lady Jane Grey, whom Northumberland would marry to his son, Guilford Dudley. The carrying-out of the plan required that Edward should be left in no doubt that he was dying and that his first duty was to ensure a Protestant succession. At the same time he was somehow to be kept alive until the Dudley marriage was solemnized. There was also the necessity of as much money as could be raised for the purchase of arms to deal with any revolt that might occur at the accession of Queen Jane.

The last was easiest. An order was made confiscating 'all the jewels of gold and silver as crosses and candlesticks, censers, chalices, all copes and vestments of cloth of gold, cloth of tissue and cloth of silver' which remained in the churches, though each church was allowed to retain one chalice and one table-cloth for the Communion Table. The Commissioners did their work quickly and thoroughly. Everything they collected was sold and the money spent on arms.

The marriage, too, was expeditiously arranged, although Northumberland encountered some opposition from Jane, who detested Guilford Dudley, a conceited and disagreeable young man, even more than he disliked her; but a good beating changed her mind and the marriage took place on Whitsunday, 25 May, 1553.

Edward was at Greenwich, so ill from 'a suppurating tumour on the lung' that the Spanish Ambassador had been told by one of the doctors that he could not possibly last till June.

Northumberland had announced, hoping to counter the people's fear for the King's life, that His Majesty would attend the wedding. When he did not, popular apprehension so increased that after the ceremony Northumberland went straight to Greenwich and gave orders that Edward was to be lifted out of bed and held up at the window so that the waiting crowds might see for themselves that he was still alive; but the sight of the wasted figure merely gave the lie to the official report that the King was now able to walk every day in the gardens of the palace.

Northumberland was now desperate and had recourse to a quack female doctor[3] who assured him that, were she given sole charge of the King, she could cure him. Edward's three doctors, who had attended him since his birth, were therefore, protesting violently, turned out of the sick room. The new practitioner gave him a dose of what she described as 'restringents', which included arsenic. The immediate effect was that the King rallied.

There now remained only to persuade him to make a new will. Northumberland took a line which he knew would be effective. 'It is the duty of a good and religious prince,' he said, 'to set apart all respects of blood where God's glory and the subjects' weal may be endangered. That Your Majesty should do otherwise were after this life—which is short—to expect revenge at God's dreadful tribunal.'

He could not have made a shrewder attack on the dying boy, whose worldly concerns had shrunk to facing the Judgement as one who had fulfilled his duty as Head of the Church. He was heard to murmur: 'I am glad to die' and then to fall to prayer: 'Lord God, deliver me out of this miserable and wretched life and take me amongst Thy chosen; howbeit not my will but Thy will be done. O! my Lord God defend this realm from papistry and maintain Thy true religion.'

---

[3] Her name has not survived. After she had served her purpose she disappeared and Northumberland was suspected of having her murdered.

It was not, in these circumstances, difficult for him to agree to make a new will, disinheriting both his half-sisters and giving the Crown to Lady Jane Grey. Fortified by his new medicine, he summoned the Lord Chief Justice, the Attorney-General and the Solicitor-General to Greenwich and addressed them, coughing and gasping for breath: 'Our long sickness hath caused us heavily to think of the condition and prospects of our realm. Should the Lady Mary or the Lady Elizabeth succeed she might marry a stranger and the laws and liberties of England be sacrificed and religion changed. We desire, therefore, the succession to be altered and we call upon Your Lordships to draw up this deed by letters patent.'

The lawyers were appalled. The Lord Chief Justice told the King that what he asked was utterly unlawful and could not be drawn up under the heading of an Act of Parliament.

Prompted by Northumberland who was standing by his bed, the King said: 'I will hear no objections. I command you to draw up the letters patent forthwith.'

The lawyers asked if they might have time to consider the matter. This was granted and they returned to London to discuss it. They unanimously decided that to draw up such a document was illegal and that to sign it would be criminal.

Next day the Lord Chief Justice, Sir Edward Montague, was summoned to Northumberland's mansion, Ely Place in Holborn. Northumberland was not present when the Councillors who had met there asked him if he and his colleagues had obeyed the King. 'I cannot,' he said. 'It would be high treason.'

Northumberland, who had been listening at the door, burst in, trembling with anger. 'You are a traitor,' he shouted. 'I will fight any man living in his shirt in this quarrel' and ordered Montague to leave.

The following day the lawyers were called once more to Greenwich. 'Where are the letters patent? Why have you not drawn them up?' demanded Edward.

Montague fell on his knees. 'To do that,' he said, 'would put all the Lords of the Council and us in danger of high treason—and yet not be worth anything.'

'Why have you refused to obey my orders?' Edward reiterated.

'That,' interposed Northumberland, 'is the real treason.'

The Lord Chief Justice burst into tears: 'I have served Your Majesty and Your Majesty's noble father these nineteen years,' he said, 'and loath would I be to disobey Your Grace. I have seventeen children and am a weak old man without comfort.' Controlling himself, he gave the King his legal reasons: 'If this new will were made, it would be no use after Your Majesty's death as long as the Statute of Succession remains in force, because it could only be abrogated by the same authority by which it was established—Parliament.'

'I will have it done now,' said Edward, in a tone which reminded all present of his father, 'and afterwards ratified by Parliament.'

The lawyers argued no more but drew up the new will and, to them more importantly, a pardon for all who signed their assent.

The only signature conspicuous by its absence was that of Sir William Cecil, till Northumberland, suspicious of his continued absence, insisted on him being sent for and signing the document. Cecil bowed to the inevitable, though he subsequently claimed that he signed only as a witness to the will.

More than a hundred signatures were subscribed, but there was still one that was missing—Cranmer's.

The Archbishop was quite clear about his duty. 'I cannot subscribe without perjury,' he said, 'being afore sworn to the Lady Mary by King Henry's will.' Northumberland argued with him, only to be met with: 'I am not a judge over any man's conscience but mine own only, so, as I will not condemn your action, neither will I base my action on your conscience, seeing that every man shall answer to God for his own deeds and not for other men's.'

But when he saw Edward, his resolution was shaken. His godson was a pitiful spectacle. As a result of his 'medicine', his legs and arms were swollen, his skin had darkened, his nails had fallen off and his fingers and toes were gangrenous. He was almost too weak to cough, but his eyes were still alive and reinforced his whispered: 'Do not be more repugnant to my plea than the rest.'

He wanted only to die, but he could not die in peace until Cranmer had signed.

Cranmer signed.

It was High Treason and, though he was not to discover it till later, the Archbishop was to die for it. All his intellect was against it, all his political sense and intuition. Yet it was his greatest act of Christian charity and, to the end of his life, he never forgot Edward's smile of thanks.

19

Nine Days' Wonder

Princess Mary was at her manor of Hunsdon when she received a letter from Northumberland saying 'that her brother who was very ill prayed her to come to him, as he earnestly desired the comfort of her presence'. She replied expressing her delight 'that he should have thought that she could be of any comfort to him' and set out immediately for London.

Edward was in fact dead but the secret was so well guarded that the new Imperial ambassador, Simon Renard, was summoned for an audience and then told that the King was in bed and could not receive him—which was true enough. The French Ambassador, Antoine de Noailles, who had invited Northumberland to dinner, received the Duke's apologies for having to break the engagement because the King urgently needed him at Greenwich. At all costs nothing must be allowed to leak out until Mary, lured by the false message, was safely a prisoner in the Tower.

The Princess had got no further than Hoddesdon, less than ten miles from Hunsdon, when she received an urgent visit from her goldsmith, who had ridden post-haste from the capital. He had been sent by Sir Nicholas Throckmorton, nephew of the Michael Throckmorton who was Cardinal Pole's faithful secretary. One of Sir Nicholas's brothers who was in Northumberland's service, had by the merest chance overheard a sentence in a conversation between his master and one of his creatures on the Council, Sir John Gates, Chancellor of the Duchy of Lancaster. 'What, sir!' Gates had said, 'will you let the Lady Mary escape and not secure her person?'

When he reported this to his brother, Sir Nicholas, who though a professed Protestant had no sympathy with Queen Jane, decided that the Princess must be warned. As it was possible that already Northumberland had taken steps to intercept any messengers, neither Throckmorton could safely go. But the goldsmith should arouse no suspicions and they could trust him.

Mary, when he had told her the true situation, was perplexed in the extreme. Was it a trap to make her commit high treason by declaring herself Queen while Edward was still alive?

'How do you know with certainty that the King is dead?' she asked.

'Sir Nicholas was there and knows it for truth,' answered the goldsmith.

Mary was silent for a moment, trying to make up her mind. Had the message come from Robert, the eldest of the three Throckmorton brothers, who had remained a staunch Catholic, she would have had no doubt. But Nicholas professed to be an admirer of John Knox and she could not bring herself to believe he was genuinely disturbed on her behalf.

'If Robert had been at Greenwich,' she said, 'I would have hazarded all things and gaged my life on the leap.'

The goldsmith tried to reassure her. Sir Nicholas, whatever his religious complexion, was a firm friend of the family and would have no part in Jane's usurpation. His love for Edward —which he won in the first place by insisting on treating him as a boy instead of as an Imperial Majesty—was as undoubted as Edward's love of him. The very circumstances of his knighthood formed a reminder of it. Edward, after a day of dutifully dubbing as knights a variety of people to whom he was either indifferent or hostile, had suddenly seized a sword of state to give the honour to one he cared for. Nicholas, professing himself unworthy, ran away, whereupon Edward chased him, brandishing the sword, in a glorious game of hide-and-seek throughout the palace and eventually found him hiding in a cupboard, where, in the presence of scandalised courtiers drawn by curiosity about the cause of the flurry, he knighted him.

Mary, remembering the incident, suddenly smiled. Sir Nicholas, whatever religious vagaries he might have indulged in to please Edward, was not a caterpillar of the court and he would serve her—had, indeed, already served her—as faithfully as he had served her dead brother. She sent him her thanks by the goldsmith and prepared to act on his information.

She decided to make at once for the comparative safety of her seat at Kenninghall in Norfolk. With only two of her women and six gentlemen of her household, she set off through the night, striking the Newmarket road at Royston. It was a longer way than the normal route through Bishop's Stortford and Dunmow but she judged it the safer. It had also the advantage that, if the worse came to the worst, that long straight road which the Romans had made led directly to Yarmouth where she could take ship for the safety of the Netherlands.

She stopped after twenty miles of furious riding at Sawston Hall, near Cambridge, the home of a zealous Catholic, John Huddleston, whose brother, Andrew, was one of the gentlemen of her party. They snatched some sleep, rose at dawn and heard Mass. As Huddleston feared that the news of her coming would be known in Cambridge, which was traditionally a centre of Protestant extremism, he advised excessive caution and Mary continued her way dressed as a market-woman riding pillion behind Andrew Huddleston. When they reached the Gogmagog Hills, they turned round and discovered that Sawston Hall was a mass of flame. A party of Protestants from Cambridge had, indeed, heard the rumour that the papist Princess was in the neighbourhood and had set out to capture her. Her absence made them think they had been mistaken but they amused themselves by plundering the Hall and burning it.

Mary, looking at the blaze, said: 'Let it burn. I will build Huddleston a better.'[1]

The proximity of her would-be captors was a warning not to be ignored. Mary remounted her own horse nor did they stop again till they had gained Hengrave Hall, another Catholic house, outside Bury St. Edmunds. They found that in Bury itself the death of the King was still not known and they explained their presence by saying that they had suspected an outbreak of the plague in Hunsdon and were therefore retreating to the depths of the country.

As soon as she arrived at Kenninghall, Mary wrote to the Council, remonstrating with them, informing them that she was aware of their designs but offering them an amnesty if they immediately proclaimed her their sovereign in London. She also wrote to Simon Renard asking him to inform the Emperor that 'she saw destruction hanging over her unless she received help from him'. Charles did not reply; and the Council's answer was to proclaim Jane Queen on the day they received Mary's letter and to send the Princess impolite information that she was a bastard and would do well to submit to her sovereign lady, Queen Jane.

In London Northumberland was making preparations for civil war. He sent one of his sons, Lord Robert Dudley, with 300 horse to scour the countryside and bring Mary back a prisoner. The Tower was made more secure as the garrison hauled up great guns to the top of the White Tower. In the Thames twenty ships lay ready and Northumberland did not really expect to be believed when he announced that they were going on a 'venture' to Barbary and the Spice Islands. A muster was proclaimed in Tothill Fields and pay of 10d a day offered to those who would accept military service with the object 'to fetch in the Lady Mary'. Throughout the city, horses and carts

[1] She built the present Sawston Hall at her own private expense as soon as she became Queen and she made Andrew Huddleston her Captain of the Guard.

were requisitioned for transport.

The heralds' proclamation of Jane was printed and copies posted up all over London and sent off to the country with orders for them to be displayed in every market square and church porch.

The unexpected Queen made a progress to the Tower and tried on the Crown. The Lord High Treasurer told her that another crown would be duly provided for her husband. Jane assured him that there was no need as, though she might possibly make him a Duke, she would most certainly not allow him to be King. Lord Guilford Dudley thereupon raged so violently against her and their mutual hatred issued in so bitter a quarrel that he left her and returned to Syon House (which his father had taken as one of his palaces).

Northumberland himself, having ordered the fleet to lie off Yarmouth to intercept Mary's possible attempt to escape, set off from London with 3000 foot and 1000 horse to capture the Princess and bring her back alive or dead 'like that rebel she was'.

Mary's force, at that moment, consisted of her steward, Sir Thomas Wharton, Andrew Huddleston and a dozen gentlemen of her Household, and her ladies among whom was Sir Thomas More's grand-daughter who reminded her that Edward had died on the anniversary of More's execution. The memory and its implications unaccountably steeled her courage. She decided to ride to Framlingham Castle, twenty miles away, which would give her at least a temporary safety in case of attack. Once there, she raised her standard over the Gate Tower and had herself proclaimed Queen-Regnant of England and Ireland.[2]

[2] Mary was the country's first Queen-Regnant. It is perhaps worth quoting the comment in Miss Strickland's *Lives of the Queens of England*: 'Had she been surrounded by the experienced veterans in arms and council that rallied round Elizabeth at Tilbury and had Elizabeth been the heroine of the enterprise instead of Mary, it would have been lauded to the skies as one of the grandest efforts of female courage and ability the world had ever known. And so it was, whether it be praised or not.'

The countryside flocked to her. Sir Henry Jerningham and Sir Henry Bedingfield, Sir William Drury and Sir Thomas Cornwallis, Sir John Shelton and Sir John Tyrrel and Lord Thomas Howard, the seventeen-year-old son of the murdered and attainted Surrey, marched immediately to Framlingham with their Norfolk and Suffolk levies. The city of Norwich had her proclaimed Queen and sent supplies of men and arms. Harwich, Thetford and Ipswich quickly followed suit. Within a very short time she had an army of 13,000 men in camp round the castle. They were serving without pay and she issued instructions that 'if any soldier seemed in need of aught, his captain was to supply his wants as if by way of gift and charge the expense to her'.

Four days after Mary had established herself at Framlingham, Sir Henry Jerningham was at Yarmouth, trying to raise more support. There had been an easterly gale and six of the ships Northumberland had sent to guard the coast were riding close inshore. Jerningham decided it was a time for boldness. He took a rowing-boat and went out to hail them.

The sailors asked him what he wanted.

'Your captains,' shouted Sir Henry, 'who are rebels to their lawful Queen, Mary.'

'If they are,' came the reply, 'we will throw them into the sea, for we are her true subjects.'

The captains discovered that they too were loyal and Jerningham was able to return to Framlingham with the captains and crews and—what was more important—the ordnance the ships were carrying.

On the same day in London a placard was posted up on a church wall saying that Mary had been proclaimed Queen in every town and city except London; the Earl of Sussex and the Earl of Bath left the Council and took their way to Framlingham; and Sir William Cecil thought the time more than ripe to betray Northumberland.

He began to regret that he had drawn up an address to the Lords Lieutenant of the counties demanding that they should 'disturb, repel and resist the feigned and untrue claim of the Lady Mary, bastard daughter of King Henry VIII'. He now started to compose a document of a very different nature, a twenty-one point exculpation of himself to be presented to Mary should she be, as now seemed at least possible, victorious. Among the items he instanced was his refusal to sign Edward's will (which was not true) and (which was not true either) 'to write the Queen's Highness "bastard" so that the Duke wrote the letter himself'.[3] He then sent his sister-in-law, who was a friend of Mary's, to Framlingham to find out how the land lay.

On Sunday, July 16, Northumberland with a considerable body of troops arrived in Cambridge where he attended a sermon by a noted Protestant divine inveighing against the 'usurper' Mary and her hateful Mass. At the service a Yeoman of the Guard exhibited, for purposes of ridicule, the very chalice which had been used at Sawston and had fallen to the lot of one of the plunderers. The Duke set the seal of his approval on the fate of Sawston Hall by sending a detachment of his men to sack and burn the houses of all known or suspected Catholics in the neighbourhood. Lord Grey de Wilton, good Protestant though he was, remonstrated with him that ravaging the countryside 'was no wise course'. The two, being both hot-tempered, came to blows. Grey rode off to Framlingham to make his submission and Northumberland led his army on to Bury St. Edmunds, burning at will as he went.

At Bury he realised at last the seriousness of the situation and sent messengers to the King of France, asking for troops and offering Calais in exchange.

[3] Cecil's draft, in his own handwriting, still exists. (Lansdowne MSS 1236. No. 15) Northumberland made a copy of it, endorsed by Cecil, two days later. (Lansdowne MSS 3, 34.)

Mary issued a proclamation of defiance, describing the Duke as a traitor and offering £1000 in land to any nobleman, £500 to any gentleman and £100 to any yeoman who should bring him in a prisoner.

The same Sunday as that on which Northumberland was in Cambridge saw unexpected developments in London. At seven in the evening, while it was still full daylight, the Tower gates were shut and locked and the keys taken to Queen Jane. The reason was that both the Lord Treasurer and the Treasurer of the Mint were suddenly found to be absent. The Lord Treasurer was eventually discovered in his own domestic surroundings 'and they did fetch him at twelve of the clock in the night from his house in London to the Tower'. The Treasurer of the Mint, however, was not to be found; he was on the way to Framlingham with the contents of the Privy Purse, of which he was Keeper.

In the morning what was left of the Council met in a mood of mutual distrust and, at the instance of Sir John Cheke, issued a private letter exhorting the Lord Chancellor and all the peers to stand firm for Queen Jane. One possible signature was missing. Cecil was temporarily indisposed and so was unable to endorse his brother-in-law's stand. He privately added to his *apologia*: 'I avoided the writing of public letters to the realm.'

He was prominent enough next day, Wednesday, July 19, when the Council changed its direction, adopted Mary's offer of a reward for Northumberland's arrest, asked Simon Renard to explain to the Emperor that only three or four of them had in their hearts assented to Edward's will, the rest having been terrorised by Northumberland—'in what peril I refer it to be considered by those who know the Duke', as Cecil put it—and wrote to Northumberland ordering him to obey Queen Mary.

That evening, about six o'clock, Garter King of Arms proclaimed Mary as Queen at the Cross in Cheapside. As soon as he pronounced her name 'there was such a shout of the people with the casting up of caps and crying "God save Queen Mary" that the style of the proclamation could not be heard'. The people went mad with joy and all the bells of London rang all through the night.

It was nine days since Mary had set up her standard at Framlingham.

Northumberland was at Cambridge again when the news reached him. He was at first incredulous but as soon as his enquiries had put the matter beyond a doubt, he took the only course that occurred to him. He declared himself a Catholic, himself proclaimed Queen Mary on Market Hill 'casting up his cap after as if he had been joyful of it' and with his own hands tore down the proclamation of Queen Jane.

After the ceremony his intimate, Sir John Gates, made an attempt to get the prize money by arresting him when he was helpless, his boots half on and half off, but the Duke managed successfully to argue illegality and remained free, too stunned to make any attempt at escape, until the following day when the Earl of Arundel and the Lord Privy Seal arrived from London to take him into custody.

20

The Monastery of Maguzzano

The monastery of Maguzzano, just off the road on the southern shores of Lake Garda, offered Pole a perfect retreat. Five miles away was Sirmione on its jutting promontory, with its warm sulphur springs rising in the lake, which had once made it a favourite summer residence of wealthy Romans in classical times, and the towers of the castle of the Scaligers, Lords of Verona, as a reminder of the non-too-distant past. The orange and the lemon groves and the vineyards and the olive plantations on the lower slopes of the hills round the lake afforded the monks a pleasant sphere for that manual work which was so essential a part of the Benedictine Rule.

The Cardinal, as Protector of the Order of St. Benedict, should, so the Abbot of Maguzzano thought, have been entertained *en prince*; but, since the Abbot was that Vincenzo Parpaglia who had been Pole's deputy in Viterbo, he immediately acceded to his visitor's request that he should remain as far as possible *incognito* and live in extreme simplicity, almost as if he were a postulant.

Which, in a sense, he was.

At last the way was open for Pole to give himself wholly to the hidden life of prayer. The duties which his birth had imposed on him were done; the distracting decisions over. Neither as

Plantagenet nor as Cardinal was there need of him. He could enjoy at last 'the largesse of obscurity', the immense freedom of not being wanted. But he knew he could only keep that freedom by giving it back to God and binding himself in the strict, simple servitude of which he had so recently written to Contarini's nephew. Obedience to God's will, henceforth, would be obedience to his religious superior. And the one reason which might have kept him in the world was abolished because Alvise would enter the religious life with him.

They were walking by the lake when the messengers arrived, clattering past along the dusty road up to the monastery gate. Neither Pole nor Priuli paid much attention. It was the Feast of the Transfiguration. A shaft of brilliant sunlight, pinpointed by clouds, on a little hill-top in the distance had led them into a discussion of that miraculous vision on another hill by another lake.

'Of all things that St. Peter did,' said Pole, 'I understand best his desire to house the vision and remain with it on the hill-top.'

'Yet I remember you once told me—it was in Viterbo I think, though it may have been in Rome when we were building your Quo Vadis chapel—that the real wonder of the Transfiguration was at the hill-foot.'

'Where they found their duty waiting for them and, because of the vision, had the courage to "set their faces steadfastly towards Jerusalem". And Calvary.'

'Then you remember it?'

'I had forgotten until you spoke of it. Yes, it was in Rome. I thought I was going back to England.'

The clouds intercepted the sunlight and the gleam faded.

'Perhaps I saw more clearly then,' Pole continued. 'I have no vision now.'

When they returned to the monastery, the Abbot gave the Cardinal the letter which the Papal messengers had just brought. It was from Innocent, informing him that His Holiness had received news of the death of 'the youth who was called King of England' and of the accession, after an attempt to prevent it, of his sister Mary. The Pope had shed tears of joy and had determined to use all diligence in helping England return to the Faith. He intended to send Pole immediately as Legate, but, the letter concluded, 'do not expect advice or instructions from us because you will know better than any of us what is to be done'.

Pole was silent for so long after reading it that Parpaglia ventured to ask: 'Is it good or bad news, Your Eminence?'

'You can construe it as you will,' said the Cardinal. 'It tells me that at last it is time for me to go home.'

London
Christmas Eve 1968

	Pope	*Emperor*	*France*
1485	Innoent VIII	Frederick III	Charles VIII
1486			
1492	Alexander VI (Borgia)		
1493		Maximilian I	
1498			Louis XII
1501			
1503	Pius III: Julius II		
1504			
1509			
1512			
1513	Leo X (Medici)		
1515			Francis I
1516			
1519		Charles V (Charles I of Spain)	
1520			
1522	Adrian VI		
1523	Clement VII (Medici)		
1533			
1534	Paul III (Farnese)		
1547			Henri II
1550	Julius III (del Monte)		
1553			
1554			
1555	Marcellus II (Cervini) Paul IV (Caraffa)		
1556			

RULERS

Ottoman Empire	Spain	England	Archbp. Canterbury	
Bayazid II	Ferdinand and Isabella	Henry VII		1485
			Thomas Bourchier	
			John Morton	1486
				1492
				1493
				1498
			Henry Dean	1501
	Joanna the Mad		William Warham	1503
				1504
		Henry VIII		1509
Selim I				1512
				1513
				1515
Suleiman the Magnificent	Charles I (Charles V of Empire)			1516
				1519
				1520
				1522
				1523
			Thomas Cranmer	1533
				1534
		Edward VI		1547
				1550
		Mary		1553
	Philip II			1554
				1555
			Reginald Pole	1556